The Celtic Quest

Andrew Clawson

**Get Your FREE Copy of the Parker Chase story
A SPY'S REWARD.**

Sign up for my VIP reader mailing list,
and I'll send you the novel for free.

Details can be found at the end of this book.

Prologue

Roman Britain, Thirty Miles Outside Londinium
AD 61

A hawk darted across the sky, its shadow racing over the massed armies gathered below. Horses stamped, and Roman soldiers offered prayers to their gods as they watched the graceful predator. An omen, but of good or bad? They would soon learn, for battle cries erupted from the throats of the tattooed, blue-painted army gathered at the other side of the field. One hundred thousand Celtic warriors were ready to attack.

Emperor Nero's horse bucked at the thunderous noise. Nero barely held on, cursing the beast. "Control this wretch," he shouted at a servant grappling with the bridle. The servant didn't look up. Nero had ordered men executed for less, though today would be different. Nero, the tyrannical emperor of Rome, stared across the field, a coldness growing in his chest as he struggled with an emotion he'd rarely felt. *Fear.*

A fear of one person. A fear he would never admit to for many reasons, though one stood above all: Nero was afraid of a *woman.*

A female barbarian, heathen leader of the rabble standing across from Rome's finest soldiers. A woman who had resisted Nero's attempts to crush the rebellion she had begun a year earlier. Her husband had been killed during the Roman conquest of Britannia, and now this woman who called herself Queen led her hundred thousand rebels against the ten thousand Roman soldiers standing before her.

Boudica, Queen of the Iceni. A real threat to Nero, and to Roman rule in Britannia. Her army had toppled cities, slaughtered an entire legion of Roman soldiers and killed over seventy thousand Roman civilians. The select few who had escaped death at Boudica's hand had come to Nero in Rome. Each carried with them the scars of defeat, and a common, horrific tale. The question was, how had Boudica's ragged army defeated the deadliest force in the world? It was rumored that she had done it with magic.

Nero shielded his eyes against the sun. He had threatened to behead the first Roman who had come to him spouting lies as cover for the Romans' defeat. The soldier had never recanted, even when Nero had pressed his sword to the man's neck. And when more survivors from the battle had offered identical claims of witchcraft, the emperor's disdain had turned to uneasy curiosity, and now fear. If what his soldiers said was true, then no horse in the world could run fast enough now to save Nero from Boudica's wrath.

Nero closed his eyes. Even now he could see the charred skin on the soldiers' bodies, hideous burns caused by the magical weapon they claimed Boudica used, one that cut through armor as easily as a scythe cuts wheat. Rumors had already spread through his troops. Rumors that the Celtic gods had come down from the skies to crush Boudica's enemies. That she could channel the elements in battle and bend nature to her will. The cold feeling in his chest threatened to overtake him, and he breathed deeply, willing himself to be still.

He opened his eyes again at the sound of hoofbeats. Nero's commanding general rode to his side and saluted. "Augustus."

Nero looked away from the seemingly endless expanse of screaming Celts. "General Quintus. You may speak."

"What are our orders, sir?"

Nero studied Quintus, a grizzled veteran of the campaigns, his most experienced leader and a man Nero trusted above all others. "Counsel me. What would you have me do?"

The stone-faced general blinked. "I follow your commands, Augustus."

Augustus, official title of the Roman emperor and the undisputed leader of all Romans. The one who ordered attacks or decided to offer quarter. But no quarter would be offered today.

"We are outnumbered," Nero said. "Ten to one, the scouts tell me."

"Correct," Quintus said. "By an enemy with little armor, no cavalry, no trained soldiers, with poor discipline, and led by a woman with scant experience."

Nero stared at the Celts. "The same enemy that overran our garrison at Camulodunum, annihilated the Ninth Legion and conquered Londinium. They have killed over seventy thousand Romans. Rumor says their leader is a sorceress who harnesses the power of earth and sky. You are not concerned?"

General Quintus spoke to Nero as few others would dare. "I am terrified, Augustus. But Roman soldiers do not run from battle."

Nero nodded. "So, how shall we attack?"

"*Cuneum formate,*" Quintus said without hesitation. "Our front line will drive a wedge through the heart of this untrained force and they will run. As we push in further, the wedge spreads them apart, splintering the troops from their leaders. This renders them incapable of any coordinated response. Once their line breaks, our reserves attack."

"And victory is ours," Nero said.

General Quintus made no reply.

"Boudica will resist our attack," Nero said.

"Our men will prevail."

"Who will lead our legion into battle?"

Quintus had spent his entire adult life in the military. There was only one correct answer. "It would be my honor."

"I would be a fool to put you at the tip of the spear," Nero said. "Remain by my side."

Quintus frowned. "As you command, Augustus."

"We attack now."

Quintus wheeled his horse around and shouted orders to his

commanders. The noisy Celts fell silent as the legion moved into position. Within minutes, the Roman soldiers were in attack formation, with reserve lines set to deploy in the second wave. Nero removed his helmet, took a cloth from a servant and ran it across his brow.

A hole opened in the Celtic line. A solitary figure stepped through, paused, and then began crossing the field. It was a woman. Dark crimson hair swirled riotously around her shoulders as she walked. Blue paint covered her face. Her metal breastplate was weathered to a dull gray, though the sword belted across her waist gleamed with a razor's edge.

Queen Boudica, leader of the Celts, had come for battle.

Nero squinted. What was she holding? A bag of some kind. Quintus moved back to Nero's side and raised an eyebrow, but Nero stayed him with an upraised hand.

"Let her come to us," he said quietly.

"Will you speak with her, Augustus?"

Nero forced the familiar cruel smile to his face. "I will kill her, then cut her troops down as well."

Boudica stopped walking. One hundred yards from the Roman front line, she stood and stared directly at Nero. An emperor in all his glory, he was unmistakable on his towering warhorse, clad in gold-plated armor polished to outshine Mars himself. The Celtic queen stared at Nero a moment longer, then set her bag down and lifted a hand, pointing one finger at Nero. She shouted his name in the harsh dialect of Britannia. Whatever she said caused the Celts to erupt in cheers that rang in the heavy air. The front-line Romans remained still, watching the rebel queen as she bent and opened the sack at her feet. Boudica lifted an object in each hand and raised her arms.

A deafening roar exploded from the Celtic army now with such force that Nero's horse rose on its hind legs and screamed. Nero fought to stay on top of the beast. The Celts fell silent again. Boudica put one object back into the bag and held the remaining one in both hands. To Nero it looked like a simple black stone, no bigger than a loaf of bread.

Boudica began shouting again as she lifted the stone skyward. Her entire army began chanting, their strange words sending dread from Nero's boots to his chest. Boudica set the dark object down on the grass and removed a metal container from the sack. She picked up the dark stone again, set it in the container, then held it aloft and turned it toward the front line of Roman troops.

The object in Boudica's hands seemed to *darken* as Nero watched. Red flashes sparked off it, faint and indistinct in the sunlight. Boudica lifted the stone and the air around her turned hazy, heat waves shimmering from her hands. The hair on Nero's arms rose. A flash of light exploded from Boudica's arms. Nero covered his eyes as his men screamed; the sickening scent of burned flesh filled the air. In moments, the front line of his troops lay dead.

The sky went dark. Soldiers gasped as the sun vanished. What sorcery was this? Nero turned in fear to see what Queen Boudica would conjure next. What he saw stunned him: Boudica's mouth hung open in shock as she stared at the sky.

The innate sense of self-preservation that had carried Nero from an orphanage to the pinnacle of Rome came alive. He grabbed Quintus by the arm and shouted.

"Attack!"

He drew his sword, pointed it at Boudica's heart, and the might of his legion thundered across the clearing toward the Celts.

One hour later, dead and dying men littered the field, precious few of them Romans. Thousands upon thousands of Celts lay sprawled in the grass, their blood mixing with the ubiquitous blue paint to turn the ground a grisly gray, the color of Celtic defeat. The first carrion birds had arrived, circling lazily on the warm air above the newly-created graveyard, waiting for the living to depart so they could gorge themselves.

Nero stood in front of his tent, watching the familiar scene unfold as he had dozens of times before. Rome conquered all. At least, until now.

Today, Rome had escaped for reasons Nero could not understand. The capricious will of the gods? His priests would say so. Or perhaps it was something else, a reason he couldn't fathom. Nero looked up as Quintus rode to his side and dismounted. "Augustus."

"Did you find her?"

"Yes," Quintus said. "She fell in battle."

But this had been no battle. It was a slaughter. Nero's troops had overrun the panicked force, ten times their size, with ease. The primitive Celts had been unable to withstand the Roman onslaught. But Nero had witnessed the power Boudica wielded, and it had shaken him.

"Did you find the objects?"

Quintus lifted a satchel. "They are inside."

Nero hesitated. "What are they?"

Quintus emptied the bag at Nero's feet, laying in front of him a pair of seemingly plain, black rocks. He did not touch them.

"This was what she used to hold them." Quintus indicated the metal frame that Boudica had used to hold the rock.

A simple, angled device forged of a metal Nero didn't recognize. "This protected her hands?"

Nero touched the dark rocks. Nothing happened. He knew what must be done to protect himself, his troops, and his empire. "Take these stones and bury them." He began to walk back toward his tent. "Far from here. These rocks must be lost forever."

Quintus spoke with care. "Is that wise, Augustus?" he called. "These stones have an incredible power. You will be invincible with them."

Nero was silent for only a moment. In that instant, he could see fires burning throughout defeated cities and hear the cries of vanquished enemies. But what he saw most clearly of all was Rome burning, and what he heard were Roman soldiers dying.

"There is nothing but misery promised in those stones. Bury them deep, Quintus. And never tell a soul where they lie."

Chapter 1

It all began with a scarab. A single scarab, crafted of solid gold, with sapphires and rubies dotting the wings. A scarab that, in the end, turned out not to be so solid. Over two thousand years after Mark Antony and Cleopatra had presented a number of the bejeweled scarabs as gifts commemorating a great military victory, a German Egyptologist had realized the scarab wasn't solid, but instead was two intricately designed halves that locked tightly together. She had opened it and discovered something incredible.

That scarab was why Harry Fox now stood in a small room in a warehouse not far from the Port Newark–Elizabeth Marine Terminal. *Why do I always end up in a warehouse?* he asked himself glumly. What was it with these antiquities traffickers? He knew the answer. Proximity. To water routes, major highways, and international airports. Places where goods entered and departed a country, occasionally without proper documentation. If Harry wanted to move items quietly across international borders, he'd operate near the same places. Except he'd have a real office, someplace where you didn't hear cranes running and ship horns blasting day and night.

A metal door banged open. Harry reached for the amulet around his neck without thinking, touching it as the man he'd spent weeks tracking down appeared. A man who specialized in acquiring items, often without proper documentation. A man Harry worried might kill him

7

because it was easier.

"Mr. Fox." The man who called himself Charles strode into the room, trailed by a single guard. "I've kept you waiting."

Harry heard everything Charles said, but only after his brain added in the missing consonants and cut through the drawn-out words. *Cha-ahles*, as he called himself, came straight out of the bayous of deep Louisiana. How he had ended up an artifacts dealer specializing in items of questionable provenance was a mystery. Though he'd relocated north, Charles sported a pale blue seersucker suit and colorful bow tie, staples of Southern style. He eschewed socks with his bespoke footwear.

"I'm sure you're busy," Harry said. He eyed the guard, who had taken up a post by the small room's only exterior door. Good thing Harry had had the sense to unlock the closest window earlier. If this went south, the window would serve as a quick exit.

"Never too busy for a friend of Ms. Leroux's." — "Never" became "Nevah" in his drawl. "How is she?"

"Well," Harry said. "Rose sends her regards."

"Tell her I appreciate the business," Charles said, lifting the briefcase in his hand. "I believe this is why you are here."

Harry watched carefully as Charles set the briefcase on a metal table and motioned Harry over. Locks *snicked*, the briefcase opened, and Harry Fox took one more step on a path laid out by Cleopatra, queen of Egypt. "That's it," Harry said.

"It is a beautiful piece, Mr. Fox."

Harry lifted a hand. "May I?" he asked.

Charles gestured at the necklace and stepped back. "You won't break it."

A pendant lay on the felt lining of the briefcase, a chain forged of golden links extending from either side of it. Harry gently lifted it from the briefcase, barely noticing the weight of the chain, which was heavy enough to tell him its links were also gold. Far too heavy for wearing comfortably. The piece was meant to impress, to make a statement. It succeeded in spectacular fashion.

"It's incredible," Harry said to himself.

Charles overheard. "A double-headed eagle," he said. "Wings spread wide. Truly one of a kind."

"Not just that." Harry angled the weighty centerpiece back and forth; it was more of a sculpture than a pendant. "There's a crown between the two heads. A crown made from a serpent."

The eagle had sharp talons; its long wings were spread out as though ready for flight. Rubies dotted the curved claws. Rich sapphires were the eagle's eyes, while emeralds colored the serpent coiled like a crown between the two eagle heads, which extended from a single body and looked in opposite directions.

"I have never seen such a creature," Charles said. "No idea what would possess a man to create it."

"How did you find it?" Harry asked, if only for the sake of appearances.

"Now, Mr. Fox." Charles wagged a finger. "You know I cannot reveal my sources."

"Fair enough." Harry turned the double-headed eagle over. The rear portion was as exquisitely carved as the front, the eagles' plumage impeccably crafted, down to the smallest feather. "I appreciate you acquiring this for me."

"Always happy to do business," Charles said.

Harry frowned. Charles knew what Harry did, which meant other people also knew. People around the world whom Harry had to view as competitors, if not outright threats. Less than a year into his new role, he thought ruefully, and already his face was known. "I assume you'll keep this transaction private," Harry said. "Mr. Morello doesn't like others to know his business."

"I always do," Charles said. "You can assure him of that."

Harry looked back at the pendant. Having the head of the New York Italian mob as his boss had proven useful for him time and time again. Once people heard Vincent Morello's name, they tended to show respect. Not surprising, considering what happened to people who were disrespectful.

"I'm satisfied," Harry finally said. He laid the pendant and chain down in the briefcase, then slowly reached into his pocket and extended his hand again. "The payment we agreed on."

Charles took the black felt bag from Harry's grasp. He opened it to reveal two diamonds worth a half-million each. A loupe materialized from inside his pocket.

"My goodness." Charles studied one of the diamonds, turning it to catch the light. "This is a beauty." He lowered the loupe. "Eight carats each?"

"Nine," Harry said. "Appraised at a million wholesale in total. A fair price."

"I agree." The diamonds vanished into a pocket. "Are you sure you don't have a pretty lady who will miss these?"

A face flashed into his mind. Harry grimaced. *Sara won't be happy.*

Charles misinterpreted his look. "She won't miss them," he said quickly. "Not when you show her that—"

A thunderous boom shook the metal building. The walls shuddered as though a bomb had gone off outside the front door. Harry grabbed the table for support, snatching the briefcase containing the necklace with his other hand.

"What was that?" Harry asked.

The guard answered for him. "The cops." He opened the exterior door and looked out. "They busted down the fence. They're coming in now!" He slammed the door shut and flipped the lock.

Charles ran toward his guard and the two of them turned towards the door, but Harry had no illusions about getting out that way. Same with the window. He took the only option left: a door behind him leading into the warehouse. Better that than the cops arresting him for trafficking artifacts. The metal door clanged behind him as Harry raced through it and into the warehouse's dark and cavernous interior.

Damp cement floors glistened in the weak light as he ran without direction, the briefcase clutched in one hand. The building stretched the length of a football field or more, with narrow flights of steps set at intervals along each side, leading up to a second level. Far above, dim sodium lights flickered like dive bar beer signs. Two external doors waited eighty yards ahead.

Doors that the cops would surely see. Harry hit the brakes, turning to run up the closest staircase a heartbeat before those two doors crashed off their hinges, courtesy of police battering rams. Harry gained the second level as the first cops moved inside, tugging on the metal handle of the first door he found. The heavy door opened just barely enough for him to slip inside.

Harry stepped into a cocoon of darkness, cut only by the faint light slipping through the cracked door behind him. He flicked his phone flashlight on. And stopped, phone in the air.

He stood inside a treasure hoard. Not gold or gemstones. *Artifacts.* Statues and scepters, scrolls and sarcophagi. An archaeologist's dream surrounded him, over a dozen incredible pieces. The sounds of his impending arrest faded as the puzzle pieces clicked into place. The heavy door. The artifacts. This was a smuggler's warehouse. Charles had left this room-sized safe of treasures unlocked, and Harry had stumbled across them.

Charles must have retrieved the necklace from in here, expecting to return in a short while with Harry's diamonds. The room's contents came into view in the beam of his flashlight; the closest object was a fiendish mask of gold. Next to it, a demon looked up at him from a felt-covered table. The mask was carved in the shape of an ape's face, its tongue lolling out to well below the jaw. The engraving around the edges told Harry this was a pre-Incan mask from South America. How Charles had come to possess it was beyond Harry. He hefted the piece: too heavy to carry with him.

Shouting came from downstairs – Charles, berating the police as they took him into custody – while a different voice yelled, "I'm going upstairs!"

Harry forgot the mask and spun around. There were more artifacts here than he could find in several years of searching, he knew, but he'd trade them all for a way out. The room's four walls penned him in, and the heavy door behind him offered only a direct route to the cops. He stepped deeper into the room. *What's that?*

A razor-thin shadow extended up the back wall, a place his phone's light hadn't illuminated. Harry stepped closer and his heart sang. There was *another* room, hidden by a door with no handle or visible hinges. But why was that door hanging ever-so-slightly open?

Harry ran toward this slim hope of safety. The door opened wider at his touch to reveal the hidden room. There was a handle on the inside of the door: at least he wouldn't be trapped in here. He stepped in and began to pull the door shut behind him, then stopped an instant before it closed. What if it had a lock secured by a passcode or key? Harry pulled the door nearly shut one breath before someone entered the outside room. He shut off his phone light and silently edged the door a tiny bit closer to its frame. A slim beam of light fell into Harry's room. He held his breath. If the intruder came close, he'd spot the hidden door. But if they stayed near the main door to the hoard room, Harry had a chance.

Footsteps pounded on the other side of the door, moving this way and that. Harry tensed.

"Clear!" came a male voice from directly outside Harry's closed door; a beat later, the sound of footsteps receding slightly. A radio squawked. "This room is clear. But tell the boss to come up here. She's gotta see this."

A drop of cold sweat ran down Harry's back. *I'm still trapped.* He kept his ear to the door as the radio barked to life again. A woman's voice this time.

"What's up there?"

"All kinds of stuff," the cop said. Harry's thin line of light flickered as a flashlight beam ran directly across it. "A mask, a big coffin, some kind of gold stick. You'll know more about it."

"Don't touch anything," the woman said. "I'm on my way."

"Understood." The man's footsteps moved away again and his boots clicked on the metal walkway outside the room's door.

Harry's situation had not improved. The artifacts had bought him time, but how long could he really hide in here? What if Charles had turned this space into a panic room – one only Charles knew how to exit? Then he'd be lucky to get out of here at all. Holding the door in place, he turned his phone light on again, shielding it so it didn't alert anyone to his presence.

There was a table behind him in the very center of the hidden room. The sounds of Charles and his guards being arrested faded as Harry walked to it and set the briefcase down. A book rested atop the table. One without a cover. Harry leaned closer and the breath caught in his throat. *Papyrus.* The pages were papyrus, the paper of ancient civilizations – the Romans, Egyptians, Persians, and Greeks. Which was the language flowing across the visible first page? He leaned in closer and shined the light carefully on it to reveal precise handwritten Greek letters, large enough for him to make out a few words he recognized in a dialect not spoken for thousands of years, and printed in a book that held a place of honor in Charles's secret vault. Harry didn't think twice.

The Greek book disappeared into his briefcase, settling beside the necklace. He gritted his teeth as a single page slipped free from the book. Harry slid it back among the others before latching the briefcase.

Noise filtered into the hidden room from outside. Harry lifted an ear to the words of a woman speaking in the room behind him. *I know that voice.*

He listened. Yes, he did. Pausing to confirm no one was answering the rhetorical questions the woman was posing herself, he pulled up a number on his phone. A number he had never expected to use again. *Life is funny.*

Harry hit *SEND.* A moment later, the woman outside fell silent. There was a faint sound of rustling, as though she were digging in her pocket. A grunt of surprise. "I can't talk right now," she said. "You cannot imagine where I am."

"You're in a warehouse at Port Newark." Harry spoke softly, his voice scarcely a whisper. "You just busted a trafficker."

"How the hell do you know that?"

"And you found a hidden room," Harry said. "With enough artifacts in it to get your anti-trafficking team on the front page of tomorrow's paper."

For once, the woman was speechless. Harry stepped closer to the door. "Do you have a gun?"

"Do I – what? Of course I have a gun."

"Then don't shoot me. Turn around."

Agent Nora Doyle, head of the Manhattan District Attorney's Anti-Trafficking team, spun around and went still. The phone stayed pressed to one ear while her mouth formed an oval. She didn't make a sound.

Harry raised a finger to his lips. "I'm not here," he whispered.

"How did you get in there?"

"Remember when you said you owed me? I'm calling in that favor. Get me out of here."

Nora didn't move, even when Harry stepped closer and put a hand on her elbow. "Nora? I need your help."

That snapped her out of it. "You want me to get you out of here?" She blinked rapidly. "You're crazy, Harry. My team has this whole building covered."

"Did Charles say I was here?" Harry asked.

"No."

"Then nobody else knows except you. Make it happen. You owe me."

The familiar hard edge in her eyes came back. She pointed to his briefcase. "What's in there?"

"Nothing."

To his surprise, Nora didn't push it. "You'll tell me later," she said.

He grinned. "You gonna bust me out of here or what?"

"We'll see," she muttered, pushing him aside. "What's this room?"

"A secondary storage area," Harry said as he followed her to the nearly-invisible door. "I haven't had time to check it out."

"You can't see the door unless you're in front of it," Nora said, impressed. She pulled it open, noted the handle on the inside only. "There must be a pressure latch or trip switch to open it from the outside."

"It was open when I walked in," Harry said. "I didn't see it at first, not with your crew showing up. Speaking of that, why are you here?"

"This warehouse is a front for an illicit antiquities dealer. My team has been watching him for months, after we received a tip from my counterpart in Paris." She glanced back at Harry. "They learned of an Egyptian sarcophagus being smuggled out of Egypt on a ship that passed through Marseille en route to here. The French missed their chance, so they warned me." Nora pointed over Harry's shoulder to the sarcophagus. "Looks like they were right."

Of course she picks today of all days to bust Charles. "Congratulations on your success, Agent Doyle," Harry said. "Keep your eyes open for a small black bag when you search Charles. You'll want to see what's inside."

Nora lifted one eyebrow. "Will those *things* hurt me?"

Harry shook his head. "They'll hurt Charles's bank account when you toss them in the evidence locker. Just a heads up."

Her eyes fell to the briefcase, then back to his face. "I see."

The sounds of cops moving about in the warehouse caught Harry's ear. "How are you going to get me out of here?" Harry asked. "Have an extra cop uniform I can put on?"

"Hardly." She walked into the hidden back room and flicked on a penlight.

What the heck was she doing? Harry followed her into the room and found Nora playing her light over the back wall of the hidden room.

"Can you send all your men outside while I slip out the back door?" he asked her.

Nora ignored him. Her light fell on the empty table. "What was sitting here?"

Harry gave his very best blank stare. "Beats me."

"I don't believe you."

Voices filtered into the room; the cops were closer than before.

"We'll talk later," Harry said, looking back toward the noises. "An exit?" he said, giving her a pointed glare.

Nora ignored him again, waving her light back and forth over the rear wall. "This wall is along the back of the warehouse," she said. Now she leaned against the wall, so close one cheek touched it. She closed an eye and squinted the length of it. "None of my men are back there."

"Which means nothing unless I can walk through a brick wall," Harry said. "Stop joking."

"I'm not," she said. "I've been in rooms like this one before."

"What are you talking about?"

"Hidden rooms in smugglers' home bases," she said. "Charles put an extra room inside his safe. A room with an…" Now she looked at him. "…*empty* table in it, and nothing else. Why? The larger room outside this one is an actual safe. You saw the door. There's no way you could break into it with anything short of a bomb. So why the need for this other, even more hidden room?" She leaned back against the wall. "Because this isn't only another room. It's a backup plan for when people like me show up." She dropped to one knee, ran her hand along the floor, then stood. A rare grin creased her lips. "Found it."

The briefcase bounced heavily in his grasp as Harry threw his arms out. "Found *what?*"

"Charles's escape route. Look." Nora's foot played along the floor where it met the wall, then she kicked a spot *just there*, and Harry understood.

A previously unseen door swung open. Outside, a fire escape overlooking an empty lot, and freedom.

It took Harry a second to find his voice. "How did you know?" he finally managed.

"I deal with men like Charles every day," she replied. "Illicit trafficking attracts a certain kind of person. Good with numbers, unconcerned with the law, and always untrusting. They always have a backup plan." She stepped back and pushed the door open wider. "I wouldn't wait if I were you. If my team walks in, this gets much harder."

"I won't forget it," he said as he slipped past her, careful to keep his body between Nora and the briefcase. "Remember, look for that black felt bag. It has two sparkly rocks inside."

Her eyes became as hard as those diamonds. "Don't make yourself hard to find," she told him coolly.

"I'd never." With that, he moved lightly down the steps of the fire escape, momentarily turning to admire how Charles had altered the door so it looked to be boarded over. A fine escape route if you managed to get to it.

Harry's feet hit the asphalt, and he forced himself to walk normally as he headed back to his car. He couldn't stop his thoughts from turning toward the Greek text in the briefcase. His gut told him that, whatever else it contained, the book promised one thing – the words were only the beginning.

Chapter 2

A knock sounded on Harry's apartment door. He stepped back from the kitchen counter. Two clean glasses rested beside the sink, atop a recipe he had no intention of attempting. He took a deep breath. *She's going to be pissed.*

Harry walked over and opened the front door. "Hey."

"Hey yourself." Sara Hamed ran a hand through her dark hair. "I've been on an airplane for the past eight hours." She spied the glasses on the counter. "A glass of wine sounds heavenly."

For the first time, he noted the carry-on suitcase she held. "You came here straight from the airport? I thought you were going to your hotel first."

"I'll take that as an invitation." Sara walked past him, the roller wheels *thunk-thunking* over his reinforced doorframe. "Do you really think I'd stop at my hotel when we're going to pick up Cleopatra's necklace?" Her eyes practically glowed. "That's a once-in-a-career type of piece. You still haven't told me how you found it."

Harry's stomach twisted. "Right. About that." He gestured to his living room. "Have a seat. I'll get you that wine." Through opening the bottle, two healthy pours, and offering her a glass, he didn't come up with a good excuse as to why he already had the necklace. Before she left Germany, Sara had made it clear she wanted to be with him all the way. Sure, he could have been more precise as to *where* he'd had to go to get the necklace, but telling her he planned to buy it using a million dollars' worth of untraceable diamonds didn't seem like the best idea. Despite all they'd been through, Sara still didn't know what he did for a living. Not exactly, anyway. It was one of the items on his list to tell her about. Eventually.

She smiled as she tasted her wine. "You remembered I like pinot."

"I do listen when you talk, you know." He flashed a grin. "And you're welcome." Harry sipped at his own glass, wishing it was a beer. "So… about the necklace."

That was as far as he got. "What about it?" Sara's eyes narrowed. She went on before he could respond. "You're going to tell me something I don't want to hear. I can see it on your face."

"You can… what?" He'd spent all of two weeks with her in total. How could she possibly know?

"I can just tell," she said. "What is it?" Her face fell. "You already have the necklace." Not a question. She shook her head. "Why? I asked you not to do that."

Inspiration struck. "The seller had something come up unexpectedly. He changed our appointment at the last minute. I was lucky to get it while I could." At least part of that was true.

"Another buyer?" Sara asked.

"I'm not certain." Now he was flat-out lying. It wasn't the first time, but he hoped it was among the last. "The seller gave me two hours to buy or pass." Harry nodded to the briefcase on his kitchen table. "I bought it."

The hard cast to Sara's face held firm. "I see." She took a drink, loosed a sigh, crossed her arms. "You made the right choice. We couldn't let this get away."

"No," Harry said. "We couldn't." *Phew.*

Sara moved to the briefcase faster than he could blink. "Is it locked?" Harry gestured that it wasn't. Sara reached toward the handle, yet didn't touch it, her fingers brushing gently over the metal. "Did you solve it?"

She meant had he figured out what the inscription on the necklace *said.* Not what it *was.* They both knew that well enough – a huge necklace, one meant to last down through the ages, a piece made to impress. Yet it was more than that. The double-headed eagle centerpiece was no mere pendant. Even the rubies and sapphires decorating it were not the true prize, whether it had belonged to Cleopatra or not. The necklace was not just a collection of precious metals and gems. It was a message. A way for this ancient royal couple, Mark Antony and Cleopatra, to communicate, just as they had done through the golden scarab Harry and Sara had found not long ago, one crafted at the behest of Queen Cleopatra. A scarab that contained a hidden message telling the finder to seek out this very necklace.

Two thousand years later, someone had finally read that message, and now they had the necklace.

"No," Harry said, getting up to stand beside her. "I still have no idea what the necklace is trying to tell us." He winked. "I hope you do."

"Me too." Sara opened the briefcase. "What's that?" she asked, pointing to the Greek book beside Cleopatra's necklace.

"Another piece," Harry said quickly as he grabbed the necklace and set the book aside. "I'll explain it later."

The full force of Cleopatra's necklace knocked any other thoughts from Sara's mind. "It's magnificent," she said. Hefty praise coming from an Egyptologist whose work took her to the world's finest museums. "The craftsmanship is impeccable. Any hidden compartments?"

"Nothing yet," Harry said. "Believe me, I tried."

"That scarab was a work of art," she said. "The message inside wasn't discovered for several thousand years."

"I'm not sure anyone was looking for one."

Sara lifted an eyebrow. "Which makes it even more impressive."

"Fair point." Harry's eyes fell to the Greek book. "Be careful. I won't tell you how much that necklace cost."

Sara gave him a look that suggested the price wasn't what worried her. "Do you have a magnifying glass?" she asked.

Harry produced a jeweler's loupe from inside a drawer, then watched as she inspected the piece from every angle. The exact same way he had, twice over. Ten silent minutes later she laid the necklace back down. "I'll need more time for a thorough inspection," she said. "The pendant may be hollow in certain areas."

"That's one possibility," Harry said. "Another is that Cleopatra didn't hide a message inside it."

"Or that." Sara crossed her arms on her chest. "If that's the case, we need to take a step back."

"That was my next thought," Harry said. He leaned toward her. A faint hint of lavender hung on the air. "Eagles have been symbols of various attributes to nearly every civilization in history. In Ancient Egypt, it stood for—"

"—protection, as associated with the goddess Nekhbet. Or with other gods, such as Isis and her sister Nephthys." Sara switched into full professor mode. "Then we look to Egypt's conquerors, the Romans. They mistook Egypt's patron deity, Horus, to be an eagle, when in fact he was in the form of a falcon. Rome appropriated this symbol as their own to show strength and power."

"Which is why Roman legions carried a golden eagle into battle," Harry said. "And losing it was the ultimate shameful act."

"Correct." Sara turned back to the necklace. Her elbow brushed against Harry's arm and stayed there. "None of which helps me understand why Cleopatra would leave a message pointing from the scarab to this necklace." Sara rubbed a hand over her eyes. "There's something else about this necklace. I can't tell you exactly what I mean, but there's more to this."

"What is it?"

"I can't put my finger on it, not right now. It will come to me."

She'd been traveling for the better part of a day. A little brain fog was understandable. "Are you hungry?" Harry asked. He considered and immediately discarded thoughts of the recipe on his counter. "There are plenty of good takeout places around here."

Sara didn't answer. Instead, she put a hand on his arm. Harry looked at her hand, which promptly pushed him out of the way. "Order whatever you think I'll like," she said.

A recipe for disaster. "What are you in the mood for?"

"That sounds good," she said, clearly not listening.

Harry frowned, then realized what had her eye. The Greek book. "Do you want to look at that?" he asked.

"First, I want to know how you got it." Sara reached out to the cover, stopping short of touching it. "This book is *valuable*, Harry." Her face had changed when she looked up at him. Subtly, like when a storm's coming from far off and you can sense it in the air. "Where did you get it?"

"From the same buyer," Harry said truthfully. "And I know someone who's in the market for a book like this."

The storm drew closer. "You want to flip it for profit."

"It's what I do," Harry said. "I buy and sell antiquities, remember?"

Sara blinked. The threatening clouds blew over. "I understand." Then her lips turned down, but in a playful way. "You should have it in a protective case," she scolded him. "Not lumped in with a heavy Egyptian necklace."

Harry breathed a silent sigh of relief. "I'll get one tomorrow," he said. "The book caught my eye too. Not just because I can turn a profit. First, it's in great shape. Second, you should read what's inside."

"My ancient Greek is a bit rusty," she said. "Do you have a translation?"

He opened a leather folder sitting on the table, removed a sheet of paper and handed it to her. "Before you ask, that's all of it. It's more of a pamphlet than a book."

Sara snatched it from him. "Even so, it's fantastic." That's all she got out before her eyes began scanning the page.

Harry counted silently to himself. He made it to nine before she visibly started.

"This can't be correct," Sara said.

"It's a first-hand account of his story."

Sara looked as though a nudge would send her tumbling. "A first-hand account of the story he told. 'He' being *Aristotle*."

"Plato's brightest student. Alexander the Great's tutor." Harry was taking an inordinate amount of pleasure in knocking her socks off. "Yes, these are his words. Transcribed by someone, then perhaps copied again, but accurate. It's a first-hand account of a story he told," he said again. "The author signed it, and he was well known as one of Aristotle's personal scribes."

Sara was ignoring him again, absorbed in the story. And quite the story it was. "You understand what Aristotle is talking about, don't you?" She asked when she finished reading.

"His time spent studying mystical tribes far from Greece."

"Not just any tribes. Celtic tribes. The Celts lived in what we call Europe. Ireland, Wales, parts of Great Britain. A long way from Greece."

"Two thousand miles, give or take." Harry tapped the paper in her hand. "He traveled a long way just to hear a bunch of magical tales."

Sara's jaw tightened. "He's talking about the Celtic belief system."

"Their *myths*," Harry said. "Like with that Dagda character they mention. I had to look him up. Dagda is a god in Celtic mythology. Or *Keltoi*, as Aristotle calls them. Dagda is tied to strength and their version of magic in that he can control life or death, the weather, or even time. Pretty powerful guy."

"Ask me about Egyptology and I'm your girl," Sara said. "Celtic mythology isn't my strength."

"Dagda is alternately depicted as a big, bearded guy or even a giant, nearly always carrying a magic staff or club."

That made Sara's ears prick up. "Aristotle's story mentions a staff."

"A *broken* staff," Harry said. "Here – let me see that." She handed him the transcript. "Aristotle traveled to the Celtic lands," Harry said. "Which later became Britannia under Roman rule. His intent was to immerse himself in the Celtic tribes and learn as much as he could."

Sara stepped closer. "To him, the Celts would have been a tantalizing window into unknown knowledge. He wrote treatises on practically everything. He would have jumped at the chance to learn from them."

"The most interesting part of this little book reads like a myth." Harry pointed to a specific paragraph. "Starting here. Aristotle arrives, and the first thing he studies? Celtic *magic*. That's the correct translation. Listen." Harry began to read the translated page.

Within two days of our arrival in Keltoi lands, their priests shared a forbidden knowledge of their gods, a power from the heavens I cannot comprehend. Their god Dagda gifted the Keltoi with his broken staff. Keltoi priests use this staff to commune with Helios, channeling his fiery strength into the land of mortals.

It is terrifying, yet the Keltoi respect this power. I thought to use the entire staff to make twice the inferno, yet they resist, fearing his wrath. The priests say mortals were not meant to possess such power. Dagda smiled upon them, as though Zeus sent lightning from Mount Olympus in a test of our inner strength. To resist such temptation is to reach for the divine.

"The rest of the text is fascinating, but it's exactly what you'd expect. This part about Dagda and forbidden knowledge is different."

She crossed one arm over her chest, holding the empty wine glass. "I assume there's a reason you're calling it to my attention?"

Was he really that obvious? "Yes."

He pulled out a sheath of thick plastic, heavy enough to protect the fragile document inside. "I bought this at the same time as the Greek book." Not exactly true, given it had fallen out of the Aristotle document when he picked it up. "Recognize the writing?"

Sara set her glass down and grabbed the sheath with both hands. "It's Latin." She held it to the light and started reading silently. This time Harry made it to eleven before Sara spoke.

"This is signed by Nero. As in *Roman Emperor* Nero."

"Two points for Sara." Harry inclined his head to the somewhat ragged Roman parchment. "Do you recognize the other name?"

"Of course I do," Sara said. "Boudica, Queen of the Celts. She led an uprising against the Romans during Nero's time." A look crossed Sara's face, as though the ground had just rumbled beneath her feet. "Are these two artifacts connected?"

"I think they're a package deal," Harry said. "I believe anyone interested in the Aristotle text would also want to buy a letter from Nero talking about the Celtic queen who tried to throw Rome out of Britannia."

"This letter talks about the battle between Nero's forces and the Celts. Boudica's last stand. The Celts were routed, Boudica died and the rebellion was crushed." She tapped the page. "Did this come out of a journal or a diary?"

"I'm not sure. To your point, the Romans won the battle, but read it again. Nero was afraid they would lose. He was terrified of Boudica and her army. These were *Romans,* fighting a ragtag band of rebels. But Nero was scared to death. Why?"

He gestured for Sara to lay the single sheet down on the table. "Listen to his words."

Harry ran a finger under the Latin text as he read aloud. Sara leaned in close, her chest on his arm.

The pagan Queen's army offered ten pagans for each soldier of Rome. Ten thousand soldiers faced the rebels of Britannia. Queen Boudica had destroyed Camulodunum and Londinium, burning each city and slaughtering all resistance. A single survivor of each battle came to me before this final battle with identical tales of their defeat — the pagan queen prayed to her gods, who stole the power of Sol and vanquished the Romans. Each survivor appeared dark, their skin charred by this vicious power.

Queen Boudica possessed a weapon not of this world. A force unlike any I have known. The ground trembled as her monstrous power began to unleash, yet I stood firm with my legions, and such was my strength that Sol turned from my face and spared us all. Boudica's assault failed when Sol blinked. She suffered the full wrath of Rome's might.

Despite my victory, defeat cooled me with its dark shadow. Had Sol not favored my courage, it would be my army lying on the field. The pagan queen's magic was taken far from that field by General Quintus. Quintus traveled to the tin isle to dispose of this monstrous weapon.

No man may possess it. Not even a Caesar, for if this force should ever be captured by our enemies, Rome is certain to fall. Queen Boudica's wrath must never be unleashed.

Harry's words faded to nothing.

"I believe these two documents are intertwined," Sara said. "In the letter Nero talks about a weapon Boudica possessed, a terrible power that could destroy his legions. Boudica, a *Celtic* queen. Nero is referencing the same Celtic power Aristotle describes. They're describing the *same thing.*"

"It's a ghost story," Harry said. "A Celtic legend, carried from Aristotle's time to Nero's. Aristotle lived three centuries before Nero and Boudica. Whatever connection seems to exist in these letters is likely from the disturbed mind of a tyrant. Nero ordered his own mother's death, burned part of Rome to make room for his palace, massacred the city's Christians for their faith and was eventually overthrown by his own government." Harry took a breath. "Not the most stable guy."

"Yes, Nero eventually lost. He also ruled as emperor over the world's foremost power. You cannot discount anything that scared him enough to memorialize it in here." She tapped the page. "Whatever *it* is." Now she peered at him again. "You acquired these pieces from the same seller?"

"He had global contacts," Harry said, then quickly moved on. "This has your attention."

"I'll admit it does. And I could use a break from the necklace. Perhaps I'm simply missing something obvious, but I cannot see anything in that necklace pointing us to the next part of her message."

"The necklace has a message," Harry insisted. "We just have to figure out how to read it."

She nodded. "We will. We have before." The edges of her lips curled up for an instant. "The letters from Aristotle and Nero. Harry, they're fantastic. Too bad I'm not an expert on this subject material."

"Come on, Sara. You know more about the past than anyone I've ever met."

Her cheeks might have colored a smidge. "Flattery will get you everywhere, Harry. Except to the answers we need right now." She lifted a finger. "I know someone who can help. She's an expert on the Roman Empire, including Roman Britain."

The doorbell rang, and both of them looked up sharply.

"I'm not expecting anyone," Harry said as he moved to the briefcase and closed it, covering the two documents and the necklace.

Sara frowned. "You don't think that man could be back, do you? The one who attacked you before Saqqara?"

Several months earlier Harry had been readying to leave for Egypt and the necropolis of Saqqara when a man had assaulted him inside his home. A man with ties to another mob family. A desperate man who owed the wrong people money. Only a desperate man ever moved against a member of the Morello family, and Harry Fox was protected by Vincent Morello.

If nothing else, Harry knew that whoever was knocking on his door wasn't the man who assaulted him. That man would never darken his or anyone else's door again. "It's not him."

Sara raised an eyebrow. "Do you want me to answer it?" she asked.

Harry shook his head. "I'll get it." Harry hid his briefcase in the dishwasher before going to the door. The doorbell rang again, this time accompanied by heavy pounding on the door. Harry didn't want to alarm Sara, so he passed on retrieving his pistol from his bedroom and instead slipped his fingers into the familiar knuckledusters nestled in his pocket.

Harry stood to one side of the door, gritted his teeth, and flung it open.

Nora Doyle stood outside, fist balled to hammer the door again. She did not look happy. "Why didn't you answer my calls?" she asked. "After what just—"

Nora caught sight of Sara standing in Harry's apartment and stopped talking. Her eyes narrowed, and then Nora Doyle did something completely out of character. She smiled. "Sara?" She pushed Harry aside and strode into the room. "What are you doing here?"

Sara opened her arms and embraced their guest. "It's so good to see you. Did you know I was coming?"

Nora stepped back and fixed Harry with a stare. "I didn't."

"Why didn't you tell her?" Sara asked, turning to Harry.

"I haven't seen Nora in a while," Harry said. "She's busy these days, what with running her own unit on the D.A.'s Anti-Trafficking squad."

"Speaking of your new role," Sara asked Nora, "how's it going?"

"Busy," Nora said. She did not look at Harry. "I don't have to tell you stopping antiquities trafficking is a never-ending task."

"Hopefully you're beating the bad guys more often than not," Sara said.

"I'm trying," Nora said, then changed the subject. "How is Germany? I've had my eyes open for new research papers on King Xerxes or Hippocrates. Haven't seen any yet."

Sara laughed. "The Egyptology department chair wouldn't be happy if I focused on them. Universities can be rather stodgy when it comes to unconventional ideas."

"Trier University can buck the trend," Nora said. "You're certainly qualified to write about those two."

Sara had been with Harry and Nora when they uncovered a number of Ancient Persian relics several months earlier, proving Hippocrates had interacted with King Xerxes II, ruler of the Achaemenid Empire. The artifacts were ground-breaking in their own right, but paled in comparison to what they had discovered later.

"Time will tell," Sara said, then looked at Harry. "My paper would be infinitely more compelling if I had the second tablet."

"The first one will have to do," Harry said. "I was lucky to get even that."

All Sara knew was that Harry Fox hunted for artifacts on behalf of others. Occasionally he worked with Nora and her unit. At other times, he worked for people who preferred a more private search. This was all true, to a degree.

Sara would never speak to Harry again if she learned the whole truth.

"The second tablet shouldn't be kept locked away," Sara said. "I hope one day it comes out from behind whatever wall is hiding it."

Harry shrugged, his eyes on the floor, until Nora came to his rescue. "It's great to see you," Nora said, touching Sara's arm. "Could I have a minute with Harry?"

"Of course," Sara said.

"We'll go outside," Harry said, and led Nora out to the sidewalk. "I didn't tell you Sara was coming because she wasn't supposed to be here yet," he said, once they were out of earshot. "She arrived early."

"Who visits you is none of my business," Nora said. An actual yellow cab buzzed past on the street. Nora's hands found her hips and Harry took a step back. "Where is the briefcase?" she demanded.

He knew better than to lie. "Somewhere safer than on my table."

"And why is Sara here?"

"To see me." It was the best kind of lie: one close to the truth. "We've been staying in touch."

"Did you tell her what you really do for a living?"

The question caught Harry off guard. "She knows what I do," he said. *Weak, Harry. Very weak.*

"Does she know the whole story or only half of it? I'll bet she's never heard of Vincent Morello." Harry's silence confirmed it. "Want a piece of advice? Be honest with her. Better to start now than have her figure the truth out on her own. You'll lose her if that happens."

"I technically do work for you," he said. "We have an agreement. If it weren't for me, you'd have been left in a Cairo hotel room while the private security team supposedly liaising with your office stole the artifact from a Persian tomb. They used you, Nora. I helped you get out of that mess."

Everything he said was correct. If it weren't for them working together, Nora Doyle wouldn't be in charge of her own team in the anti-trafficking unit. Reminding her of that was not bright, he knew. "Correct," she said. Her words were eerily calm. "I needed you – a thief – to help me outmaneuver a team of thieves."

Hard to argue with that. "I still have an immunity agreement with your office," Harry reminded her. "So what do you want?"

"The briefcase."

"I paid for it. Did you find the diamonds?"

"We did." A skateboarder whizzed past, wheels rattling on the concrete. "Whatever you bought, I'm not pressing you on it. My team broke down Charles's warehouse door because of a tip. We were told he had a stolen ancient Greek book tied to Aristotle. One we've been tracking for a long time." The hard edges to Nora's face softened. "Did you take that book?"

Her question told him two things. One, she wasn't certain the book was here. Two, she wanted it. Which made Harry want it even more. So he lied. Again.

"No. I didn't see anything like that. I'll look for it if you want me to. We're on the same team, remember?"

Nora looked down to the sidewalk. Her shoulders drooped. Harry began to reach for her arm when she looked back up. Her eyes burned with a hellish fire. "If I find out you're lying to me, I'll throw you in a jail cell where even Vincent Morello won't be able to help you." She turned on her heel and walked off. "One more thing," Nora called over her shoulder. "I lost your immunity agreement."

She wouldn't, Harry thought frantically. *She couldn't tear up the agreement.* Harry clenched his hands into fists. *She offered the immunity agreement and I signed it. I don't care if she's the head of the whole NYPD; she can't do that.* He took a step, ready to chase her down. *We had a deal, and if I ever need that, she can't—*

"Harry?"

Sara's voice stopped him mid-stride. He watched Nora go.

"Everything okay?"

"Yes," he said. "It's fine."

Chapter 3

Bethlehem, Pennsylvania

The thousands of worshippers who filled the amphitheater were on their feet, chanting and swaying to upbeat music. Many in the undulating crowd waved sticks as tall as a person. A lone figure stood at the center of the stage. The faithful had gathered to see one man, to commune with their deity however they wished, each person channeling their inner beliefs through their one chosen leader.

"The time has come." The man standing onstage wore a crown of leaves interspersed with purple flowers. His long white robes flowed as he moved. "All are welcome here, a place of faith and harmony. Ours is a world filled with disorder and haste, with no care for the land that gives us life."

The man lifted one sandaled foot. The music stopped. An invisible string seemed to thrum in the still air, ready to snap, if only the man would put his foot down again. Yet still he stood, as he spoke in a soft voice. "It is time for our leader to join us. To show us the path to harmony, where all are welcome." Now his foot slammed down. "Grand Archdruid Peter Brody!"

The crowd exploded. The long sticks hammered a beat on the ground as feet stamped in time.

"Welcome to our henge, my fellow Druids." Pete stepped briskly onstage with purpose, accepting a bear hug from the man who had introduced him. "Thank you to the Grand Herald for that welcome." The Grand Herald made his exit as the roaring increased, and Pete

Brody, leader of the Celtic Order of Druids, lifted his arms. "You are all welcome here."

Cheers and shouts filled the air for the next hour as Pete alternately wove stories of the power their beliefs would bring as they banded together as one, interspersed with warnings of what might come if they failed to keep the faith. Sweat glistened on his arms, and the black shirt he favored clung to his torso. "Always remember. All are welcome, yet we defend our right to believe as a force of nature."

A camera in the media production booth zoomed in on his unassuming face, beaming it to the oversized screens in the amphitheater as well as to the tens of thousands watching around the world.

Pete stopped moving, standing completely still as the crowd's anticipation was primed to explode. The seconds stretched out as he seemed to regard every person in turn. At last, he spoke again, and the fifteen thousand in front of him joined in. "Honor our ancestors, respect nature, and hold fast!"

With that, Pete turned and walked offstage to a tumultuous ovation. The Grand Herald returned to lead the congregation in their closing song. By the time it ended, Pete was back in his private office on the other side of the Celtic Order of Druids' complex, C.O.D. for short. He peeled off the sweat-soaked shirt and hopped into a steaming shower. Scrubbed clean, he pulled on an identical clean shirt and pair of jeans. Some of his flock went in for the whole robes and nature-crown look, and they were welcome to it. Druids didn't judge how you dressed or what you believed, as long as you didn't push your beliefs on them.

Peter Brody led the world's largest modern following of practicing Druids because he understood what mattered. Not his clothes, the songs or the cheers. No, what mattered was the *message*. A strong message all could relate to and believe in; that's what mattered. Pete had a vision to offer, and he couldn't share it if he walked around looking like a caricature of a Druid.

Pete leaned against his modest desk, waiting for the knock. Punctual as always, his secretary rapped on the door right on time. "Come in," he said.

"The list of participants for your media call, ^sir." Stan Cobb walked in and handed Pete a manila folder. "You'll find notes on their organizations and any prior concerning questions as well."

Pete took the file but didn't open it. "Nice tie."

Stan acknowledged the compliment with a reserved nod. "Thank you, sir."

Where Pete kept his wardrobe a calculated casual, Stan was formal. Stan kept track of everything in the world of C.O.D.; no small feat considering their company budget ran well over ten million dollars annually. Part of tracking everything included keeping Grand Archdruid Pete Brody ready for any challenging reporters.

Pete opened the folder now, sighing as he glanced through it. "Wonderful. Our old friend from *The Religious Times*. I can't imagine what Anthony's question will be."

"Would you like me to remove his access?" Stan asked.

"No. That will only make him put my name in bigger font on whatever article he spews out next. I don't understand why so many people are interested in the same story over and over." He dropped the folder on his desk.

Stan maintained his most diplomatic face. "Agreed, sir."

"We have a few minutes before the call." Pete turned around and looked out the floor-to-ceiling window behind his desk at the old Bethlehem Steel plant, now part of a sprawling casino and entertainment complex that drew thousands of visitors daily. What had once been a testament to how the world had passed by this once prosperous manufacturing town now helped keep that same city afloat. Real jobs, with real opportunities. Not the false hope of religious charlatans, a band of silver-tongued snakes offering papier-mâché dreams where your only reward came too late. The sort of person Pete knew well.

He laughed without humor. If it weren't for men like that, Pete

Brody wouldn't be sitting here today, giving hundreds of thousands of followers the means to push through their problems, to connect with the world, all without wasting a single day hoping and praying for miracles that never arrived.

Stan raised an eyebrow. "Is anything wrong, sir?"

"No," Pete said. "Any news on my purchase order?"

"The one from overseas, sir?"

"Our man said it should be here any day."

"Correct, sir." Stan pulled a phone from his pocket and inspected it. "No word yet. As I understand it, these private acquisitions can take more time than expected if the authorities become involved."

Pete clenched and unclenched one hand. "The seller came with quite the reputation for success. Let's hope he doesn't decide to get careless now." Pete's voice dropped. "You know how important this is for me. For all of us."

"I'll make inquiries, sir. Discreetly, of course."

"Do that." Pete pointed at a massive television hanging on the wall. "Let's see what the media has to say today."

Stan tapped a button and seconds later, twenty faces filled the screen, each in a little box, all neat and orderly. Reporters from news outlets around the world, all of them looking for a quote from the Grand Archdruid, the man who had taken an overlooked faith and turned it into an international movement. These reporters could ask all the questions they wanted, try to peel back the layers to find out how Pete Brody had done it, but the answer sat right in front of them.

Pete offered people hope, real hope, not the snake oil sold by priests, imams or rabbis. Waiting in misery your entire life for the promise of a heaven made no sense. Instead of the pointless delay, Pete told people to live in the moment, enjoy what was in front of you. Appreciate those who came before you – if they deserved it – and take care of the amazing gifts all around you, right here on earth. That was Pete's secret, but no matter how many times he shared it, people always thought there was more.

He freely shared those beliefs, just as he shared nearly everything about himself. Pete kept one thing hidden, a truth he knew in his bones, born from half a lifetime of suffering and lies. One truth the world would soon see. When that time came, Pete would be ready. As long as the seller in Newark delivered.

"Connecting now, sir."

Pete took a drink of water, his elbows found the desk, and the call connected.

"Good to see you all again." Pete offered the journalists his stage smile. "I hope you enjoyed the gathering. Anthony, from the *Times*. You go first."

Anthony Castrovilli never missed a chance to grill Pete Brody. Too bad it was always a variation of the same thing. "Grand Archdruid, would you care to comment on the sermon delivered last week at Grace Baptist in Atlanta?"

Everyone on this call knew it was coming. No matter who Pete called on first, chances were they would have asked the same thing. Why did it matter so much to them? He'd never risen to the bait, not once. Did they really think this time would be different?

"I missed that lecture," Pete said.

Anthony was undeterred. "The minister spoke about false idols. Specifically, when those idols are not other people, but objects."

"Is that so?" Pete shrugged. "Then I think he wasn't listening to me today."

The group laughed dutifully. Anthony, however, did not. "That minister's congregation is growing, Grand Archdruid. His message seems to carry weight with not only his followers, but the larger community as well. Would you comment on how such pointed sermons are impacting your flock?"

"We may call ourselves Druids," said Pete patiently, "but we're just people, same as you. I admire your persistence, so I'll say this." He took a sip of water, wondering if these reporters had any idea how soon everything would change. "This minister has made no secret of his contempt for our beliefs. Every week he tells his — what is it now, forty thousand followers? No matter. He tells them why he's right and everyone else is wrong.

"Of course, he's free to believe anything he wants. But when his beliefs infringe on our ability to live as we choose, when those beliefs threaten all of us, then we have a problem. I'm not just talking about the people who listen to me every week. I'm talking about all of us." Pete's hands went out. "We're in this together. We have only one world, and we all have to share it. Normally I'd say we should sit down and talk, just this minister and me, but that won't work. You know why."

A moment passed before Pete spoke again. "It won't work because I spent my entire childhood sitting at a table with that minister — my father — and I can assure you he will never listen to anything I have to say again."

Chapter 4

Brooklyn

The man wore a baseball cap pulled low. Eyes on the ground, he moved with purpose, avoiding fellow pedestrians with the quick gait of a lifelong New Yorker. It wasn't a disdain for casual conversation or interacting with strangers that drove him. He was in a neighborhood where he wasn't welcome. Which, to be fair, was justified.

The man skirted a streetlight's weak pool of yellow light. Apartments and single-family homes stretched blocks ahead on either side, broken by the occasional green park or asphalt basketball court. He turned a corner and looked up. *Good. Right where she should be.* A woman sat on a bench ahead, one hand on a baby stroller, the other holding a book. Trees heavy with green foliage formed a backdrop behind her. Stefan sat down beside the woman, leaning over to kiss her cheek. He whispered a question as his lips brushed her skin.

"Any activity?"

The woman smiled as though happy to see him. "Less than an hour ago a woman went inside carrying a suitcase. She was dropped off by a cab. Then a second woman arrived, went inside, and left again a few minutes ago."

"Describe them." She did, though only one sounded familiar. "The second one could have been Nora Doyle. She has worked with Harry before."

The woman knew better than to question Stefan Rudovic. His dark hair, deep eyes and tight expression didn't invite conversation. Stefan kept the world at arm's length, though for the woman beside him, that arm often held money. Her name was Iris, and she did odd jobs for Stefan. When Stefan wanted to watch someone and he couldn't do it himself, he called Iris, and she followed orders. She was pretty, but not overly, and smart like a girl who'd been forced to grow up too soon. Iris had proven adept at handling the requests, so they kept coming. Of all those who worked for Stefan, Iris was the most reliable. Which was why he'd asked her to watch Harry Fox's apartment.

"Look at this picture." Stefan pulled up a recent *New York Times* article heralding the recovery of a missing Egyptian artifact. A group of men and women were pictured, all agents of the New York District Attorney's Anti-Trafficking Unit who pursued the criminals who stole and sold historical artifacts. He pointed to one of the women. "Is that her?"

"Yes," Iris said. "Auburn hair and mocha skin."

"Why is Nora Doyle coming to Harry's place?" Stefan wasn't looking for an answer, and Iris didn't offer one. "What about the other woman?" he asked. "Is she in this picture?"

"No."

"She is still inside?"

"Unless they have a third exit."

Yesterday Stefan had sent Iris on a walk around the block that had taken her behind Harry's building. She'd verified what he'd already seen for himself – that the rear exit led into a fenced yard. Harry could go out that way, but the fence gate led to an alley that would send him out to one side or the other. Either way, a person sitting on this bench would see him. "Then she's still inside," Stefan said. "Good work."

He reached into his pocket, removing a folded stack of bills. "Your fee."

Iris slipped the money into her purse. "Please tell Mr. Cana I am grateful."

"He knows," Stefan said. He didn't need to tell Altin Cana what Iris said. The head of the Cana Albanian crime family knew everyone who worked for him was grateful. That, or scared to death. "Take the baby for a walk."

Iris looked into the stroller and smiled at the empty blankets. The stroller was an effective prop. Nobody suspected young mothers pushing a stroller of being anything except tired. They certainly weren't paid help running surveillance for mobsters. Unless they were.

"Do not be long."

She stood and walked off slowly, pushing the stroller and Stefan relaxed, but only slightly. Anyone sitting alone for too long might attract attention, because this was a Morello family neighborhood, and they watched out for their own. Harry Fox was a Morello man, as his father had been before him, and Vincent Morello must be jumpy, with his only son having nearly been killed recently a scant few blocks from here. Stefan grimaced at the *nearly* part of that statement. He'd been so close.

His phone vibrated. Pushing thoughts of Joey Morello's luck aside, he pulled it out and frowned. Nora Doyle was calling, and Stefan didn't believe in coincidences. "Agent Doyle."

"Can you talk?" It was always business with Nora. Which, as an occasional informant, Stefan appreciated.

"Yes."

"What do you know about an artifacts trafficker, first name Charles, who operates out of the Port Newark–Elizabeth Marine Terminal?"

More than he would admit. "I've heard of him," Stefan said. "I also heard he has had a difficult week. Which you already know."

"What has Charles sold lately?"

"I don't know."

As Altin Cana's trusted lieutenant, Stefan kept money flowing into the Cana family operation. On occasion, that money came from stealing and selling valuable cultural artifacts, so Stefan made it his business to stay in touch with the antiquities market around New York. Charles was a big player, an acquaintance of Stefan's and clearly someone on Nora's radar. Stefan had no idea what Charles had been hawking lately. It appeared Nora did.

He threw a line in the water. "Why do you ask?"

"I'll find out if you're lying."

"I have no idea what Charles is moving right now." Occasional cars buzzed past as Stefan kept his eyes on Harry Fox's front door. His shadow had grown in the minutes since he'd sat down. "Tell me what you need to know and I can ask around."

Silence from Nora. She never gave anything away for free unless she had no choice. Which, it seemed, she didn't. "Have you heard anything about a Greek book tied to Aristotle?"

Stefan's spirits lifted. "No. Which means nothing. As I said, I will ask around. I would ask him, if he were free to talk."

"Don't bother with Charles," Nora said. "Just find out what you can about the Greek text. You owe me."

A debt he planned to pay as he always did: with information on his competitors. They had an arrangement. Stefan stayed away from big-time artifacts and occasionally supplied Nora with information, and she let him slide. It had proven to be an excellent way for him to get rivals out of the way. All he had to do was tell Nora where to find an artifact and she took care of the rest. At least until Harry Fox, the Morellos' hand-picked artifacts hunter, had begun to get in the way.

"I will be in touch," Stefan said. "Any suggestions on where to begin?" He paused for a breath. "Harry Fox may know."

"Don't start a war over this. But yes, he may."

"I am a businessman, Agent Doyle. Not a thug. Anything else?"

Nora clicked off. Her dropping Harry Fox's name told him two things. First, that Harry was involved. Second, this was big. Nora wouldn't have called him unless she was in a tough spot, and she wouldn't have encouraged him to look at Harry Fox unless this Greek book she'd asked about was important. Harry Fox played into it in some fashion, and if Stefan could figure out why, there might be a chance to get at Harry and make a lot of money along the way.

Stefan had put a tail on Harry not long ago after a plan had gone wrong. A plan that his boss, Altin Cana, had been assured wouldn't fail. Yet fail it had, and Stefan was left standing alone to pick up the pieces. Given Altin had little patience for failure, Stefan was now desperately trying to get close to Joey Morello, son of Vincent Morello, the *capo dei capi* of the New York crime families. Vincent was the man other family bosses asked to settle disputes before the disagreement turned into all-out war. Too much bloodshed was bad for everyone's business. Vincent watched over every mob boss in the city save one. Altin Cana.

Despite Altin's unwillingness to get into line, Vincent hadn't come down on the Cana family. He had used a more subtle tactic. He'd tried to starve the Albanians of money so their enterprises would collapse. The small pocket of town Altin Cana operated in wasn't large enough to fund a serious threat to the Morello rule, so now, Vincent tolerated the Cana's drugs and gambling operations with little worry. He let them be, barely surviving and never big enough to be a real threat.

That was where Stefan came in. His task was to find new sources of revenue, money enough to make the Albanian Canas a real threat to the Italians. For several years now Stefan had succeeded. One of his biggest money-makers? The black market for art and historical artifacts. Stefan stole, bought and sold relics, paintings or other artifacts, making a handsome profit for Altin Cana along the way. For years a man named Fred Fox had made Vincent Morello rich by hunting artifacts for the Italian mob. Then two years ago Fred had died mysteriously in Rome. Which pushed a new man into Fred Fox's role as the Morellos' artifacts hunter: Fred's son Harry.

A crumpled newspaper spun past as the breeze picked up. A bicyclist whizzed in front of Stefan, veering across traffic before skidding to a halt outside Harry Fox's door. The cyclist rang the doorbell and set a paper bag on the stoop. Stefan fought the urge to stand and walk closer. The door opened and Harry Fox stepped out. A bit short, with dark hair and the frame of a guy who kept in shape. His mother's Pakistani heritage was evident in Harry's face. A mother long since dead, from what Stefan knew. When Harry bent down to pick up his food delivery, Stefan glimpsed a flash of metal around his neck. A necklace Harry never took off. A medallion Stefan believed was more than just a favorite piece of jewelry.

Stefan believed that medallion could be the key to knocking Vincent Morello from his position at the top. If only Stefan could figure out what it meant. A woman's face appeared above Harry's shoulder, and Stefan snapped a quick photo of the pair before Harry closed the door. The first order of business was figuring out who she was. Identify her, and he might have a new way to get at Harry.

Stefan sat a moment longer. *Food.* The outline of an idea took shape in his mind, nothing but rough edges at the moment, but rough edges with promise. He stood when Iris re-appeared from around the corner.

"Time to take the baby home," he said. "We are going out for dinner."

She didn't ask questions. After stowing the empty stroller in her car, Stefan had her drive them to a Mediterranean restaurant not far from Harry's, a place that had recently experienced a renaissance. A few months earlier it had been on the verge of closing, a victim of poor location. Amazing food wasn't enough to save Sanna from the fact it sat on a street that was the dividing line between Morello and Cana turf. Given the sheer number of people who either worked for or had strong feelings about the family controlling their respective area, it was no surprise that neither the Italians nor the Albanians felt safe patronizing Sanna. Even Brooklyn's best baba ghanoush wasn't enough to entice them through the front doors, because they inevitably ran into people with ties to the other family. Vincent Morello's power had sealed Sanna's fate, as patrons had stopped coming rather than risk offending him. The restaurant had been set to fail, until Stefan Rudovic realized that establishing a foothold in enemy territory could be invaluable. To that end, he had connected with the owner, a man named Ahmed, and offered an interest-free loan to keep him going. When Stefan began spreading the word that Sanna was a neutral, Albanian-friendly restaurant, business boomed.

Iris held the door for him as they entered Sanna's front doors. Ahmed was standing near the entrance, and his face lit up, though some would say the smile never quite reached his eyes.

"Mr. Rudovic, welcome." Ahmed shook Stefan's hand. "It is so good to see you." Welcoming, yet reserved in the manner of one owing a debt he'd never wished to incur. Stefan did not take note. "Your normal table?"

"Yes. I need to speak with you," Stefan said. "Please serve Iris at the bar."

Ahmed and Iris both followed orders without question, and Stefan quickly found himself seated at his usual table in the rear corner, close to both side and emergency exits. He surveyed the room, finding only friendly faces as Ahmed hurried over with quick, short steps.

"What do you wish to speak about, Mr. Rudovic? I have not missed a payment."

"I see business has been good." Stefan pushed a fleeting grin across his lips, the unfamiliar look there and gone in an instant. "I am here to tell you the loan has been forgiven. You do not owe me any more money."

"Mr. Rudovic," Ahmed sputtered. "I owe you thousands of dollars. Why?"

"Because we are partners, Ahmed. I helped you when you needed it." Stefan lowered his voice. "Now you will help me."

"What can I do for you?"

"Keep making good food, and keep guests happy," Stefan said. "No matter who comes in, make sure the service is excellent. I want everyone who comes here to talk about it."

"I understand."

"Remember. No matter who comes in."

"I will remember."

"Then we are finished." Ahmed started to thank him again, gratitude Stefan waved away. "One more request. I have a friend who needs a

job. A place to start again. He is a hard worker and will follow orders."
Stefan raised an eyebrow. "Understood?"

"I will be happy to assist."

"Good. Now I need to make a call." He waited until Ahmed was
gone before pulling his phone out.

Altin Cana answered after several rings. "What is it, Stefan?"

"I need your help." Stefan explained his request, and despite the
oddity of what he asked, Altin Cana did not hesitate.

"I will do this."

When Stefan clicked off, the faint sparks of hope that had flared in
his chest not an hour ago began to kindle. If this worked, soon the
Cana world would be set right, and Stefan Rudovic would be the man
who did it.

Chapter 5

Brooklyn

Empty takeout containers sat on Harry's kitchen table. A six pack of beer was down to one can. Harry sat in a chair, head in one hand, the other flipping through a book thicker than his arm. Sara held Harry's golden eagle necklace to the light, the rubies sending a spray of fire across his walls. The glow of a streetlight slipped around Harry's closed curtains.

"I need a break." Sara set the necklace down, then stood and stretched. Harry couldn't help but note the slice of exposed midriff. "I'll go cross-eyed if I stare at this necklace any longer."

"Do you want me to get you a cab to your hotel?" Harry asked.

"I didn't come all the way to Brooklyn to go to bed early," Sara said. "Though the idea is appealing." She grabbed his arm and hauled him from the chair. "Why don't we go out for a bit? Show me the neighborhood."

He couldn't resist the playful smile on her lips. "I know a place not far from here. A local place."

She ran a hand through her hair. "Let's do it."

Harry ordered them a ride. "Five minutes," he said. No sooner had he confirmed it than his phone rang. Joey Morello was calling.

"I have to take this," Harry said, and Sara waved a hand as she opened his briefcase to look at the Greek book yet again.

Harry connected the call. "Joey, how are you?"

"Busy," Joey said. "Which means business is good. Did Sara make it into town?"

Harry had told Joey of Sara's scheduled arrival, along with his plan to acquire the eagle necklace from Charles. Harry hadn't shared any update other than that the deal was done. Updates like Nora Doyle's team showing up, or his improvised escape from the warehouse. "Sara's here," Harry said. "We're about to head out for a drink." Harry cleared his throat. "I need to talk to you about an item. The one tied to my Egyptian interest."

One of Vincent Morello's rules was to always assume your phone was bugged. "Do you have any time tomorrow? I can come by."

"A drink sounds perfect right now," Joey said. "Mind if I tag along? If not, I understand."

Harry glanced at Sara. She paid him no mind as she studied the Greek text, one hand on her chin, one on her hip. His first instinct said no, don't bring her into this. She had no idea about the true nature of his work, though he could only keep that from her for so long. Maybe it was better to give her a glimpse into his world. He wouldn't tell her Joey Morello would one day run a crime family, but it couldn't hurt to have them meet over a drink. Could it?

What the hell. "You're always welcome. Join us."

"Thanks," Joey said. "I have something for you. From my father."

From Vincent? Harry left it alone and told Joey where to meet them. When he clicked off, Sara still had eyes only for the Greek book. "I didn't think anything would take your attention off the necklace," Harry said. "Even a story about Aristotle."

"It's a first-hand account of his time with Celtic tribes," Sara said. "Not to mention the letter from Nero. The letter is a magnificent find, yet my instincts tell me it's the less interesting of the two."

"Why?"

"Honestly? It's hard to say. The Celtic story involving Dagda is one I'm not well-versed on, though it's fascinating. Dagda connects to a range of topics including fertility, magic, Druidism and agriculture."

"A jack of all trades."

"You do have a way with words. Yes, and I know there are groups that still incorporate the idea of Dagda into their beliefs today."

"Druids?"

"That is the most prominent one," Sara said. "Druidry has recently experienced a resurgence around the globe."

"Why?"

"A number of reasons," Sara said. "People's increased mindfulness about how we live and the impact humanity has on the planet. Druids were some of the first people to advocate a green lifestyle. They believed in both a spiritual and a physical connection between humans and the planet. The lessons from Dagda and the Druids have never been more relevant."

Harry's phone buzzed and he checked the screen. "Our ride's almost here."

"Do you know of any Druids in New York?" Sara asked as she followed him outside.

"If they're around, I've missed them." Harry looked past Sara's shoulder, checking for anything out of place. A habit he'd learned to live with. "We have lots of people doing all kinds of things in the city."

"I haven't heard of any specifically in the New York area," Sara said. Her eyes narrowed. "Is everything okay?"

"Just keeping my eyes open."

"I read about a new Druid movement in Pennsylvania," Sara said. "It's grown exponentially in recent years. Their numbers rival some Christian denominations."

"Maybe we should ask these Pennsylvania Druids about Dagda," Harry said. "Here's our ride." As he slid into the rear seat behind her, he tucked the metal chain around his neck out of sight. His father's amulet, a last connection to Fred Fox. Harry wore it everywhere.

"The story piqued my interest," Sara said. "But we don't need to talk to modern Druids. Think about what the book says. Aristotle talks about a gift from Dagda, a *staff* wielding incredible power. Normally I'd be skeptical, but then you look at the letter from Nero." She jabbed his arm. "I know there's a reason Nero's letter was with the Greek book. They are related."

"I think so too," Harry said. "Nero claims Queen Boudica used some sort of *monstrous weapon* that defeated the Roman legions in two battles before Nero nearly lost again. Only Sol's interference saved him. Being saved by a sun god tells me Boudica's weapon must have been powerful."

Harry tried very hard to keep a neutral face. "The sun god must be a metaphor, right? But for what?"

"Who says it's a metaphor?"

Harry didn't know what to say, so he wisely kept his mouth shut.

"I'm only having a little fun. Yes, I do believe it's a metaphor. For what, I have no idea." She grabbed his hand and squeezed. "Perhaps we'll find out."

"I thought you came here to look into Cleopatra's mystery," Harry said. He touched his shirt overtop of the amulet. "That's the reason you're still talking to me, isn't it?"

"Mostly. Though I'll admit you do live an interesting life."

Harry could only laugh. "What's the curse? *May you live in interesting times.*"

Their driver slowed for a red light.

"Your amulet is not why I'm here. It *was* the second thing I noticed about you."

The situation of their initial meeting couldn't have been much worse for Harry. He had been alone and about to get his ass kicked by a trio of skinheads outside a bar in Germany when Sara stepped in and verbally laid waste to the drunken goons itching for a fight. The men had slunk away, tails between their legs, and Harry Fox's life had never been the same.

"What was the first?" he asked.

"I'll tell you later." She gave him no chance to argue. "I still want to unravel the mystery behind your amulet. It's a riddle from the time of

Cleopatra and Mark Antony."

"Hard to pass up."

"I'm an Egyptian and an Egyptologist." She ran a hand through her hair. That familiar note of lavender came back. "So, yes, the journey you are on is impossible to pass up."

"There wouldn't be a journey if it weren't for you," Harry said. "You're the first person who actually understood what was written on this." He touched the hidden amulet.

"Right place, right time. A man cursed to live in interesting times." She winked. "Often of your own making."

"I had no intention of acquiring a Greek book and a Roman letter when I purchased the necklace."

"Yet here we are. I'm not a Greek or Roman scholar, though I know someone who can help us."

Harry pointed out the window. "That's our stop ahead," he told Sara. "Who can help us?"

"A woman I know in Scotland. She's a history professor at the University of Edinburgh."

"Do you have any friends who aren't professors?"

"No." She winked. "I'm joking. I'm not always a buttoned-up academic. But Jane is in academia as well."

Harry opened the door as their car stopped. "Jane?"

Sara stepped out behind him. "Jane White. If you're serious about looking into Greek and Roman artifacts, she's the person we call. You have two entirely unique items, written centuries apart, both referencing the same object. That's enough to pique her interest."

The car pulled away. A street light flickered overhead. Without thinking Harry reached for Sara's hand. One finger brushed her hand. He stopped as she looked at him, down to his hand hanging in the air, then back up. He blinked. Sara grabbed his hand and squeezed, then pulled him after her down the sidewalk. The edges of his lips turned up and he squeezed back, falling into step alongside her as they walked, the streets in this up-and-coming neighborhood not quite busy, but steady with foot traffic. His phone buzzed. "Joey will be here in a minute."

Sara's shoulder brushed his. The noise of people enjoying themselves drifted out of the bars they passed. Ahead of them a man walked out the door of a bar, fumbling in his pocket until he produced a pack of cigarettes. He struggled to make his lighter touch the tobacco, looking none too steady on his feet. Harry touched Sara's elbow, trying to guide her around the guy.

They almost made it before two other men barged out, spilling onto the sidewalk and shouting at their friend. Harry's hand tightened on Sara's elbow as he pulled her behind him to avoid the trio. Eyes ahead, he took a long step and suddenly Sara's elbow vanished.

"Whoa, look at this little treat."

The slurred words came from one of the men who'd just stepped out. He had a hand wrapped around Sara's bicep.

Sara smacked him. "Get your hands off me."

The one trying to light a cigarette started laughing. "Feisty. Be careful – Daryl likes 'em when they're mouthy."

Daryl laughed, keeping his hold on Sara's arm. "Come on now, pretty girl. Have a drink with us."

"What's wrong with you?" Harry quick-stepped to Daryl, popping him in the chest with a two-handed shove.

Daryl's mouth fell open. Harry backed away, out of range of the haymaker he knew was coming once Daryl gathered his wits. He dragged Sara behind him again, ready to shove her out of harm's way when this went down. Yet no fists flew. Harry reflexively dug in his pocket before remembering this was supposed to be a fun night. The kind where you left your knuckledusters at home. Like a fool.

"You think you can push me?" Daryl shook his head. "You damned raghead, coming here like you belong. Your girlfriend forget her burka?" Daryl took a step closer. So did his friends, one on either side of the red-faced Daryl.

"Let's go." Harry grabbed Sara's hand and turned to leave. One of the men stepped into his path.

"Not so fast." The guy had six inches on Harry. "We want to talk to her. Go blow yourself up."

Harry had no time to respond before a shove to his back sent him into the man's chest. He bounced off, and with Sara's hand still in his, pushed her away, up against a car parked alongside the street. Surrounded and outnumbered, he had no chance against the three boozed-up punks, not even if he fought dirty. Sara needed to get away from this.

"Go!" Harry shouted at Sara before dropping down low in case the guy behind him tried to swing. Harry kicked, connected with something solid and was rewarded with a grunt. An instant later Harry shot up from the crouch and landed an uppercut on one assailant's jaw. In the evening darkness and peering through a haze of drink, the guy never saw it coming.

Harry's punch sent the man reeling. Pivoting, Harry swung at Daryl, the jackass who'd started all this, but his fist found nothing but air. Daryl was already on the ground with another man standing over him. "Joey?"

"You wanna mess with us?" Joey Morello shouted at the prone figure of Daryl. "You're messing with the wrong guys." Joey kicked Daryl in the gut. "Not so tough now, are you?"

Harry and Joey both turned to face the third man, the one Harry had kicked in the leg. He had gained his feet and took a step toward Harry before he screamed, clutching at his knee as he dropped to the sidewalk. Sara Hamed stood behind him with her fists up, one of her legs having just connected with the inside of the fallen man's knee. A hard, direct shot. The sort of kick you learned in kickboxing.

"He's not getting up soon," Sara said. She kicked him in the ribs for good measure. "You deserve that."

Harry reached for Sara's hand. "Time to go." He nodded to the few people who had stopped to watch the scuffle. One person already had a cell phone out and was recording.

Sara took Harry's hand as they darted through the small crowd gathering around the three men lying on the sidewalk in varying states of distress. Joey led until they stood in front of their original destination. Then he turned to Sara, flashed the smile that had gotten him into trouble many times, and offered his hand.

"Joe Morello. Nice moves back there."

Sara actually blushed. "Sara Hamed."

"Harry told me he met you on the way to kickboxing class," Joey said. "I can see it."

"It's better to attack when they least expect it."

Joey's laugh filled the street. "My kind of lady." He slapped Harry's shoulder hard enough to rattle his brain. "Keep your eyes open with Sara around. Now, how about a drink?"

They found an empty table in the bar and soon had a round in front of them. Music played in the background while the well-heeled crowd went about their drinking, some here to see and others to be seen. Sara took a long drink from her wine glass.

"Does that sort of thing happen to you often?" she asked Harry.

Harry was halfway through his beer. Punching jerks was thirsty work. "Not really. Brooklyn's pretty diverse." He nodded to Joey. "Look at the riff-raff I hang around with."

"You're lucky this Italian showed up when he did," Joey said. He sipped his beer, then frowned. "Or maybe it's those three guys who were lucky. No telling what Sara would have done to them if she let loose."

"Aren't you the charmer?" Sara asked. "Please, continue."

"I'll let Harry go next," Joey said. "Seriously though, we don't get much of that in our neighborhood. Ask Harry. He knows a thing or two about being an outsider, mainly because of assholes like the guys we just met."

Harry Fox had grown up in an Italian neighborhood, gone to school with mostly Italian kids, and learned to speak the second language at an early age because he heard it as often as English. All because his father had saved the life of a man he didn't know. Fred Fox could never have imagined all that his split-second decision would bring for Harry, who had spent his youth trying to fit into a world where he didn't look like the other kids, didn't know why some kids never accepted him, and had spent years trying to join a world determined to keep him an outsider.

One of those kids who hadn't accepted Harry was Joey Morello. The reason? Jealousy. Joey's father Vincent owed his life to Harry's father. In Vincent's mind, that debt could never be repaid, so he treated Fred and Harry as his own family, which had made Harry the brother Joey had never had and didn't want. Vincent didn't know how Joey truly felt about having a surrogate brother, but Harry had felt it every day – until a short while ago, when Joey had finally embraced Harry for who he was. A guy who kept getting up in a world that never stopped knocking him down.

"It can't be easy being a mixed-race man in a neighborhood of Italians," Sara said.

"Joey and I are both familiar with the neighborhood boxing gyms," Harry said. "We may not look like it, but we're harder to land a punch on than you think."

Joey laughed. "We've each taken our share of punches. Given them too." Joey spread his arms out wide. "Despite what you saw tonight, our neighborhood is diverse. We have Italians, Pakistanis." He nodded at Sara. "Even Egyptians. Those three guys must have come in from the city. They're not from around here."

The way Joey said *the city* spoke volumes.

"Agreed," Harry said.

Sara looked at Joey. "How do you and Harry know each other?"

Harry signaled for another beer. "Joey and I go back a long way," he said.

"Our fathers knew each other," Joey told her. "I've known Harry for nearly twenty years."

"I assume this isn't the first time you had to bail him out of trouble."

Joey laughed, long and hard. "It's not. If I'm being honest, Harry's had my back a few times as well." He tilted his glass to Harry. "In both personal and professional matters. My father is a collector. On occasion he'll rely on Harry to acquire new pieces for him."

"Speaking of which," Harry said, "I have a lead on a new piece. Actually, two pieces that are linked." Harry detailed the Greek book tied to Aristotle and the Roman letter from Nero. Joey didn't react outwardly, merely listening to Harry's tale, but Harry knew better. Joey couldn't help but be excited, because he saw only one thing. Dollar signs, and lots of them.

"Interesting," Joey said when Harry finished. "I assume these weren't cheap?"

"Not as bad as you'd think," Harry said. "I practically stole them."

"Good man." He crossed his arms on his chest. "You know my father is a discerning collector." His eyes flicked toward Sara, so fast only Harry could see it. Sara might have come with Harry, but Joey didn't trust her. No way would Joey spell out what Harry truly did in front of her. "Do you think it's wise to look into this further? Fascinating, but two letters are hardly proof."

Sara interjected. "Rarely is there *proof* in the historical record. Most of what we have from the past has filtered through numerous sources, so very few of them are first-hand accounts." She tapped the table in front of Joey as she spoke. "Two distinct sources hinting at the same concept. Sources separated by three hundred years mention the same incredible power, a power wielded by Druids. It's far more than fascinating. The Druidic faith is a common thread linking the two documents. It isn't merely the story told in each. It's the details. Those are what matter."

Joey swirled his drink on the table. "So, in your professional opinion, the coincidence of two people experiencing the same power or artifact three hundred years apart is worth investigation."

Sara nodded. "In each story, the Greek and the Roman, the power is described in a strikingly similar manner. Each time it's wielded by Celtic Druids, and both Aristotle and Nero are afraid of it. Aristotle because of its raw power, Nero because his legions have been decimated by it."

"Why haven't I heard of this legend?" Joey asked. "You'd think if a weapon like this ever existed, there would be other accounts of it."

"Good point," Sara said. "One that might make our case even stronger. If the weapon first resided with the Druids Aristotle visited, they kept it to themselves. Perhaps the Celtic Druids used their weapon before, but very little information has survived from pre-Roman Celts."

"Let's say your idea is correct," Joey said. "Where does Harry go from here?"

"*Our* destination is England." Sara pulled out her phone and fired off a message. "First, the person I trust to help us in this search lives there now. Second, Nero's letter references the *tin isle*. I'm not certain which isle he means, but Great Britain isn't just one massive island. It's hundreds of tiny *isles* as well."

"Nero's talking about one isle," Harry said. "We can't check them all."

"One reason Rome invaded Britannia is that Britain is rich in minerals, tin being one of them." Her phone lit up. "That's why England is our first stop. And speaking of England, this is my Scottish friend. I have to take this."

Sara scooped up her phone and ducked outside. "What do you think?" Harry asked.

"You tell me," Joey said. He signaled for another round of drinks. "Could she be right?"

"She could. At the very least, there's more to find out about this story. It's worth a conversation with her colleague."

"Any idea who the colleague is?"

"Her name is Jane White," Harry said. "She's a professor in Edinburgh. And that's everything I know."

Their drinks arrived. Joey kept quiet until the waitress departed. "Listen, Harry. If you think this is worth pursuing, I'm on board. And you know my father will support you."

Whereas six months earlier that could have been a subtle dig, now it was a compliment of the highest order. Harry inclined his head. "I don't do anything without his blessing."

"You'll have it. But do me a favor. You nearly died the last time you went off with Sara. I'm technically your boss, so I'm giving you an order. Don't do this alone. We can't afford to lose you." Joey took a long pull on his drink. "That health scare my father had last month wasn't serious, thank the Lord." Joey crossed himself. "He's not getting any younger. Next time it could be more."

"Your father will outlive us both," Harry said.

"That's the truth. Still, you don't go out there alone. There's a new guy in our crew. He's reliable, quiet. Not one of the loudmouths. Bonus, he's fluent in Italian and Spanish."

"So am I."

"Take him. He's a smart kid. And he's tough. Italian tough."

"I don't need an assistant. Another person only makes it harder. I've always worked alone."

"By alone, you mean other than Sara, right?" Harry had no response for that. "He's going with you." Joey removed an envelope from inside his jacket. "My father wants you to have this. Don't open it here," he said when Harry made to do so. "Later."

"What's in it?"

"Everything my father found out about your mother's death," Joey said. "You asked him about it, so he made a few calls. That's what he found."

"I don't know what to say."

"Say you'll take my guy with you. Now put that away. Sara's back."

Sara sat down at the table, all energy now. She grabbed Harry's hand. "I told Jane about what you found. She's agreed to help us."

Chapter 6

Brooklyn

A nurse sitting at the front desk looked up when the door opened. She ran a hand through her hair, smoothed her scrubs, and flashed a set of white teeth. Tony Cervelli stepped into the doctor's office the same way he walked everywhere: with broad shoulders and a smile. He liked this nurse. She was kind to his mother.

"Hello, Mr. Cervelli."

"Come on, Gina. Making me sound old. Call me Tony."

"Okay, *Tony*." Her eyes lingered on Tony as she pecked at the keyboard. "Your mother is ready to go."

Tony gripped the reception desk, his forearms tensing. "How did she do?"

"Very well, considering what she's been through. You should see how quickly she moved around with the cane. Almost as though she didn't need it."

Tony exhaled. "Great news."

"She's a tough old girl," Gina said. "I know it's just you and your sister to help her get through this."

"We owe her a whole lot more than a helping hand," Tony said. "She raised us on her own. You might find this hard to believe, but I could be a handful."

"Oh, I bet you were." Smiling, Gina pressed a call button, then walked around the front desk. "Here's her discharge paperwork. And here are the names of the contractors you asked about, ones who specialize in remodeling apartments for people with mobility issues."

"Thanks, Gina. You've been such a help since her accident. Hard to believe she doesn't have to come back again until next year."

"It's my pleasure, Tony. Don't be a stranger."

Tony didn't have time to digest that before a door opened to reveal one of the only two women he'd ever loved. "Look at you move, Mom. I hope that cane can handle your speed."

"Very funny, Anthony." Tony's mother was the only person in the world who called him by his full name. "I can't move like I used to."

She practically vanished when Tony hugged her.

"You look great," he told her. "Ready to go home?" He held his arm out.

His mother refused to take it. "I'm perfectly capable of walking on my own." She pushed him away, and Tony pretended it sent him back a step. "Why don't you stay for a moment and talk to this nice young lady?" She inclined her chin at the nurse, making no effort to keep her voice down. "She's single, you know."

"Mom, will you stop it? I bet Gina has work to do, and she's sure not interested in a lug like me."

Gina leaned on the counter. "I can spare a minute."

She could, like so many of the other girls who crossed his path. Problem was, Tony couldn't. Not when he could spend that minute with his mom. "See you soon," Tony told her.

But Adriana Cervelli didn't give her son *suggestions*. "Stop being rude, Anthony. Go ask Gina for her number."

Tony knew better than to argue. Gina pretended not to have heard Tony being ordered to chase her as she scribbled down the phone number he quietly asked for. Tony shoved the slip of paper in his pocket and moved as quickly as a man could when escorting a mother with a bad leg. "How's your wheel feeling, Mom?"

"Remember, Anthony." His mother completely ignored the question. "It is rude to keep a young lady waiting. You need to call her."

Once again, this wasn't a suggestion. "Yes, Mom. I'll call her." And he would, because if he didn't, Adriana Cervelli would find out and it wouldn't go well for Tony.

The sidewalks were crowded at this time of day. Tony gently guided his mother along, using his sturdy frame to keep other people at bay as they made their way home. His mother moved as quickly as she could, which wasn't quick at all. He lifted one hand to hail a cab.

"Put your hand down," Adriana said. "It's only a few blocks. Don't waste money on a cab when we can walk."

She'd been saying that his whole life. "That's what got you into trouble in the first place, Mom. I can afford it."

"You won't be able to afford it for very long if you keep wasting money. We walk." That settled it. Adriana was moving at what passed for full steam ahead now, forcing Tony to keep up if he wanted to continue warding off other pedestrians. He didn't argue with her. If nearly getting killed by a car after slipping on an icy curb hadn't put fear into Adriana's heart, her only son sure wouldn't.

Adriana Cervelli had taken everything life could throw at her with her chin up and no complaints. Tony's father had left them shortly after Tony's younger sister was born. Adriana worked day and night at a clothing shop in Brooklyn, sewing for a kind man from the old country, a man who had watched out for Adriana and whose clothing shop was the reason Tony and his sister always had a roof over their heads. The old man had fallen ill less than a year ago and been forced to sell his clothing store, leaving his sole employee at the mercy of new corporate owners who'd never even visited Brooklyn and only cared about getting a foothold in the New York market.

In a cruel twist of fate, Adriana had slipped while walking to work on the very last day before the sale was finalized. The compound fracture took far longer to heal than expected, and without health insurance, Adriana was left jobless while facing a pile of debt, just when Tony's younger sister, Elisa, was about to graduate from high school and head off to college. A college education her mother could no longer pay for.

Maybe it was the painkillers, but Adriana had faced the injury with her lifelong secret weapon: humor. "Now you can get the best rate on loans," she told her daughter. "Your mother lives on social security." She didn't mention her savings, all in cash and stored in a safe deposit box. "Have your brother help you with the loan papers. You know how I am with computers."

A car horn blared. Tony jerked involuntarily, nearly taking his mother down as he did. "What is wrong, Anthony?" Adriana held his arm more tightly.

"I'm fine, Mom." He patted her arm. "Just thinking."

"Young men should not worry so much. It will all be fine."

They crossed an intersection, bringing the familiar front door Tony Cervelli had spent his entire childhood walking through into view. Except now it wasn't a young Tony opening the door for his mother. Tony Cervelli, man of the house, reached for the door as it swung open toward him and the light of Tony's life stepped out: Elisa.

A weight Tony didn't know had settled on his shoulders lifted. Elisa was safe.

Adriana noticed, as only a mother can. "Stop worrying, Anthony. Everything will be fine. Your sister is leaving for school soon. Do not let her remember you being sad."

"I'm not sad, Mom." Tony squeezed her shoulders. "Stop saying that."

"I'm your mother. I know."

Any further debate was swept away when Elisa hugged them both. "What did the doctor say?" Elisa asked. "Is your leg better?"

Adriana tapped a finger on her bad leg. "As healed as it will ever be. Which is good enough."

Tony helped his mom up the new ramp that had been installed a month ago to give Adriana the smoothest entrance possible to her home. "The doctor said she's a tough old bird. No running," here he smiled at his mother, "but the more walking the better."

"Worry less about the doctor and more about that pretty nurse," Adriana said as they went inside. "You need to settle down."

"Get out of here, Mom. I just finished college last year. I have plenty of time."

Elisa's eyebrows lifted. Tony bit his lip as Adriana wagged a finger in his face. "I told you to study what you loved, and I still believe it. Your art history degree will not get you the job you deserve here."

"I know, Mom. I know."

"Then move to where you can find a job. If you stay to take care of me, I will throw you out on the sidewalk."

Tony wisely kept quiet.

Elisa swooped in to save him as usual. "Someone needs to keep an eye on you while I'm away. Besides," Elisa shook her head as though delivering grim news. "Tony's no good with girls. He's hopeless."

Mirth sparkled in their mother's eyes. "I have faith in you, Anthony." She touched his cheek. "The girls will line up for such a handsome man."

Tony rolled his eyes. "Thanks, Mom. Let's get you upstairs."

Adriana took one unsteady step after another up to the second floor. Her bedroom was there, along with the family's lone bathroom. She held Tony's arm, unwilling to voice that she needed it, yet leaning on it more with each step. If Tony didn't value his life, he would have picked her up and carried her. "Your leg hurting?" he ventured.

Adriana responded only after reaching the last step. "It's better than ever. Didn't you hear the doctor say so?"

No, because he didn't say that. "Good, Mom. That's good."

Adriana shuffled off, and Tony turned to head back down the steep stairs. His mother needed a new bedroom downstairs, one with an en suite bathroom, which wasn't cheap. About twenty-five grand, money Tony didn't have.

"Where are you going?" Elisa asked as Tony headed for the door.

"Sit outside for a bit. I have to make some calls."

Elisa's face lifted. "Did anyone call you back from the interviews?"

"Not yet. The rich kids with their Ivy League degrees take all the museum jobs."

She did an admirable job concealing her true feelings. "Don't worry, big brother. You'll get a job. I know you will."

"Thanks, sis." He pushed the door open and sat heavily on the stoop. An ice cream truck crept past, that awful carnival music blaring. He reached into his pocket right as his phone buzzed. This could be good – maybe Joey was calling with another job.

Joey Morello, his old pal from around the neighborhood, a guy Tony had known forever. To the neighborhood kids he was just Joey, a decent guy, a little quiet. But outside the neighborhood he was Joey Morello, son of Vincent Morello. A guy who would be somebody. The kind of guy who could give you work if you needed it. The kind of work that paid cash and required only one skill: your complete loyalty.

A while back, Tony Cervelli had needed cash, so he'd started taking bets for the Morello family. Soon Tony was drumming up business and keeping a portion of what he collected. Being the man holding illegal gambling money was dangerous, the kind of thing that could get him a criminal record. Joey Morello never got within a hundred feet of the dirty cash. No, handling it was Tony's job, and it had earned him enough to pay for the new entrance ramp and to make a dent in his mother's medical bills. The major home renovation she needed remained out of sight, however, until more lucrative work came Tony's way.

He pulled out his phone, read Joey's message and frowned. Joey wanted Tony to go meet a different man on the Morello team. Not just anyone. Harry Fox. *Damn.*

Tony got to his feet, opened the door and called back inside. "Elisa, I gotta run out for a bit. You okay?" She assured him she was, and Tony skipped down the steps, headed for Harry Fox's house. A warm breeze slipped under the cuff of his jeans, yet nerves kept his skin cold. Why Harry Fox?

The nerves jingling up his leg twitched harder when Harry Fox's apartment came into view. Tony was prepared to bust his tail to earn the money he needed, but until a few months ago he'd never expected Harry Fox to enter into this equation. Harry was unique in the Morello world, a man who operated on his own, handling a line of business few Morello men understood. Harry had grown up around the crew, much as Tony had, but the Pakistani blood running through Harry's veins had stopped him just short of being accepted. Sure, Harry did what the other guys did, boxing at the local gym and cheering on the Yankees, yet he did so at arm's length. Harry Fox had been part of the crew, but only just so.

At least until Harry's father had died, and Vincent Morello had made it clear Harry was one of the family. The new artifacts man, Harry traveled for weeks at a time, returning as quietly as he left, usually with a package in tow. Most of the crew didn't understand Harry or his relic hunting. And they didn't care to. You practically needed a history degree to understand what Harry did.

Which Tony had. Art history, barely one step removed from archeology. Tony's background made him unique in their crew. Harry was older than Tony, which meant their paths rarely crossed, but Tony knew Harry was different. To Tony, different in a good way. Which made what he'd done so hard.

Tony stopped in front of Harry's door. He lifted a hand to knock just as his phone buzzed. Tony lowered his hand and pulled out his phone. His stomach clenched. *Not now.*

The message was clear. *Stay inside Harry's place at least twenty minutes. Look across the street. Now.*

Across the street? Tony looked all around. Nothing. Someone walking two dogs, a kid on one of those motorized scooters, a woman on a park bench. Tony skipped over her, then looked back. The woman was waving at him.

Who was she? And how did she know he was here?

"Hey, Tony."

He spun around and found himself staring down at Harry Fox. The phone nearly fell from his grasp, and Tony fumbled to catch it.

"Good hands," Harry said. "I didn't hear you knock."

"Knock? No, no, I didn't." Tony ran a hand through his hair, shoved his phone into a pocket. "I just got here."

"Thanks for coming over." Harry stepped back. "Come on in."

Tony glanced over his shoulder. The woman was still sitting on the bench across the street, her head now buried in a book.

"You want a beer?"

Tony spun back around. "Yeah. That'd be great."

The phone was a brick in his pocket as Tony stepped inside. He managed not to turn and look back.

Chapter 7

Brooklyn

Harry Fox set his empty beer bottle down. "I'm not sure where else this will take us," he said. "But your background is an asset. You interested?"

He eyed Tony Cervelli across the table. Eager, a bit nervous, but that was to be expected. The kid was barely out of college, yet Joey Morello wanted Harry to take him along as they chased this Celtic legend across an ocean. Tony was built, sure, the kind of guy you'd want on your side in a pinch, but he was more than brawn. Over the past twenty minutes Harry had poked and prodded Tony on a variety of subjects that might come in handy on an artifacts hunt. Tony knew his stuff. He spoke fluent Italian and Spanish, knew art history, and, more importantly in Harry's view, Tony Cervelli was determined. Tony had a fire burning in his belly. How else could you explain him getting out of the neighborhood and returning with a college degree?

And all without a father in his life. Harry couldn't imagine keeping his head on straight as a teenager without Fred Fox to guide him.

Tony's forearms rested on his knees. He hadn't stopped kneading his fingers the whole conversation. "I am," Tony said. "Just being honest, but I'm still digesting it all. This isn't what I thought Joey had in mind when he sent me here."

Harry laughed. "I was surprised too." Harry looked out of his window, watching cars roll by. "I have one more question."

Tony stopped the kneading and leaned forward. "Shoot."

"Why did you ask Joey for work? You have a degree that will get you a job. Why not use that?"

Tony shrugged, offering an easy grin that didn't quite reach his eyes. "I haven't found the right fit yet. My family is here. It's nice to be close to them."

Harry looked at the floor. "I understand. Things can change quickly."

"Like today. Look at the curveball you threw me."

Harry looked up and found himself nodding in agreement. "You never saw it coming."

"Like a Mariano Rivera cutter."

"Good reference," Harry said. "He was a little before your time."

"Are you kidding?" Tony asked. "I've watched the Yankees since I could walk. Rivera is the best closer to ever play."

"Can't argue with that." Harry made a snap decision, something he'd found could get him into trouble as often as it got him out of it. "Come with us. Chase this Celtic legend, wherever it takes us."

Tony's shoe beat a rhythm on the carpet. "Any idea how long it will take?"

"It's hard to say. Most of the time when I go after an artifact, I'm gone for less than two weeks. By then I've either found what I'm after or realized I can't get it." He paused. "For any number of reasons."

Tony bit his lip, chewing on it for a long while. "Fair enough. Mind if I ask you another question?" Harry gestured to fire away. "How did you first find out about this trail?"

Harry told him a version of the truth. "I acquired the two documents from a dealer not long ago."

"Didn't the guy realize what he had?"

"I don't think he did."

Tony stuck a hand out. "Okay. If it was enough to get Aristotle and Nero's attention, I'm in."

"Good man," Harry said. "Pack light, and for cool weather. You ever been to England?" Tony shook his head. "Rains all the time. I'll take care of your ticket and any money we need while we search."

"Does Dr. Hamed mind if I come?"

"Sara? She'll be glad to have someone other than me to talk to."

Tony laughed, then promised Harry he would pack as soon as he got home.

"Keep your phone handy," Harry said. "I'll be in touch with flight times."

Harry stepped onto the sidewalk and watched Tony walk away, a cell phone held to his ear. Working for Joey Morello wasn't easy, never mind agreeing to uproot his life for who knew how long, traveling across an ocean with a man he barely knew and a woman he'd never met. Tony Cervelli had the quiet confidence of someone who'd taken life's punches on the jaw. If Joey said take Tony, so be it.

The evening's first streetlight flickered on across the street. A woman sat on the bench beneath it, book in hand. She looked up as she turned a page, checking her watch. Harry cast a wary eye down the street in either direction before sitting down on his front porch. Not a minute later, movement to one side caught his eye. Harry couldn't exactly say why, but the two men coming his way made the hairs on his neck stand up. They were walking toward him on the sidewalk, heads down, not talking, but moving with what he could only describe as *purpose*. Instinct made him glance in the other direction. A single man, young and fit like the other two, approached from that side.

Harry stood. The men were thirty feet away on either side and closing. He stepped back toward his door, closer to the shotgun he kept inside the coat closet. A 20-gauge ace up his sleeve. One of the men called out.

"Harry Fox." The lone man on his right stopped walking. "Need a word with you."

Harry twisted to see the other two men had also stopped. Ten feet away, they stood side by side, watching him watch them.

The single one to his right spoke up. "We're not here to cause trouble."

"Then leave."

"I'm serious, Fox. Look."

Harry risked a glance back to his right and found the lone man had his hands out, spread to either side. They were empty. Dark tattoos edged out from under each shirtsleeve.

"No trouble," the guy said.

Harry watched as the other two men did the same: showing their empty hands.

"What do you want?"

"To talk," the tattooed man said.

He must be the leader. Harry took a step back. "Not interested."

"Listen. That's all."

"Go stand beside your buddies," Harry said. "I don't like being surrounded."

The man didn't argue, walking halfway out into the street and then back in again as he moved to join his mates. All three were strangers to Harry. Dark hair, average height, though the tattooed leader was skinny as a rail where his two friends were thick with beef. After the three were standing together on the sidewalk, Harry spoke.

"You have two minutes."

"I only need one," the leader said. "You stole two documents. The owner wants them back."

"No idea what you're talking about." Charles was in jail. How could he know Harry had taken the documents?

"Both documents are tied to Celtic history. The owner wants them back," the man said again. "Now, we're asking. Next time we won't."

"Is that a threat?" Harry asked. Tattoos shrugged. "Who's this owner I supposedly stole from?"

"It's not your property. You have one chance to give them back."

"Or what?" Harry asked. The man again made use of his expressive shrug. "I don't know what you're talking about."

"Think hard and try to remember." Tattoos turned and started walking away, his two buddies following him. His head turned and he called over one shoulder, "See you around, Harry."

Harry watched until they were out of sight. He glanced up and down the street. The seated woman was still reading her paperback, seemingly oblivious to what had transpired. Harry stepped inside, bolted the door, and grabbed two things. The first was his shotgun. The second, his phone.

He dialed Sara's number and headed upstairs. He needed to pack a suitcase.

Chapter 8

Brooklyn

Stefan Rudovic sat at the only table in his apartment, a phone to his ear. "He's leaving?"

"Yes," Iris said. "He left in a hurry ten minutes ago with a suitcase."

"Alone?" Stefan asked. Iris said he was. "Did he notice you?"

"No."

"Then go home." Stefan clicked off and sent a text message. Coffee long gone cold sat in front of him. He took a sip. The wheels were in motion. Now he could only wait and see if his plan worked. Tony Cervelli was the key.

Tony Cervelli had fallen into his lap and given Stefan a chance to redeem himself after failing Altin Cana several months ago. It was Stefan who had organized the failed hit on Joey. Morello's bodyguards had died, but the Morello heir had escaped.

Leaves about to turn rustled outside his window. Not long before those same leaves first appeared, Stefan had started passing money around for inside information on the Morello family. One of the informants had given him a name. A guy in the Morello crew, a local kid named Tony Cervelli.

Stefan did some digging on Tony. Turned out he was a recent college grad with an art history degree, a guy who sounded like he might get involved with what Harry Fox did – stealing, buying and selling artifacts for Vincent Morello. Something told Stefan Tony could be useful. Turned out Tony's mother had quite literally fallen on hard times, and Tony *also* had a younger sister about to enter college. With no father in the picture, Tony watched over the two women in his life like a guard dog.

It only took a few photos of Tony's sister out and about to get Tony's attention. *Hey, Elisa is a nice girl. I hope nothing bad happens to her.*

Tony had stood his ground, telling Stefan what he'd do to him in no uncertain terms. That was, until Tony had realized who he was dealing with. Then he'd folded. No more macho tough guy, not when Elisa might get hurt. Just like that, Stefan had his chance. Leverage Tony's background, force him to share information on Harry Fox, and Stefan was one step away from Joey Morello. More importantly, he had an inside track to stealing anything Harry Fox came across. Not a bad way to show Altin Cana you were a man to consider when it came time to name a successor.

He'd posted Iris outside Harry's apartment, then told Tony to let Joey know he'd finished his degree and was having trouble finding work. Do that, then see what happens. What happened was that Joey Morello had sent Tony to Harry Fox's apartment, giving Stefan a man on the inside. A chance to track and manipulate Harry.

Then, Stefan had sent the three toughs to Harry's apartment. He wanted to rattle Harry, push him to move up his timeline and get out of town faster. The gambit had worked beautifully. Harry looked to be headed out of town with Tony Cervelli in tow.

Stefan's phone buzzed. He read the message, then smacked a hand on the tabletop. *Perfect.* Tony Cervelli confirmed that Harry Fox was headed to England today and Tony was going shortly thereafter. Harry might as well have invited Stefan along for the trip. He typed a reply.

I'll be in touch. Don't worry about your family – I'll keep an eye on them.

That would keep Tony in line.

Stefan fired off the message and walked with confidence as he left his apartment, making the short walk to Altin Cana's headquarters, a sprawling building that used to be several residences until Altin had combined them into a fortress. Stefan didn't break stride as he passed the ever-present guard inside the door, weaving his way through the wide halls to Altin's open office door. Low-hanging clouds of cigar smoke stung his nose. Altin sat at his desk reading a newspaper.

"Stefan." Newsprint crinkled as Altin set the paper aside. "You have news?"

"I found another way to get to the Morellos."

The impressive lines creasing Altin's forehead deepened. "I have heard this before."

"This is different," Stefan said. "From the inside." He gestured to the chair in front of Altin's desk. "May I?"

Altin waved at it. "I hope you have planned more carefully this time. Our opportunities to show Vincent Morello this is no longer his town are limited. Before, he had grown careless. Now, he is alert."

Stefan didn't need to hear about his last failure again. "My plan to surprise them did not work. Now I have a more subtle approach."

The ember on Altin's cigar glowed red. "Go on."

Stefan's elbows found his knees, and Altin's cigar burned to ash as he laid out his plan. The old man listened in silence until the very end. When Stefan sat back, Altin rubbed his jowls, looking out one of the bulletproof windows, turning the plan over in his mind. Altin hadn't come to run one of New York's most successful non-Italian crime families by being rash.

When Altin finally spoke, the two gravelly words were music. "I approve."

"I will keep you updated," Stefan said. He stood and strode from the room. He had a kingpin to take down, and it started now.

Chapter 9

A digital Grand Archdruid Pete Brody wiped the sweat from his brow. Painfully intense stage lights lit him up for all the world to see. He looked over the thousands in attendance, raised a hand, then froze. The real Pete Brody had pressed *PAUSE* and the recording of his recent sermon froze on-screen.

Pete always reviewed his sermons, taking notes as he watched. Where did the narrative lose steam? How could he tighten his message? His was a world where poor messaging was unacceptable, not only a way to lose your audience, but an opportunity for another preacher to get your flock's attention and distract them from the true message. For that message to truly resonate, image and delivery were paramount, because, as Maya Angelou said, it wasn't what you said that people remembered; it was how you made them feel.

Pete had to be flawless. No missed opportunities to make people feel the message. Pete took notes on everything from his body positioning to his inflection and use of the stage. Pete didn't hear his office door open, looking up only when Stan Cobb coughed. "Stan." Pete stopped the video. "You have the latest numbers?"

Pete's personal assistant squinted suspiciously at the tablet he held. "Yes. Overall viewership is up eight percent over last month. That is above our projections, and new member surveys indicate the largest increases are in the over-twenty to under-fifty age group." Stan looked up. "This is the age group that consistently provides the highest level of donations. Positive news."

"It's about more than money," Pete said. "I know, I know. Creditors don't accept prayer as payment. The new member numbers are fantastic." Pete gave a thumbs-up.

Stan, of course, had already run the numbers. "If we continue to exceed projections by at least five percent monthly, we will be the largest Druidic organization in the world early next year."

"Ten years ago, the Celtic Order of Druids didn't exist," Pete said. "Look at us now." He waved toward a window framing the entrance to their facility. "A beacon for Druids, many of whom never knew they were. In ten more years?" Pete shrugged. "We'll be an international destination."

Stan coughed discreetly into his fist. Pete laughed. "That's never a good sign. Out with it, Stan. What did I say?"

"The *international* aspect, sir. Did you review the email I sent today?"

"Probably not."

"It details allegations by the European Council on Druidry."

Pete's eyes narrowed. "What did they say – that I'm a televangelist looking to capitalize on the gullible masses with a shiny stick in one hand while picking their pockets with the other?"

"Words to that effect, sir."

"Notice how they only make those statements as a group. What are there, five on the Council?" Stan said there were. "Put together, they have more members than I do. But alone? Not one of them holds a candle to our numbers. They're afraid of what we're building here, so they lash out. They're more right about the shiny stick part than they realize." Pete drummed his fingers on the desk. "Once our contractor delivers those artifacts, I'll have a real surprise for them. No more sad jokes about us after that."

Another cough. Less discreet this time. "I received a message minutes ago from the contractor's solicitor."

"Charles's attorney?"

Stan nodded. "His facility was raided by New York authorities recently. Charles was arrested."

"What about the artifacts?"

"In a positive development, Charles had already acquired both the account of Aristotle's journey and the Nero letter referencing Queen Boudica."

"That's what we paid him for." Pete frowned. "What aren't you telling me?"

"I'm told the two items are now missing."

Pete prided himself on keeping a level head. He sat very still. "Do they have any leads?"

Stan shook his head. "Charles was not entirely forthcoming with the authorities regarding his inventory."

"The cops have no idea those documents are missing." Pete's jaw tightened. They had paid handsomely for Charles to recover those artifacts. Pete's generous congregation put millions in his coffers annually, more than enough to risk paying Charles to chase a legend Pete had heard about from an elderly Druid at a recent gathering in England. A legend about two artifacts tied to Queen Boudica, which had turned out to be true. Charles had delivered on his promise to find them.

And now the artifacts were missing.

"The police don't know Charles had and has now lost our documents," Pete said. "What does that tell us?"

Stan didn't respond. "First," Pete said, "Charles is either lying to us, or he truly did find the artifacts. He couldn't have known the authorities were raiding his warehouse. Second, Charles hasn't sold us out."

"Agreed."

"Is he still in custody?" Pete asked. Stan said he was. "No bail?"

"His attorney indicated his assets have been frozen."

Pete picked up a mug, took a sip of tea and then set it down on the desk. "Call Charles's attorney. We'll put up the bail money."

"It's one million dollars in cash."

"Pay it."

A tinge of red crept up around Stan's collar. "He could leave the country."

"He won't. You know why? Because Charles is in a tough spot right now and he needs a friend, a friend with money. And if that friend is us?" Pete tapped his desk. "Then Charles will do anything we ask to get those documents to us."

"Those documents are still only conjecture at this point. It's far too risky until we see them."

"The risk isn't in helping Charles. It's in letting those documents go. We need them. We're under attack from multiple directions. Our fellow Druids. The Catholics and Protestants and Baptists."

"Especially the Baptists."

Pete's fists clenched. "They see what I'm building and they know it's a threat." He closed his eyes, pushing away the tightness in his chest. "I've spent most of my life fighting that garbage. This is my chance to take the upper hand."

Pete had faced this particular challenge inside his home every day of his life, until he'd finally realized it was hopeless. His father was a convincing, successful fanatic with the platform to amplify his distorted views and spread them around the world.

"Call Charles's attorney. Pay his bail."

"As you wish, sir. I expect Charles will recover the documents in short order."

"No." Something in Pete's tone made Stan twitch. "Charles won't recover them. *I* will. And when I do, all those voices shouting that we aren't the true way will be silent once and for all."

Chapter 10

London

It was a whirlwind day, one in which Harry had woken in Brooklyn and now found himself riding shotgun in a rental car as Heathrow Airport disappeared in their rearview mirror. Sara drove with the recklessness of those for whom cars are meant to be enjoyed at speed. Unfortunately, Harry didn't splurge on rental cars, so she was currently flooring it in a mid-sized Volkswagen. The results were less than impressive.

Harry held on to the grab bar as Sara swerved through traffic, making up in risk what she couldn't get in speed. "You know we won't get there at all if you wreck," he said.

"Relax." Tires screeched as she whipped into the slow lane to pass someone before she jerked the wheel back over. "This is how everyone drives in Europe."

Harry noted the distinct absence of other maniacs on the road. "How far is it to Jane's place?"

Jane was Jane White, the Scottish professor and associate of Sara's who had agreed to help them uncover any connection between the Aristotle and Nero documents. Even if they were authentic, the odds were stacked against Harry finding anything other than an emptied wallet for his troubles.

He knew this, yet here he was, chasing a legend. Why? Simple. The pursuit made him feel like his father was still alive, watching him every step of the way. It wasn't just the life he'd been thrust into any longer.

Now it was the life he chose.

"Jane's family has property outside the city," Sara said. "We'll be there in about twenty minutes."

"Do all Scottish people have summer homes in England?"

"Of course not. Her family is fortunate." Sara paused. "Old-money fortunate." Sara paused again. "Jane lives in an honest-to-goodness castle in Scotland. Her father is a nobleman. I visited her once. It really is a castle. The place is so big it has a caretaker."

"How did a rich girl like that become an academic?"

"Because Jane's one of the most down-to-earth people I've ever met. I didn't know about her privileged background until we'd been friends for years."

"I can imagine that kind of money attracts unsavory characters."

"And yet she still agreed to help you."

Harry laughed before he could stop himself. "Anything I should know about Her Royal Highness that you haven't told me yet?"

"She's smarter than both of us put together. So listen to her."

Minutes later they exited the highway and maneuvered through suburban streets. The house they stopped in front of was partially hidden by tall shrubbery designed for exactly that purpose. A black metal gate surrounded the property. Sara reached for her cell phone. "She's expecting us. I don't – oh."

The gate swung inward of its own accord. Sara pulled through and started down the tree-lined drive, a long circle that brought them to a front door painted black in the style of Number 10 Downing Street. The doors looked to be designed for siege warfare. If Jane wasn't at home, they had no hope of getting inside.

"I think this is what rich people consider a 'getaway home,'" Sara quipped. "But don't judge Jane before you meet her. She's the least pretentious rich – I mean truly rich – person I've ever met." Sara considered. "And one of the only ones, to be honest."

Harry stepped out. One of the imposing front doors opened to reveal the lady of the manor. Jane White. Clad in a light sweater and jeans, she wasn't what Harry expected.

Her brunette hair floated out behind her as she strode over to Sara and embraced her. "My goodness, it is wonderful to see you." Harry picked up Jane's words even though her face was smooshed against Sara's. "You look positively lovely."

Sara returned the compliment, holding on to Jane a beat longer before turning to Harry. He didn't fight it when she grabbed his arm. "Jane, meet Harry." Sara jerked him closer. "Harry's the man who found the artifacts."

"Charmed, Mr. Fox." Jane offered her hand, giving him a firm shake. Her arms were muscled. "It's a pleasure to make your acquaintance. Sara has told me much about you. Which is more than I can say about the other men in her life."

"Other men?" Harry asked.

"More than Sara would ever let me tell you about." A red blush spread across Sara's cheeks, deeper than any Harry had ever seen on her before. "I'm joking, of course. Our Sara isn't one to return affection lightly."

Sara fired back. "Your first important lesson, Harry. Jane is not always to be believed."

"Then we're doomed from the start, but we'll have fun." Harry nodded to Jane's house. "Nice place."

Jane waved the comment away and pulled a lock of brunette hair behind an ear. "One of my parents' homes. I'm in London lecturing at King's College for part of the semester, so I stay here. I'm sure Sara told you my home in Edinburgh is a castle."

"I'm more impressed that you've put up with Sara for so many years," Harry said. "Shows character. Or a lack of judgment."

Jane glanced to Sara. "You're right. I *do* like him." Jane ushered them inside before Harry had a chance to puzzle through that one. "Forgive the decorations," Jane said as they walked into a spacious foyer. "My mother furnished this house. Her tastes run toward modern pieces."

The mention of Jane's mother reminded Harry of the unopened

envelope he'd left in his safe deposit box back in Brooklyn: the fulfillment of Vincent Morello's promise to inquire about Harry's mother and her death. Harry's jaw tightened. He pushed the thoughts away. He'd deal with it after he unraveled this mystery. "Nice room," he said as Jane showed them into what could only be a library. "You read all of these?"

Row upon row of shelving lined the walls. Wood so dark its coloring could only have come from a century of cigar smoke and polish made up the walls and ceiling, with a towering window allowing what little sunlight fell on London's outskirts to light the room. This was the kind of room Harry could only have imagined as a boy.

"Yes. Some of them twice," Jane said. "I spent many summers here, avoiding my father's orders to get outside and play." She gestured toward the hundreds of volumes. "I visited the world without ever leaving this room."

A shadow crossed her face. Jane's eyes lingered on the shelves a moment longer before she sat on a high-backed chair, while Harry joined Sara on a couch that looked far more comfortable than it actually was. "Would either of you care for a drink?" Jane indicated an elegant drinks cart beside her chair holding a dozen different bottles and a full ice bucket. Harry hadn't ever seen one like it outside of the movies, and told her so. "English law stipulates you're required to have a drink if you've never seen one of these," Jane said. "What will it be?"

Harry glanced at his watch, still on New York time. "Beer if you have it."

"I do." Jane leaned over and opened a drawer, which turned out to be an ice chest with bottled beer inside. She pulled out a bottle, deftly removed the cap, and passed it to him. "Sara?"

"White wine," Sara said. "I can't say no to such a wonderful hostess."

"Nor should you." Jane filled two glasses, handed one to Sara, then raised hers. "To friends, old and new."

As Harry raised his bottle, he couldn't say why Jane's words set him on edge. Maybe it was the inquiring way she looked at him as she sipped.

She took a sip from her glass now and began to probe. "Sara gave me precious little information about your adventure," she began. "How did you come to possess the documents?" She nodded to the well-worn messenger bag he'd barely let go of since they walked in.

An internal alarm dinged. Jane was a stranger. Didn't matter how long Sara had known her. One rule that had kept him alive thus far was that people had to earn your trust. He hid behind his beer bottle to buy time. Sara trusted Jane. Harry needed both of them to decipher these documents. If he ever wanted to be truly open with Sara, he needed to start acting like a normal person, not a gangster. That meant trusting people. Sometimes.

"I work for a private collector," Harry said. "My father began the relationship, and I've been fortunate enough to keep it going."

"Who is your client?"

"This client prefers to remain anonymous."

"Does this client have anything to do with why you and Sara were attacked in Brooklyn?"

Sara jumped in. "No. Those morons came after us because we look different."

"It's appalling," Jane said. "Even in the most diverse cities, such travesties still occur. Including London."

"Maybe it's *because* of the diversity," Harry said.

"Excellent point," Jane said. "Forgive me being direct, but you don't look or sound like an immigrant. Your skin's not that dark, and you don't have an accent. Sara, on the other hand, is more mocha and has a bit of one. So why would they single you out to attack because of your heritage?"

"Put the two of us together and it's more apparent," Sara said. "I'm just happy Harry's friend came along at the right time."

"And I'm happy you take those kickboxing classes," Harry said.

Sara smirked, and Jane raised her glass again. "Nicely done," she said. She turned back to Harry. "I'm sorry about your father."

"Thanks. How did you learn about it?"

"I read several articles he coauthored on antiquities. It's unfortunate he became involved in such… trouble."

Harry's stomach went cold. Jane was talking about his father being arrested and having his reputation ruined – not about being murdered. "Yes, it was."

"His intellect was obvious. I can see why people involved in artifacts trafficking would be drawn to him. I'm certain he was a good man."

The cool wall Harry had so carefully constructed over the years to hide his feelings cracked a little. "He had no idea who he was dealing with," he snapped. "We don't all have money to protect us."

The air seemed to go out of the room. Sara choked quietly on a mouthful of wine. And Jane just watched him, the silence drawing on.

"No," Jane said at last. "We don't. My own father is a philanderer, well-intentioned but clueless when it comes to how his wanderings impact our family. In his mind, such choices are concerns for others. He believes his money insulates him from repercussions. My mother knew what she signed up for by marrying him. His money is also why they're not divorced – their prenuptial agreement would cut her off from the money. Instead of divorce, they live separate lives in different countries, making me the center of their failed, ongoing marriage."

Harry couldn't respond. Sara barely reacted. This story wasn't new to her.

"Forgive me if my questions were intrusive," Jane said. "I meant them to be. Sara is one of my dearest friends, and you are a man she met on the street and whom she has seen two times. Each of those times involved verbal or actual fisticuffs, so you'll understand if I wonder about you."

"Fair enough," Harry said. The heat in his gut vanished. "I'm sorry I said what I did."

"Don't be. If you want to solve this Celtic mystery, you'd better be ready to fight for it." Jane paused, her eyes going to a massive sword hanging on the wall. "You'll never survive if you don't."

Harry followed her gaze and his eyes widened. The thing was *terrifying*. "What does that mean?" he asked.

"It means I have some experience in this sort of thing," Jane said. "A story for another time." She drained her wine glass. "Sara and I had a long conversation earlier."

"A *private* conversation," Sara said, anticipating Harry's protest.

"She trusts you," Jane went on. "I, however, am not a naturally trusting person. I had to find out for myself." Jane aimed a finger at Harry. "You're handsome, which immediately worried me."

Sara was not amused. "*Jane.*"

"Not that Sara would let you get away with anything just because of that," Jane said quickly. "But in my experience, pretty packaging can hide internal defects. I think you're a decent guy. One who's playing a dangerous game."

Harry played his best card and kept his mouth shut.

"Regardless, you have something here, and I'll be darned if I let you gallivant across England without my help."

"I appreciate that," Harry said. "What sort of experience do you have dealing with artifacts?"

"In my academic work in Edinburgh, my job occasionally leads into the world of antiquities. Buying and selling, trafficking, hunting. And interacting with the sort of people who inhabit that particular ocean. I don't need to tell you there are sharks in the water."

Harry finished his beer, then leaned back on the most uncomfortable couch money could buy. "No, you don't."

"I have a friend who's chased a prize or two. He has resources. More than my family does, but even that sort of support didn't stop the chase from taking away the best thing he ever had." Again, Jane's eyes went to the sword. "Parker never thought it would happen to him or someone he loved, yet it did."

The tone of her words did not invite question.

"I know it can be dangerous," Harry said.

Jane blinked, snapping out of whatever had taken hold of her for an instant. "It can be, which is why I'm going to help you any way I can." She pointed to his messenger bag. "Starting with figuring out what those two documents say." She nodded to the table in front of them. "Do you mind if we look at them here? The books in this room may help our review."

Harry opened the bag and laid out the two documents. "This is the account of Aristotle's visit to study the Druids, and here is Nero's letter."

"May I touch them?" Harry gestured for her to have at it. "Their condition is fantastic," she said as she carefully picked up the Aristotle text. "Where did you say you acquired these?"

"From a collector."

Jane didn't push it. "I could study these for days, but we don't have that luxury right now." She leaned over the pamphlet written by one of Aristotle's scribes. "Aristotle traversed Europe to study Celtic myths. According to this, the Keltoi myth caught his eye. Today we call this god Dagda. He appears as a robust man with control over life and death, weather, and even time. Dagda carries a staff, which is interesting given Aristotle claims the Celts used Dagda's broken staff to commune with the sun god Helios. It fits."

"That's what drew me in too," Harry said. "A staff channeling *fiery strength,* which terrified Aristotle. A man of science and logic, not superstition. His fear gives credence to it being more than a myth."

"It's possible," Jane said. "But this account is thousands of years old. We're talking about a story that may have changed entirely since it was first written."

"Or it could be identical to it."

"It could. What we need is another source to verify the content."

"Lucky for you I'm here," Harry said. "And I brought another letter with me."

"A letter written by a Roman emperor. You've done this before," Jane said. Harry didn't take the bait. "We need specifics."

"Nero says one of his generals took the weapon after Boudica's defeat and hid it where no one would find it," Harry said.

Jane held up a hand. "We'll get to that."

Sara crossed her legs and leaned over. Her hair lifted as a breeze filtered through an open window. "The Aristotle text has precious little information to verify. The geographical references are consistent with what Aristotle would have seen at that time, and the tribes inhabiting those lands are ones mentioned, but the important part reads more like a warning than the facts we need: forbidden knowledge, Zeus's lightning and a broken staff."

"Aristotle wasn't known for hyperbole," Jane said. "He wrote about astronomy, biology, and philosophy. This isn't Homer we're talking about, with Achilles or the Trojan War. Also, you have to consider that to Aristotle, advanced though he was, some of this could have seemed like magic."

"Any sufficiently advanced technology is indistinguishable from magic," Harry said, quoting Arthur C. Clarke.

Jane turned to Sara. "You were right. He's an interesting man."

Sara glared at Jane, who kept talking. "Two thousand years later, it's hard to know what Aristotle thought or saw. Aristotle met Druids, the same people who three hundred years later formed a peasant army and nearly defeated Nero. *That* makes me believe there's more to this story." She paused. "I might know where to find the truth."

"Where?" Sara and Harry asked together.

"In Nero's letter. History verifies Boudica's victories in two supposedly un-winnable battles. The first could be chalked up to a surprise attack, the second to Rome's overconfidence. But when Nero faced Boudica, even though he was outnumbered ten to one, it wasn't a mismatch in favor of the Celts. Despite their superior numbers, it's no surprise the Celts were slaughtered. Their raw troops were no match for the Romans. Those legions ran riot over the known world. The odds were worse than when a handful of angry farmers started shooting the British in Lexington and Concord."

Nobody had to remind her how that had turned out.

"What did you see in Nero's letter that we missed?" Sara asked.

"Nothing, but let's look at what Nero said regarding the two prior battles. One survivor from each battle told Nero about the battles, and how were survivors described? They were said to be *charred*."

Harry rubbed his chin. "Charred as in burned would line up with how both Aristotle and Nero describe the terrifying power at play here. Aristotle talks about the sun god Helios, and Nero mentions Sol – the Roman sun god."

"It's all tied to the sun's power," Sara said.

"The overlap gives credence to the idea there's *something* to find here," Jane said. "Nero's next words may tell us *where*."

Jane reached onto a lower level of the drinks cart and removed a book Harry hadn't seen. "Nero routed Boudica despite her superior numbers. The mere mention of his doubts about the outcome tells me he came close to losing. Doubt and fear weren't in his vocabulary."

"What part gives you an idea of where to look?" Harry asked. "I can see Nero is afraid of what Boudica had. I can't see where he gives a direction we can actually use."

"Yes," Jane said. "Whatever Nero witnessed was more than powerful. It frightened him. Just like when Aristotle mentions a *terrifying, fiery strength*."

Jane indicated another line in Nero's message. *"The pagan Queen's magic was taken far from that field by General Quintus, to a place I know not. Quintus traveled to the tin isle to dispose of this monstrous weapon.'"*

"A helpful line if those are actual directions," Sara said. "The *tin isle* he references could be anything – there are thousands of islands in Great Britain. Even if you narrow the list down to those within a few days' ride from the battle – a site never positively identified – there are still hundreds of possibilities."

Jane tapped the book she'd retrieved. "This atlas illustrates the various incarnations of Great Britain from before Boudica's time through today."

A bookmark stuck out from the pages. Jane continued speaking as she opened to it. "When Nero fought Boudica, Britannia was a part of the Roman Empire, a commercial hub providing the raw materials to sustain the Roman economy. That included a great number of mines that produced the metals Rome needed to equip soldiers, shoe horses, mint coins – and pay for all of it."

"Copper, iron, gold, silver and lead," Harry said. "Salt. And tin."

"Yes, including tin," Jane said. "It was mined in only a few parts of Britannia – almost exclusively in its southernmost areas."

"That's not far from where Boudica's army was defeated," Harry said.

"Yes, though even if we narrow it down, there's no way to know which specific island he means." She frowned. "And Nero could be referring to Britannia as a whole."

"Valid points," Jane said. "It *could* be a feint to mislead anyone searching for the source of her magic. Another possibility is he's telling the truth and there's a specific island tied to tin production Nero's talking about, and that I've figured it out."

"Where was the majority of British tin mined in Nero's time?" Harry asked.

"Hold that question," Jane said. "The Celts occupied Britannia for eight hundred years, beginning in seven hundred BC. We know large populations concentrated in the southern lands in Nero's time because archaeologists have discovered massive hoards of coins, which we use to pinpoint dates. Many of the Celts who made up Boudica's army would have come from this area."

"Why does that matter?" Sara asked. "Nero wrote this account, not Boudica."

"Nero would have taken prisoners and interrogated local villagers as he chased Boudica's army. Regions of the land were often named for the materials they produced." She took a breath. "One of those areas is an island that produced massive amounts of tin. So much that they referred to it as the *tin isle*."

Harry nearly jumped out of his seat. "Would Nero have known about this?"

Jane said he would have.

"Where did you learn about this?" Sara asked.

"Partly from reading this atlas," Jane said. "And partly from studying Britannia's history during that era in all forms – the written word, visual media, and the most common way: shared oral traditions."

"You mean their stories," Sara said. "Told around the campfire."

"Passed from generation to generation," Jane said, nodding. "Stories were how Celts kept their ancestors alive, how they defined their cultural identity and shared it with their children. And those stories still exist today."

"Do any of them talk about a *tin isle?*" Harry asked.

The atlas lay open. Jane's finger hovered over an island on the southernmost tip of Britannia. "The *tin isle* that Celts sang about in Boudica's time is here. The Isle of Wight."

Sara had no response to that. Harry did. "Impressive." He flipped the book around to get a better look. "Assume you're right. Our best bet is to identify places that existed during Nero's time. If it's tied to Boudica or Nero, even better." He shook his head. "Wait. Nero wouldn't be dumb enough to send Quintus to hide Boudica's weapon somewhere people could find it."

Harry thought for a moment. What could still be around today that he could use as a beacon, a place to start? "What about the Celtic myths?" Harry asked. "That's another common thread from Aristotle to Nero. They each talk about the god Dagda a lot. Does anything on the Isle of Wight tie back to Dagda or the Celtic religion?"

Jane sat back in her chair, smiling. "You don't even need me to go along," she quipped. "That's the same thought I had." Her face grew serious again. "Unfortunately, I don't have an answer. What I can tell you is we need to go to the Isle of Wight, and we need to go before those men from Brooklyn make good on their threats and follow you here."

"We?" Sara asked. "I thought you were teaching this semester."

"The students won't complain if I cancel class for a few days." She shut the atlas. "Do you really expect me to sit by the phone waiting for a call while you two have all the fun?"

"We could use your expertise," Sara said.

Harry opened his mouth to tell Jane it could be dangerous; he was also tempted to tell her how he had really come to have these two relics. Jane looked at him. Harry closed his mouth. *Not yet.* "You're welcome to join us," he said. "Any trail out there won't be in plain English."

"I should hope not," Jane said. "Otherwise, the chances are someone would already have found it. The deeper it's buried, the better." She stood. "I'll pack my things."

Harry looked out of the window as Jane left. Sara remained behind. "Are you really okay with her coming?" she asked.

"No matter how smart we think we are, Jane knows more than both of us about British history." A tall red flower waved lazily back and forth outside the window. Was that a rose? It was. "Think about what happened to us at Persepolis. If you hadn't been in Megabyzus's tomb to decode those clues, I'd never have found the emerald tablet. It's about having the right people for the job."

"Good." Sara jumped up. "We agree." She squeezed his shoulder, then vanished as she went after Jane.

Harry finally got to study the library. This was the sort of place you could get lost in for *weeks.* What exactly did she have on these shelves besides incredibly useful atlases? The flitting red flower again grabbed his eye as he started snooping. A rose, planted outside the window, a brilliant dab of red in the middle of Jane's flowerbed. For Harry, it was an impossible-to-miss reminder of a certain older woman in New York. Rose Leroux, the city's most formidable fence, who had moved most of his father's finds over the years. A woman Harry trusted and who had offered to look into his mother's death using her contacts in the police force. Rose had more connections than even Vincent Morello. It had only made sense for Harry to ask both of them to look into what had happened to his mother all those years ago. A story his father had never shared.

Harry walked down the hall and out the front door, a rare English sun warming his face as he fired off an email to Rose. He didn't tell her where he was. He did ask her for an update on her research into his mother's death. Harry hadn't followed up with her before this for several reasons. One, Vincent was looking into it for him too. Two, he didn't want to rush her. The fact was he still had a job to do for Vincent. And perhaps another reason, one he wouldn't admit at first: he might learn something he didn't want to know.

His phone buzzed. A reply from Rose. Harry's thumb wavered over the phone. He'd promised himself this could wait. The universe intervened as a call came in. Harry squinted at the name in disbelief. Charles was calling him. Which was impossible, because Charles was in prison.

Charles, from whom Harry had stolen two artifacts and who had sent three men to Harry's home with a warning. Except Charles couldn't know for certain Harry even *had* those documents.

Harry rolled the dice. "Hello?"

"Harry." Charles's languid New Orleans drawl filled Harry's ear. "I am so glad you took my call. I'm afraid you have a problem."

Chapter 11

Port of New Jersey

Locations exist inside national borders that, by a unique trick of the law, do not exist when it comes to certain taxes. Owing to the financial wizardry – or chicanery – of enterprising tax experts, items in such facilities are not subject to import duties or formal customs entry procedures. Created with the intent of making the country more appealing for international trade partners, such locations also appeal to businessmen who take a dim view of regulations such as taxation, border inspection, or the legal system in general. Unsurprisingly, nearly all of these locations are near international ports of entry.

It is because of these loopholes that one moment Pete Brody was walking through a chaotic shipping yard in the Port of New Jersey, and a moment later he was on international ground. He stepped into a small warehouse that looked like a dozen others surrounding it, yet this warehouse was unique. In this building, imported merchandise was taxed only when it left the facility, not upon entry. Of course, a customs officer had to be aware an item had left in order to impose taxes on it. That didn't always happen.

Such murky international facilities attracted citizens from around the globe, and they paid well for their privacy. Some of these same citizens also had the resources to pay million-dollar cash bails to get out of jail – perhaps with a little help from their friends.

Charles was such a citizen.

Pete Brody stopped inside the warehouse door. He'd never met the man Pete had promised a small fortune if he could acquire two particular artifacts. The man's name was Charles. A few generations ago, people might have called him a dandy. Charles didn't exactly fit the image Pete had of an international smuggler.

Charles offered a hand laden with diamonds that sparkled in the well-lit warehouse. "It's a pleasure to meet you," he said. No full names, of course. Charles looked over Pete's shoulder to the drawn face of Stan Cobb. "Both of you. I appreciate what you did. My liquidity isn't what it used to be. Temporarily, of course."

Pete took the proffered hand. "Nice to meet you, Charles." He stepped back and surveyed the room, his eyes lingering on the two beefy men standing back, leaning against a wall. "This is a clean warehouse. Do you polish the floor?"

The place was immaculate. Wood and metal containers of all shapes and sizes lined the walls. One nearby container no larger than a jewelry box sported a retinal-scan lock. Directly beside it, a rectangular object with a tarp draped over it leaned against the wall. Pete nodded toward the little box. "Neat lock."

"You asked to see me today," Charles said. "And I owe you an apology."

"You had the artifacts we paid you to locate?" Pete asked.

"I did," Charles said. "But now I do not. You can thank the local authorities for that."

"What happened?"

Charles detailed how, not long after he'd "located" Pete's relics, the District Attorney's Anti-Trafficking unit had smashed down the doors of his warehouse and seized everything. "I'm happy they didn't come to this facility," Charles said. "That would have been a total disaster."

"As opposed to just losing my artifacts."

"Forgive me. I'm truly sorry for what happened."

"What *did* happen to my artifacts, Charles? Where are they now? I'm not clear on that part."

The two beefy men behind Charles stood straighter. "I wish I knew," Charles said. "I was in the process of conducting business when the cops showed up. Next thing I know I'm in jail."

"How do you know my items are missing?"

"My lawyer demanded an inventory of the warehouse. The police provided it, and your two pieces are missing."

"Was anything else missing?"

"That's the confusing part. Every other piece is accounted for."

Years spent sitting first in front of a pulpit and then behind one had given Pete incredible control over what emotions he showed the world. And more importantly, the ones he didn't. "You think the police stole my artifacts?" he asked with surprising calm.

"I doubt it," Charles said. "They wouldn't know what they were stealing. Any corrupt cop would have had little time, and there were much shinier jewels to take if they were of a mind."

"It's unlikely the police stole them. You have no reason to withhold either document." Pete's words hung in the air for a moment. "Unless you intend to sell them again for another fee. You're not doing that, are you?"

The two brutes were definitely paying attention now. Charles put his hand out, staying them. "Come now." Charles spread his arms out. "Look around you. I acquire objects. I do not keep them. Cash is my beloved artifact." A hint of steel underscored his next words. "I will ask you never to accuse me of stealing from you again."

Pete nodded. "Had to ask, Charles." Now Pete tapped his chin, a slight frown on his lips. "You mentioned you were handling some business when the doors burst open?" Charles said he was. "What sort of business?"

Charles went still. Just for an instant. "I respect every client's privacy," he said. "Yours included."

Interesting. "Which I appreciate. Could this business have had a connection to the police showing up and my items going missing?"

Charles swallowed. "I couldn't say."

"Charles." Pete stepped closer. "I bailed you out, remember?"

Charles may have been smiling, but there was something else in his expression Pete hadn't yet seen. *Fear.* Pete leaned closer to catch Charles's reply.

"Trust me, you don't want to know who was here. I'll give you the money back. Even the retainer, along with my apologies. But take my advice and let this go. There are other artifacts for you out there."

Pete spoke low so only Charles could hear it. "True, but I want *my* artifacts."

Pete knew those artifacts represented the turning point, the chance he'd been waiting for his entire life. He'd been lied to by the man he trusted most – his father. A man who had turned out to have nothing but false promises and empty truths.

"Take your money back and forget those two papers." A vein on Charles's neck bulged out. "Go after them and you won't live long."

Pete put a hand on the man's shoulder. "Tell me who you were conducting business with. That's the person who can help me find my artifacts."

Charles barely moved his lips in response, the words so soft Pete nearly missed them. "I'm trying to warn you. I'd say I'd kill you myself if you tell anyone that I gave you this name, but I won't have to. You're already going to be dead." Charles whispered a name, then stepped back and spoke loud enough for all to hear. "It's unfortunate about your artifacts. I'll have my banker refund your deposit." He clapped Pete on the back, then turned him toward the exit door. "I hope we can do business again."

The two hulking guards took the cue, coming up close behind Charles in case Pete didn't get the message. Pete offered his hand. He didn't want any trouble. He had what he'd come for. "Hard luck with the police, Charles. Take care."

Pete and Stan walked out into a waiting car. "Back to the helicopter," Pete told the driver.

By the time they pulled to a stop in front of the rented chopper, Pete had a plan in place. He waited until the rotors powered up before telling Stan about it through the aviation headset, using a channel the pilots couldn't hear.

"Find out everything you can about this man." Pete handed Stan a slip of paper on which he'd scrawled the name Charles had whispered to him. "Whoever this guy is, Charles was afraid of him."

"Understood. And when I locate him?"

"We'll send a man to tail him until I can get to him. Use our network. Pay whatever it costs. These artifacts are worth it."

Long ago, Pete had realized you were better off with allies, not enemies. Most religions didn't get along, even with people who basically thought the same as they did, and in the end everyone lost. That's why Pete had tried to unify the factions of practicing Druids around the world. They might not have the same doctrines, but they could stand together for what mattered.

His efforts over the years had led to the creation of an interwoven network spanning six continents, devout men and women dedicated to spreading Druidic beliefs. Pete's circle included everyone from new followers to leaders with massive followings. A diverse group of like-minded Druids dedicated to the common good as they saw it.

However, Pete's network ran even deeper than that. He had cultivated a select group of Druids willing to take whatever steps were needed to ensure the success of their global goal. Now Pete needed their help. Once Stan located the man in their sights, Pete would leverage his group of believers to help find the man. The druids who followed Pete came from all walks of life, including a number of people with the technological skills to locate practically anyone on the planet. Give them a single piece of information, and within hours they'd tell Pete where to find who he needed. After that, he would take charge of getting his artifacts back. Also, and he didn't say this out loud, Pete wanted to meet the person who could make a man like Charles so afraid for his life. A fear Pete didn't share because his path was righteous. He couldn't fail.

###

Stan started making calls when they touched down, putting the tech geniuses who followed Pete into action. Twenty-four hours after Pete and Stan landed back in Bethlehem, they had not only a name, but a destination.

Pete was exercising when Stan came to him with the news.

"Harry Fox is protected by the mob. Specifically, the Morello family, headed by Vincent Morello, the acknowledged leader of the mafia in New York."

Even Pete had heard stories of Vincent Morello. No wonder Charles wanted nothing to do with Harry Fox.

"We just want to talk with the man," Pete said. "Maybe Harry Fox saw those documents and can help us figure out where they are now. Maybe he took them. Either way, we'll deal with it."

"Vincent Morello convinced five warring crime families to work with each other, under his control. He started out working with Carlo Gambino – the head of the family who gave the world John Gotti."

Pete stood from the bench. "If I didn't know better, I'd say you were trying to frighten me away."

"I provide information," Stan said. "It is your decision whether to act on it."

Pete shook his head. "There's no alternative. We need those artifacts. They're *ours*. Harry Fox is our only lead. That he can scare a man like Charles doesn't bother me. We just need to be smart about it. You said Harry is in England."

"We have a man tailing him," Stan said. "One of our members who is in private security. A former British Army Special Air Serviceman."

"An SAS man? Well done, Stan."

"His instructions are only to follow Harry Fox." Stan paused. "Though it may be wiser to have our SAS man handle the questioning."

"This is my search." Pete walked out of the gym, rubbing his neck with a towel. Only when they were in his office and Stan had closed the door did Pete go on. "I'll find those artifacts because the most impactful way for this to happen is I do it. Understood?"

"Yes. I also understand the mob does not follow rules. No one can guarantee your safety if Harry Fox realizes you're chasing him."

"I survived a childhood living with a despot. I can handle a mob lackey."

Stan opened his mouth to speak, hesitated, then closed it again.

"Listen to me," Pete said. "Either you are in, or you're not, and that means you're working for someone else. I need your full support. Do I have it?"

No hesitation this time. "You do."

"Good man. Get our SAS friend on the phone. I'm going to England."

Chapter 12

London

Harry stood outside of Jane's suburban château, phone pressed to his ear, feeling as though the ground had shaken beneath his feet. Something about what Charles said had set him on edge. "What do you mean, a problem?"

"Listen, Harry. I'm doing you a favor."

"I'm listening."

"A man came to me today asking about two specific pieces that are missing from my inventory. A pair of documents tied to Aristotle and to Nero. This man had retained me to acquire them."

"Sounds like high-quality inventory."

"I located both of them. And now they're missing."

"How did that happen?"

"During the raid," Charles said.

Harry knew Charles might be baiting him. Otherwise, why not cut to it? He'd already sent men to Harry's doorstep. Fine; he would play along for now. "Do you think a cop stole them?"

"I doubt it," Charles said. "Those chumps aren't smart enough to realize what I had. Those documents were far from my most attractive pieces."

"Then why take them?"

"Good question. Maybe one of the cops has it in for my client. Or they could have just been destroyed during the raid."

No accusations yet. "Who's your client?"

"You know I can't say, Harry. That's why people do business with me."

"You say a guy comes asking about me and you won't tell me who it is? Some people might say that's a threat."

"I'd never threaten you, Harry. You know why."

He did. A threat to Harry was a threat to Vincent Morello. Which no smart person did. "Is this guy connected?" Harry asked. "At least tell me that."

Charles actually laughed. "Not like you mean. His connection is to a higher power."

Who the hell was higher up the food chain than Vincent? Nobody on the East Coast. And who would care about two ancient documents badly enough to start a war with the Morello family? Nobody Harry knew.

"Enough, Charles. I talked to your three men. They came to my place."

"My men? I never sent anyone to your place. I want to stay healthy for a long time."

"Three men came to my place asking about documents I supposedly stole. I bought a necklace from you, Charles. I didn't steal anything."

"I have no idea what you're talking about." Charles sounded genuinely frightened now. "I never sent anyone to your place. Did they say it was about my warehouse? Specifically, *my* warehouse?"

Harry replayed the scene in his head. "They said they had a message from the owner. Which would be you."

"No," Charles said. "I was retained to acquire the documents. I was only the owner until my client paid me. *He's* the owner."

"This person you won't tell me about."

"I've already said too much. If word gets out that I'm talking about my clients, even to you, I'm through."

Harry connected the dots. "You gave him my name. That's why you're warning me. You already sold me out."

Now Charles sounded desperate. "Don't accuse me," he said. "I'd never sell anyone out."

"Save it," Harry said. "Tell me who the guy is. If he's as connected as you say, maybe he can save you from Vincent." A lie, but a terrifying one. Harry wasn't ratting Charles out. He was better than that, even if Charles wasn't.

"I didn't sell you out." Charles was shouting now. "Vincent would kill me." He took a breath. "I'm warning you, as a favor. This guy is serious about getting those documents back, and he thinks you took them."

"Do *you* think I have them?"

"I don't care if you do. All I'm saying is watch your back."

A delivery truck rumbled past on the street, though Harry only spotted the distinctive dark blue van when it passed Jane's metal gates. He kicked at the ground as Charles kept talking.

"You already knew I thought you took the documents," Charles said flatly. "Why didn't you say anything when I called?"

"I wanted to see if you were going to accuse me of stealing from you," Harry said. "Good thing you're not. I'm not calling Vincent. I can watch out for myself." A door opened behind him, and Harry turned to find Jane standing on the porch. He held up a finger. *One second.* "Though it will be a lot easier if you tell me who to watch for."

"Look for the most dangerous kind of man," Charles said. "A true believer." With those cryptic words, he clicked off.

Harry looked at the phone. A true believer? Gangsters only believed in money and family. Whoever he was, this guy had serious pull if Charles was afraid of him. Harry made a mental note to ask Joey if any other families had a beef with the Morellos.

"That's beautiful."

Harry spun, nearly losing his balance. Jane had come to stand beside him without Harry noting her approach. He realized his hand had moved to the amulet around his neck.

"What is it?" she asked.

Sara was nowhere to be found as Harry slipped the amulet back beneath his shirt. "An heirloom," he said. Damn his habit of touching the thing when his mind wandered. "It was my father's."

"I've never seen anything quite like it."

Harry hesitated a bit longer before he lifted the piece from beneath his shirt. The light caught it just right; its golden fire roared to life. He did not slip it over his head. "I really don't know that much about it. The only thing I'm sure of is it meant something to my dad."

"I can see why." Jane leaned close. Harry caught the faint scent of jasmine. "Has Sara seen this? She may be able to help identify what it is."

"I have." Sara had walked out and overhead the last bit. "And I will, but that is for another time."

Harry slipped the amulet back out of sight. He didn't want to get into the story of his father's amulet right now. An image popped into his head of the unopened envelope waiting back in Brooklyn. Whatever Vincent had found would wait. The same went for anything Rose might send him. What had Fred Fox so often told Harry when they were in the field? *Focus on the problem in front of you. Do that, and maybe you'll live to figure out the next one.*

"Where's your car?" Jane asked. Sara pointed to the Volkswagen. Jane frowned. "You can't take that unreliable German machine to Wight. What if we have to go through a puddle?"

"Very funny," Sara said. "You have a better option?"

"Yes." Jane pointed behind them. "Take my car."

A light gray Range Rover was parked further down the driveway. Harry immediately turned to Sara. "It's not black."

"It's not," Sara said. "I wouldn't drive it if it were."

Jane eyed them both with suspicion. "What's wrong with black cars?"

"Bad memories," Sara said.

"Very bad," Harry added.

Jane shook her head. "If you say so."

"I'll get our luggage into your car," Harry said. "I can sit in the back."

"No need," Jane said. "I'll take the other one."

Harry looked at the car, back to Jane, then to the postcard-perfect house behind her. Of course Jane had two Range Rovers.

Sara marched to the vehicle. "I'm driving."

Harry didn't argue. Jane went inside to grab her kit and the keys to her birthright Range Rover, leaving Harry to get his bag from the rental car. His phone vibrated as he tossed it into the rear hold. Tony Cervelli had texted – he was about to leave Brooklyn for London and needed to know where to go after landing. Harry told Tony to head directly for the Isle of Wight, though his thumb hovered over the green *SEND* button. It could have been decades of his father warning him to be careful, or the countless times Vincent had told him to be careful who he trusted. Not that Harry thought Tony Cervelli would sell him out. A Morello man didn't do that. No, it was something else, a newfound wariness. It came from how Nora had been betrayed by her colleagues in Iran.

Harry deleted his message and keyed in a new one. *Call when you land. You'll need a car.* He fired it off, wondering how it had come to pass that he didn't entirely trust a man who had sworn loyalty to Vincent Morello. The world was changing, he told himself, and if you didn't see that, it could get you killed.

As they set off, the second gray Range Rover barreled around the bend in the driveway, nearly clipping their mirror as Jane raced through her estate's gate and onto the road. Sara gripped the wheel. "Hold on."

Rubber chirped on asphalt, Jane's moneyed home grew small in the rear window, and Harry couldn't help but smirk. With these two women on his side, the Celtic mysteries around Queen Boudica stood no chance.

Chapter 13

Brooklyn

A miracle was underway in Brooklyn. Honking horns and hanging exhaust fumes had been replaced by cheerful organ music and the sweet scent of cotton candy. Street sweepers had cleared the refuse and tow trucks had moved the most recalcitrant vehicles, a team of city employees transforming this four-block stretch of the borough into a blank canvas. Moments after they completed their task, the carnival descended.

Brightly colored tents sprouted overnight. An entire block filled with food vendors hawking all manner of overpriced heart attacks, while the next blocks offered games of skill or chance, flashing lights and caffeinated barkers vying for attention in front of their over-stuffed toy animals, the biggest of them dingy from years of never having been won. Children squealed as they pulled their parents along behind them, entranced by the magic. The local green park had been overrun by small-scale rides that promised a brief, terror-filled experience for anyone willing to risk their life on the mechanical skills of carnies.

Stefan Rudovic briefly considered abandoning his journey. Where had all this come from? He'd left his apartment to put the next part of his plan in motion, and had actually been looking forward to the short walk he'd take on the way. Crisp night air had been appealing, a change of scenery, perhaps a soda from the corner bodega. Stefan wanted a quiet walk. Not this mess.

A nearby screeching child made the hair rise on his neck. He lived alone for a number of reasons, one of which was so he never had to worry about another person bellowing in his face. Stefan half-turned, and then the thought of his empty apartment forced him to turn back around again. Perhaps they had a fresh lemonade stand. Stefan soldiered on, sliding past adults and around running children with the quickness of a man who'd spent his entire life one step from the streets. His gaze passed over a woman with hair so dark it gleamed under the lights. A boy stood beside her, doing his best to eat an entire slice of pizza in one bite. The woman touched the boy's arm, and as Stefan walked past, he heard what she said to him. *"Njeriu im I vogel."*

Stefan nearly tripped. She was speaking Albanian, the language of his homeland, using words he couldn't possibly forget. *My little man.*

That was what his mother used to call him. Stefan went still, the flashing lights and droning generators forgotten as a memory drew him back to being a young man high in the air, looking down on the sprawl of a city too big to comprehend. Stefan's first plane ride. Nose pressed to the plane window, he had watched New York City come into view. He hadn't understood what the Kosovo War was or why he'd been forced from his home. All Stefan knew was that New York was a place where his mother promised they would start over.

Her fingers had rested on his shoulder as she leaned close, her voice carrying over the rumbling engines. *"Ne jemi ketu, njeriu im I vogel."*

We are here, my little man.

Scarcely a year later his mother had abandoned Stefan, leaving him in the care of a woman he barely knew, an immigrant like them. The old woman had looked after him, somehow keeping them both going even though she never worked.

Stefan pushed the memories back into the box where they belonged. His chance was at hand, an opportunity to redeem himself to Altin Cana and change his future. Altin was the only person whose opinion he cared about now. Head down, he passed a teenage boy standing on the sidewalk, a small table in front of him. An impressive selection of purses was on display. The teen called out to Stefan as he passed.

"Hey, mister. Wanna buy your lady somethin' nice?"

Stefan pressed on, though he had to admit the teen had his attention. Hustling for a living, a kid trying to make a buck in a tough world – just like Stefan had done when he'd latched on to Altin Cana's crew as a teen. His first gig for Altin was selling stolen merchandise on the streets. Make a couple bucks, give most of them to Altin, pocket what was left. Heady stuff for a Balkan kid with few friends and fewer options in life.

A neon yellow and green sign caught his eye. Lemonade for sale, fresh-squeezed and a steal at only nine bucks a cup. Stefan plunked down the extortionate fee and took a barrel-sized vat of the concoction. What came through the bendable straw would probably rot a few of his teeth, but by God, it was delicious. He took another long pull as he continued walking and ran through the plan in his head once more, looking for weaknesses, poking holes in the logic. Months spent laying the groundwork would either pay off or fail spectacularly. He hadn't gone through all of this trouble, compromising people and luring others into doing his bidding, only to see it fail. This had to work.

The black-haired mother and her child appeared in front of him, walking his way. Stefan watched as they passed the teen hawking purses on the corner, close enough to hear the kid rehash his pitch.

"A beautiful lady needs a nice purse." The teen held one up. "How about it? Half off, just for you."

The woman pulled her child in close, as though the entrepreneurial teen was contagious. "Get away from me." Her sharp footsteps echoed like a hand slapping a mosquito. "Hoodlum."

The teen didn't bother to reply, already having moved on to a more likely mark. Stefan stood still, watching the woman leave. Why was she so hostile towards the teen? Perhaps his parents had abandoned him, by choice or fate. Perhaps the kid had to help pay this month's rent, and one more purse bought his family another four weeks with a roof over their heads.

All around Stefan, people walked and ate and drank and ignored the teen. A young man who reminded Stefan a lot of himself not so long ago, a kid with one shot and no second chances.

Stefan turned and strode quickly back to the kid's table.

"Hey." The kid looked up at him, wary. Stefan pressed a hundred-dollar bill into his hand, then turned and walked away without a word. He didn't need to see the kid's reaction – it would be the same if someone had randomly handed him a hundred bucks at that age. Suspicion, then elation. Hopefully it kept the kid going for another day, week, however long it took for his fortunes to change.

The garish carnival lights were behind him when Stefan's phone buzzed. An update from Tony Cervelli. Stefan read the message twice. Harry Fox hadn't given Tony a final destination, instead telling him to rent a car when he landed in London, which meant the possible destinations included several more countries within driving distance of London.

Stefan fired off two text messages before slipping back into the light pedestrian traffic, most of which flowed against him as people made their way toward the carnival. The noise faded as Stefan neared his destination. A place that not long ago had teetered on the edge of ruin, but was now thriving and known as one of the local gems of Middle Eastern cuisine. Sanna, a restaurant Stefan had helped rescue from financial troubles brought on by the Morello and Cana families. A familiar hostess greeted him inside.

"I need to speak with Ahmed," he told her.

"I'll see if he is available," she said. "Would you like a seat at the bar while you wait?"

"He won't make me wait."

The hostess disappeared through the swinging kitchen doors. Stefan barely had time to take in a buzzing dining room and full bar before Ahmed appeared from inside the kitchen. He offered Stefan his hand.

"My friend, it is good to see you."

"Busy night?"

Ahmed surveyed the room proudly. "Lots of repeat customers these days. It's fantastic."

"Good to hear." He meant it, though not for the same reasons as Ahmed. "How are the two men I sent you doing?"

"Those two are hard workers." Ahmed tilted his head, indicating a man across the room. "There's Luka. The guy never stops working."

A barback was manhandling cases of beer behind the bar. He then moved into the kitchen at full speed lugging two full ice buckets.

"I appreciate you giving him a chance," Stefan said. "His life has been hard. Finding work was not easy for him."

Ahmed lifted a hand. "As long as he shows up on time and sober, I don't judge."

"And the other man I sent?"

"Raf? Same as Luka. Quiet too."

"I am glad to hear it," Stefan said. He glanced at his watch. "I want to place an order to go."

"Whatever you want. This will be my best year. Chances are it wouldn't have happened without you."

Stefan didn't need to tell Ahmed chance wasn't involved. Sanna would have closed if Stefan hadn't provided an infusion of cash to Ahmed several months ago. Forgiving that loan before Ahmed had barely made a payment hadn't hurt the bottom line either.

"I am happy to see you doing well," Stefan said. He refused the offer of a drink while he waited for his food. Standing not far from the hostess's stand, he felt Luka's eyes on him at one point. When he turned to meet them, Luka immediately looked down and went back to work. Luka and Raf were here for one reason: to work hard. That was all Stefan paid them to do. At least until he told them otherwise.

Stefan collected his food and headed outside, taking a different route home so he didn't have to pass through the carnival traffic. He pulled out his phone. The two text messages he'd sent earlier had been received, and now two men were heading for the airport, having purchased tickets on the same flight as Tony Cervelli. Stefan took a breath, a deep sense of satisfaction spreading in his chest. It wasn't that he didn't trust Tony. It was that Stefan couldn't leave anything to chance when it came time to finish his mission.

He had a contingency plan in place.

Chapter 14

Approaching the Isle of Wight

In just over two hours, Harry had traveled back in time sixty years. The journey should have taken closer to three hours, but Jane had proven as fond of the gas pedal as Sara was. The two women had led each other on a scenic chase to one of the southernmost British Isles. Cosmopolitan London was traded for towns along the southern tip of Britain, low-slung homes buttressing one another, interspersed with taller inns and public houses that had stood for centuries. All were a mix of dark timber and whitewashed stone fronted by narrow streets. Their destination was an island two miles south of the mainland, accessible by the high-speed ferry on which Harry and his companions now stood, the vessel churning water at an impressive rate.

Sara and Jane had remained in contact during their swift journey south, talking through possible next steps while giving Harry little chance to voice his thoughts. Though all signs pointed to the Isle of Wight as a starting point for their efforts, it was nearly one hundred fifty square miles, with over a hundred thousand inhabitants. For something to have remained hidden in Wight since Boudica's time seemed ludicrous. And both women were quick to remind him that chances were whatever Nero had ordered to be hidden here had to be small enough for one man to carry.

Harry turned to Jane, who leaned against the front of her Range Rover. "Why are you so sure we're on the right track with Brading?"

Brading, a town Harry had never heard of until an hour before when

Jane told them it existed. Jane said it was a road sign they had passed. The sign listed the upcoming towns on the Isle of Wight, and one of them had been Brading. Seeing that name was a breakthrough for Jane. "There are Roman ruins that still stand in Brading," Jane had explained. "The site dates to Nero's time and is located on the eastern edge of the coast."

"A port city makes sense," Sara said. "General Quintus would have known of the seaside town, and there would have been plenty of places to hide whatever it was Quintus needed to hide."

Harry, however, was not so quick to agree. His father had warned him of a deadly trait in the treasure-chasing business: overconfidence. As with carpentry, you should measure twice to cut once. Confirm your intelligence before jumping in. As much as you could, anyhow. "What else do you have?" he asked Jane.

"There's a church."

Harry made her go through it again now as they stood on the ferry. "What about a church in Brading makes you more certain?"

"I'm not *certain*. I'm optimistic. It's a place to start." Jane looked around, keeping her voice low. "This church dates from Roman times, and the ruins are well-preserved."

"You said these were ruins."

She tapped one finger on the Rover's hood. "Britain is filled with Roman ruins. The Isle of Wight, however, is not. Take Nero ordering General Quintus to the *tin isle* with the Roman ties of Brading, add the strategically vital seaside location, and we have a possibility."

Even Harry had to admit there was smoke here. Maybe not fire yet, but close. "Now tell me about the last part again," Harry said. "Mithras."

"Archaeologists uncovered artifacts tied to the Roman war god Mars," Jane said. "If General Quintus wanted to quickly find a place to hide Boudica's artifact, he'd likely head to a location where he could move about with impunity. A town where the locals followed Roman orders."

"A town with soldiers, men who prayed to Mars for their safety." Harry scratched his chin. "Quintus was a big deal in the army. No one would question him in a town like that."

"Which makes Brading a good choice to hide something," Jane said. "Nobody saw anything if Quintus told them not to look. It's a theory. Not perfect, but promising. It fits what we know." The ferry slowed. "A theory we can test soon enough."

Wight stood atop the sea in front of them. Private boats dotted the waters as the ferry slid into Cowes Harbor, docking alongside a long pier. Most passengers had driven aboard, and a steady stream of cars began to drive off the boat and onto Wight. Jane and Sara were still talking as Harry watched the cars go, scrutinizing the drivers one by one. The chances they had been followed were slim, but the *true believer* Charles mentioned had resources. Men with resources were to be dismissed at your peril.

Harry watched couples and a few families depart the ferry. Anyone with gray hair was dismissed out of hand: it was unlikely anyone would send their grandfather to follow them. A lone man with a cigarette between his lips several cars behind Harry's stood at the railing and looked out over the strait, having driven one of the last cars to board the ferry. He had scarcely looked Harry's way the entire trip, even when Harry had walked behind him en route to the café. No taller than Harry and slim of build, he seemed too average to be a hitman. That left one more person nearby. The only one who'd caught Harry's eye.

Thick forearms were crossed on his chest. Vividly red hair that Harry assumed had once been atop his head had migrated south, taking up residence on his face. The man looked like the kind of guy who sprouted a full beard when he sneezed. Not tall, but thick; a man whose ancestors had likely pillaged their way across Europe with axes and longships. If Harry were going to send a man after someone, he could do worse than sending that guy.

Harry slid into the Range Rover beside Sara and started the engine. "Remember that guy I pointed out to you earlier?"

"The one with the red beard?"

"I think he might be following us. Call Jane."

Sara didn't hesitate. Harry's instincts had saved them more than once in Iran. "Listen to me," Harry said into the speakerphone when Jane answered. "I think we're being followed. Just do what I say."

"I'm listening."

Harry laid out a plan as they drove off the ferry. "You got it?"

"I do," Jane said. "It's our turn to get off the boat. But I hope you're wrong about this."

Her taillights went dark, and her vehicle rolled onto the Isle with Sara at her rear. The red-bearded man was one car behind, with only the smoking man between them, piloting a small, dark sedan that looked like nearly every other car on the ship. Harry stared at a map on his phone as Sara eased off the ferry.

"Go right," he told Jane. "The first street you can take."

Jane turned right as Sara turned left, leaving red-beard with three options. Go straight and lose both Range Rovers, or commit to following one of them. The smoking man turned to follow Jane. *That's the way he'll go. He'll use that guy as cover and follow Jane.* Harry was so certain of it he repeated it out loud. A moment passed as red-beard paused at the intersection of three streets. As Sara drove up a slight rise and approached a turn that would take them out of sight, the man's car moved. To Harry's utter surprise, red-beard drove straight ahead.

Harry checked his map. "Circle around. He could be baiting us into thinking he's not following. He won't expect us to go right back at him."

Sara took a right. They drove toward where red-beard had gone, which meant they'd go directly past the man if he were feinting and had turned left after going straight. Now he wouldn't be able to do a one-eighty and turn around to follow Sara without making it obvious. Tourist shops and cafés passed mere feet away as they drove. When they reached the next intersection, they saw him.

Red-beard stood on the sidewalk, his thick arms wrapped around two small children. He lifted the kids as though they weighed nothing and leaned in to kiss a woman holding an infant. The tiny baby had hair that sparked like fire in the sunlight.

"Damn." That was all Harry could say.

Jane's voice filled the car. "What's happening?"

Sara didn't try very hard to keep the smirk off her lips. "Harry successfully identified a father coming home to his family."

"The guy with the beard?"

"A loving husband and father of three children," Sara said. "If he's after us, the biggest danger is his infant spitting up on your shirt."

Jane laughed long and hard. "All right, Harry. Let's get to Brading."

They passed through the town and headed for the Isle's interior, the road veering away from and then back toward the coastline, hard against the English Channel. The harbor and city of Cowes fell away behind them, leaving green and tan fields stretching to the water's edge, where the ground either sloped gently to meet the lapping waves or fell off a cliff. Occasional farmsteads dotted the land, some with small herds of livestock. For Harry, this was as far from home as it got. He was chasing artifacts, and he couldn't have been more excited.

"This was all Celtic land before the Romans arrived." Sara waved a hand across the sweeping vista.

"Well before Christ," Harry said. "That's a long time ago."

"Celts lived here since the Iron Age. Lush farmland, defensible coastline, natural resources for building and trade. They knew this was a special place."

Harry looked out the window. Good land to farm, plenty of food from the ground and sea, and the terrain was imposing for invaders.

"Once you consider all that the Celts were protecting," Sara said, "you start to understand why they were determined to stand up against the Roman army."

"Don't forget the force Dagda tossed down from the heavens to vaporize the Romans."

"The sentiment remains unchanged."

Tall grass waved outside of Harry's window as they drove through Wight's interior. He glanced in the mirror. Every car was some version of the same small hatchbacks or miniature sedans prevalent in Britain.

"Their passion is a feeling you should understand," Sara said.

"Because I'm a half-Pakistani guy living in Brooklyn?" Harry ground his teeth. "I'm an American, you know."

A herd of cattle grazed off to Sara's side. They veered to the east, heading toward the town where Jane hoped a Roman emperor had sent a relic that terrified him. At least a mile of asphalt hummed beneath their tires before Sara spoke again.

"I meant you should be familiar with it as an American. Your country stood up against the most powerful military in the world. You didn't have a chance, same as Boudica's army. Exactly the same, except those ragtag colonists won."

She spoke softly, yet her message hit like a sledgehammer blow. He was acting like a jerk, even playing the victim a bit. Harry cleared his throat, searching for the right words, and failed once more. "Oh."

She reached over and touched his forearm. "Living as a minority in America can't be easy. The reason I mention this is to give us a link to what the Celts felt, why they rallied behind Boudica and rose up against such odds. Yet, in the end, Nero feared the queen. We should do Boudica the courtesy of seeking to understand her." Her next words caught him by surprise. "Jane would really love to know more about it."

Harry blinked quickly. "About what?"

"Your amulet."

"What?" Only then did he realize he'd been touching it. Sara had offered an insightful take on what they needed to do. The only other person he'd known who could do that so well? His father. This amulet was a connection to Fred Fox. "We'll see." He slipped the amulet back under his shirt.

"You're right," he said, changing the subject. "About being American and understanding what Boudica was up against." He looked over at her. "You're also right about feeling like an outsider in your homeland. We can both be strangers in our towns."

"If we can understand how the Celts felt, what they were fighting to regain, we have a better chance of unraveling this mystery."

"Fear drove Nero to hide whatever Boudica had," Harry said. "The same sort of fear drove her to use it. Understanding their thinking brings us one step closer."

How it would matter, he had no idea.

Ringing filled the car. Sara connected the call. "Jane?"

"We're entering Brading," Jane said. "Now this gets interesting."

Something about the way she said it caught Harry's ear. "Why do I get the impression you've had some *interesting* times in the field before?"

"You're perceptive," Jane said. "I mentioned someone earlier. Parker Chase, an American. He was engaged to one of my best friends before she was murdered."

Sara's hand went to her mouth. "That's horrible. Why would anyone murder your friend?"

"I don't know the whole story. I met Parker through her, and since she died, I've consulted with Parker on several of his research trips. He's another one who often finds himself in interesting situations. The one story I'll share is that Parker and I were in Salzburg last year and found ourselves running from the police after we located a lost Gutenberg Bible."

"Did you say *Gutenberg* Bible?" Sara asked. "As in—"

"—the first book mass-produced on a printing press," Jane finished. "Yes. A story for another time. I want you to understand you can count on me."

"Remember to tell me that story later," Harry said.

"Will do," Jane said. "Now look alive. Brading is ahead."

The town appeared now, just a quick glimpse at first over the rolling road. Red-roofed buildings, clustered against each other, peeked over the hills before the town again dropped out of sight. Whitecaps dotted the English Channel beyond, though that was not what drew Harry's eye. He was more interested in the dark clouds that hung low over the town, heavy with the promise of rain.

Harry craned his neck to look up at the sky. "It's still blue above us. When did those dark clouds show up?"

Jane was still on the line, and she laughed. "Welcome to England, Harry. You know the saying. If you don't like the weather, wait a few minutes and it will change. You don't strike me as the type to let a bit of rain scare you off."

"I'd rather solve Boudica's mystery in the sun, if it's all the same."

"I packed proper gear for all of us. Now follow me and don't get lost."

Sara snapped on the Rover's headlights as the low-slung buildings surrounded them; the town was a throwback to midcentury in both architecture and feel. What was it with English country towns? All of them were gorgeous, and nearly all looked the same. At least to Harry's eye, which told him he probably had no idea what he was talking about and had better keep his mouth shut. They partially circled a roundabout before shooting off toward the coastline for several hundred yards. Just as Jane was about to run out of real estate, she veered north to wind along the coastline for a beat. One small inn and a roadside copse of weather-beaten trees later, Jane chirped her tires as she wheeled into a gravel parking lot.

Harry grunted. "This fits the bill." He peered through the gloom at the open ruins they'd arrived to inspect. "Hold on. Is that a *new* church?"

Sara leaned over the steering wheel as the first drops of rain plunked on their windshield. "It looks to be. And built right next to the ruins."

Jane hurried over to their car and opened Sara's door. "Put these on." She thrust a rain jacket at each of them, then handed each of them a flashlight. "This shouldn't be more than a light shower, but you never know. It could hang on for a bit."

Harry looked skyward as he slipped into the raincoat. *Light shower?* One of the bulbous clouds overhead looked like the Death Star. "You never mentioned this new church." He pointed at the falling-down structure to one side. "And this isn't Roman."

The building he indicated – or what remained of it – had been a large church constructed within the last sixty years or so. He knew it had been a church because the exterior walls that weren't collapsed had crosses etched into them, while a few windows still held dingy stained glass. The place now had no roof and two exterior walls had disappeared. Harry lifted a hand to shield his eyes against the rain, which now fell steadily. He noted a depression in the ground where there were no walls.

"I knew you were observant," Jane deadpanned. "No, this is not a Roman structure. It's British, dating to just before the Second World War. I suspect the Germans mistook this church for a depot of some sort and targeted it during bombing."

"The Germans blew this church up?"

"With great success," Jane said. "However, this loss did have one positive effect. Look here."

She marched through the steadily falling rain to the top of a well-preserved staircase leading down into the earth. A sign warned trespassers to stay back. Jane pointed ahead. "The church was built next to the ruins you saw coming up here. The church leaders either didn't realize or didn't care that centuries earlier another religion had considered this holy ground. If it weren't for the Germans flattening the new church, we never would have discovered the deep cellars underneath."

Scarcely one hundred yards from where the rear wall of the British church had once stood were the first signs of Roman ruins. It took Harry a second to comprehend what he was seeing. A network of basements had been carved into the rock beneath the ruins, most of it now exposed to the elements. "Are those Roman catacombs?" Harry asked.

"Good guess, but not quite. The Romans didn't bury their dead here." Jane pointed to the few remaining above-ground walls. "This was a supply outpost as well as a house of worship. Romans built atop natural caverns and added storage rooms. Before the German bombs fell and opened the foundation, we had no idea any of this was underground."

Water dropped from the hood shielding Sara's face as she spoke. "Which suggests this site as a likely spot for Quintus to have hidden the *monstrous weapon*. It is a secure location that the Romans controlled, with direct access to the sea."

Dark clouds scudded overhead as the rain held steady, the horizon holding nothing but the promise of continuing wet stuff.

"What makes you think General Quintus didn't just throw it into the English Channel?" Harry asked.

"A few things," said Jane. "Hope, first of all. It's possible Quintus destroyed the weapon, but we have to hope – and assume – he didn't. Quintus himself, second. He's a lifelong military man, not the sort to completely abandon such an extraordinary weapon. Also, Roman artifacts have been found here that are tied to Mars, the god of war. This is a warrior's place. All that makes me think Quintus hid the weapon rather than destroying it."

Harry admitted these were fair points. "What's next?"

"If we're lucky, there may be Celtic imagery or inscriptions to support our theory."

"Seems like a stretch," Harry said. "Though I've found treasure with the help of less promising trails."

"Good man," Jane said. "Now, let's start searching before we wash away, and for goodness' sake, you two, be careful."

Jane vaulted a waist-high fence fronting the ruins. A padlock on the swinging gate suggested this wasn't what the owners intended.

"Any chance local authorities are going to show up?" Harry asked as he followed suit. "We're trespassing."

"The site is closed because the ruins are unstable," Jane said. "They don't expect trespassers."

Great. Not just a deathtrap but a wet one. "Which part?" Harry asked.

"No idea." Jane sped up, that being the last word on the subject.

Harry motioned for Sara to go ahead. "You first."

"How chivalrous." She didn't laugh, shouldering him aside as she passed.

Climbing a small rise, Harry discovered the complex contained far more than one ruin. The structures covered roughly two acres of mostly flat land, ancient walls jutting from verdant ground like broken teeth. A half-dozen formerly imposing buildings covered the ground, most of them now reduced to a few walls amid piles of stones. Interior walls had held up better, but none of the ruins was more than one story high, all the roofs having long since fallen. The feature that caught Harry's eye in each of them was where parts of the original floors had fallen away to reveal lower levels. It was reminiscent of the Colosseum in Rome. Ruins of a building not fifty yards from cliffs had levels beneath the ground.

Jane shouted, her words lost in the worsening rain and wind.

"What?" Harry called as he ran to catch up.

"We need to split up." Jane pointed in either direction. "Sara, go that way. Harry, head over there. I'll start here and walk straight ahead."

"Look for anything tied to Nero, Quintus or the god Mars," Harry offered.

"Right. Come find me if you see anything interesting." Jane turned and continued walking along the broken ground.

Harry set off in the direction she'd indicated and seconds later wished he hadn't. What had seemed a good strategy quickly became a hazardous slog through slick grass and deep puddles. Half a dozen steps into his search, he slipped on a wet stone, hitting the ground with a *thud* that rattled his teeth. He ignored the laughter coming from Jane's direction.

"Need a hand?" she yelled.

He didn't dignify it with a response. Grumbling, he struggled soggily to his feet and continued walking toward the cliffs, the direction Jane had chosen for him. Of course she had. Send him toward an edge where, if you fell off, it was a hundred feet straight down. He pulled the jacket's hood tighter around his face and plunged into the first set of ruins, one of the few that still had its entire ground floor intact.

These floors had held up shockingly well. Small blades of grass or weeds poked through the stones, which had been worn smooth by centuries of foot traffic as well as later exposure to the elements. The building didn't have much beyond a front wall. Harry traced his finger over the Latin text carved into several of its stones. They were likely nothing more than ancient graffiti. *Lucius was here* or something along those lines.

Harry prodded, knocked on and, in more than one case, slid across entire sections with no luck. Walking was precarious, so it was with no small amount of caution that Harry moved on to the next structure, coming closer to the cliff. He glanced back at the road as a nondescript car drove past, moving slowly in the rain. Headlights washed across the site to momentarily blind him and he nearly slipped again. *Pay attention, dummy.* Even if he managed not to fall and slide off the edge, he could easily miss something important. If that happened, Sara might toss him over the edge herself.

The third building looked to be in better shape. This one had clear outlines of what had been a second level. Dark moss grew in the gaps where stones had shifted. He moved from wall to wall, finding more carvings on the side stones. He rubbed the moss and dirt away to reveal the message. *GLORIA EXERCITUS.*

"To the glory of the army," he read. The Roman army motto. He found no other writing on this level, so Harry skirted a gaping hole and stood in front of what had been a staircase to the lower level. Too bad all the stairs were gone. The thick cover of storm clouds above rendered it nearly impossible to see more than vague outlines below. He grabbed a rock and dropped it. *Splash.* Pooled water waited beneath him, the ripples giving off the faintest of light. He flicked his flashlight on, then aimed it down. Light reflected off the water's surface five feet below. He stood for a moment, debating whether to go down to investigate. Not the tallest of men, Harry figured he could still grab the lip of the first floor and haul himself back up as long as the water wasn't more than a foot or so deep. Much deeper and he'd be stuck down there – at best. He didn't want to consider what would happen if it was a long way to the bottom.

A loose chunk of stone about three feet long caught his eye. He hefted the stone and dropped it vertically into the murky depths. A geyser of water shot up. He could still see the tip of the stone breaking through the surface. Not too deep, though anything could be under the surface. Harry turned around, laid on his stomach, and slowly lowered himself into the water until his feet hit bottom.

The water came up to his thighs. He flicked his flashlight on again. This was a shallow cellar of some sort, one of what he guessed were several in the building. Perhaps cold storage for food. It had intact walls on all four sides, none of them more than ten feet away on any side of where he stood. No inscriptions adorned the walls. Deciding he was unable to get much wetter, he bent and ran a hand over the flagstones beneath his feet and felt nothing suggesting there was more to discover. This basement was just that: the bottom.

Hauling himself up and out, Harry checked two more holes in the first floor, getting nothing but dirty for his troubles. Both were the same type of shallow basement storage area, both empty of anything except for a bird that shrieked menacingly when Harry got too close. He hopped back up to the first-floor level, exiting through what was left of the front door and heading for the next building, pushing away any thoughts that all of this was futile. But still, two thousand years for Boudica's terrible weapon to have been moved, lost or destroyed, and Jane thought a few tenuous clues would point them to the correct place?

Stop it. He focused on the rain hitting his face, the faint strip of light at the horizon – maybe the storm was breaking – anything other than thinking this search would turn up nothing. *Come on, Harry. What would Fred say?* His father had told him time and again to control what he could, that this was a rough business where failures outnumbered successes. One thing you could control was your outlook. *Stay focused, stay positive.*

The next ruin was little more than a foundation, and there was no basement level. That left one more structure for Harry to check, this one thankfully farther from the cliffside. Unlike the others he'd checked, two-story pillars remained standing at the main entrance, the circular stone columns rising at least fifteen feet overhead. Remnants of a decorative arch remained between two pillars. Harry did not walk under it.

The rain lessened a tad as he inspected the pillars. No designs on the first one. He slid over to the second. Water ran down it, diverting into tiny rivulets because of what was carved into the stone. A majestic eagle was etched in profile, its broad wings lifting to take flight. The same eagle Roman legions used to carry into battle. An *aquila*. More than a symbol to Roman soldiers, this eagle embodied all they fought and died for – Rome's incomparable power.

His heart beat faster. Clearly a military tie, perhaps a place General Quintus would come to fulfill Nero's mission. One exterior wall rose to waist height across the building's front. Harry walked past it and stepped inside. The ground floor was a patchwork of holes, though the rear wall and two side walls stood high enough to show where the second floor would have been, along with frames for long-missing windows.

He skirted a hole down which a small waterfall streamed into the floor below. Harry examined each standing wall, vaulting onto the open window frames to check the highest reaches. Another pair of military-slogan inscriptions, but nothing remotely tied to the people or events he needed. If Quintus had been here, he hadn't left a marker. Wet, cold, and thoroughly ticked off, he turned to see Jane and Sara off in their own buildings, doing much the same as he was: failing.

That left the basement. He went to the nearest hole, watching the tiny waterfall plunging into the darkness below. Harry tilted his head.

Something was off here. He knelt by the hole and aimed his light into the depths to reveal not a pool of water, but stone floors. Impossible.

It had been raining steadily. Water flowed downhill. Every lower level he'd jumped into had been flooded. Except that hadn't happened here. Why not?

Harry grabbed the edge, wondered for an instant if this was the time he went down and didn't come back up, then lowered himself onto his stomach, swung his legs over the edge, and dropped. He landed, stumbled, righted himself, and then looked up in alarm. This basement was deeper than the others, and the ground floor above him was too far to reach. Jumping, he managed to get one hand on the ground floor edge, then the other. As long as the rain didn't get any worse, he should be able to pull himself out. Harry dropped back down. His light reflected off wet stone in every direction, but no pooled water. Darkness held the flashlight at bay, the basement walls far enough off that he couldn't see them. A step forward, his foot splashed, and he stopped and looked down. Here, the water rippled around his foot. No, not rippled. *Flowed.*

Water was draining out somewhere ahead of him, moving toward the cliffs, which made sense and also made his stomach clench. Could there be a hole up there waiting for him to tumble down, some kind of deadly waterslide taking him on a one-way journey into the English Channel?

What he should do, he knew, was go back and get Jane and Sara, get them down here to help, and then find out how this water was vanishing into a hole that shouldn't exist. Harry knew he should do that, just as he knew he'd never do it when he had a chance to figure this out *right now*. Harry followed the water flow. Ten halting steps later he found a wall. A giant stared back at him.

The Romans had carved a seven-foot-tall behemoth onto their basement wall. A soldier, he could see, but one unlike any Harry had ever seen, because what else would the Roman army carve onto a wall? The figure was clad in a flowing robe; a hood covered his head, though a bushy beard spilled out of it like a living thing, nearly touching the walking staff he carried. Did this depict some sort of demon? Perhaps it was a priest, a spiritual good-luck charm soldiers relied on when pagan hordes massed across a field and charged them in a frenzy, their war cries turning their guts to water and – *No. Pagans.*

Harry knew this image. It wasn't a Roman deity. This was Dagda, the Celtic god usually depicted carrying a staff. Harry stepped closer. *I'll be damned.* The staff had a crack in the middle, clear as day. A broken staff like the one described in Aristotle's text. The broken staff Celtic Druids used to channel a sun god's strength, whatever that was. Harry cocked his head, eyeing the figure. What else was he missing in this carving? The broken staff might only be the start. Heart thudding, Harry stepped closer. The floor gave way beneath him.

A thunderous crack filled the air and he went weightless for an instant as the floor caved in. His flashlight went flying as Harry threw himself backwards, away from the hole, scrambling to grab hold of anything so he didn't fall farther down, didn't disappear into a dark river that flowed out to sea. Feet scrambling, he caught a foothold and grabbed for his flashlight as it twisted round and round in the darkness, throwing light all around too fast for him to see anything. He snatched the thing, then aimed the light forward as he gulped dank air and looked to where he'd cracked the floor apart.

A massive stone at Dagda's feet had broken. It was smooth and level and had a fissure running down the center of it where Harry had inadvertently stepped. The stone placement seemed deliberate, as though it had been laid to draw attention to it. But why would the Romans put a stone that size on the floor when every other stone was much smaller? Romans were precise. It meant something, and now the thing had cracked in half. Time to find out why. Cool water was running past him, flowing toward the image of Dagda – which, like before, shouldn't have been happening. The room was a basement with four walls of solid earth. The water shouldn't be flowing – unless this basement had space beneath it.

His light revealed that the floor was merely wet, because the water had drained down into the broken stone. The massive stone beneath Dagda. So, it wasn't a solid floor stone. No, this big rock was a cover hiding an opening beneath it. An opening rainwater had been running through since the downpour began. It had been slowly draining the whole time. The stone must have had a crack in it that allowed water to seep through. When Harry trod on the weakened stone it had broken, allowing far more water to escape through the fissure, toward whatever the Romans had gone to such lengths to hide. The now broken stone covered an opening, one calling Harry's name.

One problem. He couldn't move that stone by himself. Chances were, he couldn't do it with help, either. Sara and Jane weren't that strong, and he was no power lifter. No, the way down wasn't to lift it out. That stone had to be broken apart. Harry turned, hauled himself back to ground level and looked around for his companions. Jane was closest, and he dashed over to her.

"We need your tools," he said, panting. "I found something." He brought her up to speed as they collected Sara, then grabbed the more destructive implements from Jane's Land Rover. She was nothing if not prepared. Crowbars, two pickaxes, even a sledgehammer.

"Are you certain the image is Dagda?" Sara asked as Harry handed her a pickax. "Celtic myths have no tie to the Roman military. They each had their own gods and legends. Why would the Romans carve Dagda?"

"It's him." Harry lifted the sledgehammer onto a shoulder. "The beard, the robes – it all could be coincidence if there was no staff. And not just any staff. A broken one."

Jane tossed a length of rope to him. "In case things get slippery," she said.

Harry looped it around his torso. "It's going to be soaked down there, whatever else it is." A car rolled past in the distance, dark and nondescript in the lessening gloom. Harry stood and watched it go. The driver never looked their way as he huddled over the steering wheel, eyes on the road. "At least it's not at the cliffs."

He led them back to the ruined building and over to the opening in the floor. "Down this hole."

Jane aimed her flashlight into the depths. "It's nearly dry," she said. "All the lower levels I saw are flooded." Sara told them hers were too.

"Same with mine," Harry said. "Except this one. I'll show you why." One of the women, he couldn't tell who, gasped as he lowered himself back into the murky hole. "It's not a long drop," he called up. "Grab my hand."

Sara kicked his hand aside as she lowered herself to the ground beside him. Jane accepted his offer with a smirk.

"You should know Sara better than that," she said. "Suggest she can't do something? Like a red cape for a bull."

"I'll thank you not to compare me to cattle." Sara knelt and put her finger in the water trickling past their feet. "This water is flowing. Do we think there's another basement beneath us?"

"Aim your light over there." He pointed into what now was only darkness.

Jane's light swung over to where he had indicated. It illuminated the bearded man carved into the far wall. "Look familiar?" Harry asked.

Jane's flashlight wavered. "That's impossible."

"It's Dagda."

"Celtic gods wouldn't be part of a Roman military installation."

"Yet here he is," Sara said. "Anything else on the wall?" She darted toward the carving before Harry could grab her.

"Wait!" he shouted, and lunged, missing her by a finger. Sara's foot slipped as she stumbled onto the broken stone.

Screams bounced off the walls as Sara dropped; the cracked stones thundered down after her. Harry went airborne, reaching out as Sara went down the hole. He grabbed her wrist, nearly lost her when he crashed to the ground and was pulled across the slick stones until he was peering over the edge with Sara dangling below him in the darkness. He scrabbled wildly at the floor, anything to stop him from following her into the hole as the force of her weight pulled him forward – remarkable, since she hardly weighed anything.

He blinked. Sara lay sprawled on the rubble below. He blinked again. She was not far below at all. "Are you okay?" he asked.

She didn't respond, her hand still latched firmly onto his. Harry pulled, stones shifted, and understanding dawned. "You landed on stairs."

She lifted herself upright as Harry gained his feet and hauled her back up to safety. Sara's breath came in ragged gasps as she fell into him. Her other hand latched onto his bicep for an instant, painfully tight, then she turned to look behind her.

"It's a set of stairs," Sara said, confirming what he had seen. "To another level beneath this one."

"Let's find out." He twisted Sara around. "Want to lead?"

"Not without looking first, you don't." Jane shouldered them both aside, her light playing over the newly enlarged hole. "There's no guarantee they're safe."

"The rock that fell didn't knock them down." Harry shrugged. "Looks sturdy enough to me."

Jane aimed her light back to the hole they'd come through. "The smart thing to do is wait until it's sunny and the water down there has drained away as much as it can. We could come back. Safer that way."

"There's no chance I'm doing that."

"Same here," Sara said.

"Good," Jane said. "We're in agreement. Now step aside."

They moved the fallen rocks aside and could see that the staircase was made not of wood, but stone. Stairs had been carved out of the bedrock below the basement level, and the three of them descended carefully to an open area ten feet high and nearly as wide.

"It's a cave," Harry said.

Rivulets of water flowed freely across the floor and down the walls. "It's not a cave," Jane said. "It's a tunnel…" said Sara.

"…that slopes downward," Harry said. "That's where the water has been going. Watch your step. Let's see where it leads."

"Stay close," Jane said.

Harry took one hesitant step, then another, Jane beside him and Sara right behind. A few yards ahead the tunnel turned sharply to the right and the ground's slope increased. Harry looked back to find the bottom of the staircase was nearly at eye level.

His foot skidded on the wet ground. "Hold on." Harry threw up an arm as they approached the turn. "Wait while I go first."

Jane's expression made it clear how she felt about that. "Only because there could be a pit ahead."

"A what?"

"I'm joking. Romans didn't build pits as traps."

"They also didn't build shrines to Celtic gods." Harry took a long step that brought him to the turn, then another step past it, then stared down the passageway in amazement.

Dagda looked back at him. Seven feet of empire-defying power lorded over the grotto hidden beneath this Roman military installation, a Celtic myth brought to life in exquisite detail. The stone carving of Dagda was meant to inspire awe, terror or devotion, depending on your beliefs. Or perhaps all three in one go.

"Come here and see this," Harry said.

Jane stepped carefully around him with Sara on her tail. The path opened as it turned into a grotto, wider and more open than the tunnel. In front of them now stood the carved Celtic god in all his fury. Dark pools where Dagda's eyes should have been reeled Harry in, while the unruly beard and thick torso spoke of a power not of this world. One massive hand gripped a gnarled staff, while the other was raised high, palm toward the congregants as though bestowing a blessing. The staff had a clear crack in the middle.

"A pagan shrine, right under their feet." Jane moved toward the statue, her hand out, but stopped just short of touching it. "No Roman soldier would have been foolish enough to carve something like this. It would have been impossible with a garrison stationed here. Carving this would have taken months."

"You're right," Harry said. "No soldier could have done this undetected."

"No," Sara said. "But a general could."

In this military town far from Rome, Quintus would have been the soldiers' Nero, the walking representation of their emperor. His word would have been above scrutiny. "The question is why?" Harry asked. "Assume Quintus built this. He was told to get rid of whatever Nero gave him. Why defy Nero and create a shrine to Dagda?"

Jane pointed to the open area in front of the statue. "Forget our assumption that Quintus believed in the Roman gods and therefore would never do this. This whole space was created for people to pay respect to Dagda, perhaps even to worship. This place would have held a decent-sized group of people."

There was, indeed, room for perhaps ten people to congregate in front of the statue. The floor was still rough, telling Harry this had not been a heavily trafficked area. This was a place of secrets. Homage to Dagda happened in this hidden, sacred space while Roman soldiers walked not twenty feet above. While Rome had officially tolerated all religions, protecting pagan worship in a military camp was risky at best, suicidal at worst.

Jane's flashlight zipped over the walls, stopping on Dagda. "Look. Behind the statue. Do you see it?"

Harry had not until Jane called it out. "Writing." He moved around the statue to find a square outline surrounding a block of text, roughly ten lines in total. Harry ran a finger over letters worn by water and time. "It's Latin. Romans definitely built this."

Sara stood beside him, her hands running over the letters as though they might vanish. "Celts like Boudica spoke Brittonic, not Latin."

"What does it say?" Harry asked. He could decipher the odd word or two, but Sara was the expert.

Sara's lips moved silently. A long minute passed. "It's odd," she finally said. "The first lines reference Boudica and Dagda. The final portion I don't understand. No mention of Nero."

"Maybe General Quintus disagreed with Nero's order," Harry said. "Getting rid of such a powerful object may have gone against all his instincts." Even as he spoke, the pieces started coming together, small clues leading to a larger idea. The grotto, this statue… "Quintus couldn't bring himself to destroy Dagda's staff. So he hid it."

"It doesn't say that," Sara said. She began reading the Latin inscription aloud.

The Roman legions are invincible, never knowing defeat. Victory honors the empire as it honors our god, the son of Jupiter. Mars, who protects us all. Mars, who traces his line to Ares, a Greek legend in the times before our gods were born.

Jane interrupted her. "Ares is the Greek god of war. He was Mars before there was a Mars."

"Borrowed, like all gods." Harry nudged Sara. "Keep going."

Dagda, a powerful being from the pagan lands, now stands alongside these powerful deities. His broken staff brought Rome's mighty legions low. Were it not for fate's hand, Rome would not stand. Dagda's power cannot be denied. Such power we praise, and keep it in our hearts and minds, hidden from mortal men who would misuse it. To destroy this power is to mock the gods of war.

We, the guardians of his power, cannot let it be. For the glory of Rome and the honor of Dagda, Mars and Ares, we hold fast. We look north to the true power, to the rodland rix, as we pray for strength in battle and honor in death.

Dripping water echoed in the grotto as Sara finished. She pointed at two specific words. "*Rodland rix.* Do you know what that is? I don't." She looked to Harry.

He shrugged. "Beats me."

"That's because it's not Latin," Jane said. "It's Brittonic. The language of Boudica."

"Is it a place?" Sara asked. "A holy town?"

"Not a town. Quintus is talking about a monument tied to burials."

"How do you know that?" Harry asked. "I've never heard this legend."

"The problem is you don't speak Brittonic," Jane said. "*Rodland* is referencing a specific monument, and *rix* describes the valley near the monument. The valley connection is important, because there are several monuments around."

"You're losing me."

"Quintus is telling us where to go."

"Why would he do that?"

"I think Quintus had to explain to the gods why he disobeyed Nero's orders. The terrible power that Nero feared and Quintus couldn't destroy was truly that. Terrible. So Quintus took it to a place no one would ever find it. *Rodland Rix* is a group of stones near Oxfordshire. It's a few hours' drive north of here."

"And it dates to Quintus's time?" Harry asked.

"It does. The stones are still standing. They're three monuments called the Rollright Stones." Jane took a step closer to them. "That's where we go next."

Chapter 15

Brooklyn

A ring of empty tables in Sanna was a rare sight during dinner rush. Except when Vincent Morello had a reservation. While diners filled the restaurant and waiters buzzed around the room, Vincent and Joey Morello had an oasis of quiet. An oasis with two tables of bodyguards nearby, but still. Even a month ago this wouldn't have been possible. A month ago, neither Morello nor Cana men came here, which meant nobody from the neighborhood did either.

Joey Morello understood. He didn't want his men starting fights, and neither did Vincent. It seemed Altin Cana wasn't spoiling for a fight, either.

Vincent swirled red wine in a long-stemmed glass. Joey had just finished telling him a story. "Ahmed has paid off his loan from the Cana man?"

"In full, about six weeks ago." A tanned brunette at the bar caught Joey's eye and smiled. He did the same, then turned away. Nothing came before business with his father. Even that gorgeous woman at the bar. "Then the Cana men stopped coming around the place. My guess is they didn't like having to pay for their food."

"Free meals are not good for business."

"Ahmed said the same thing without actually saying it. Now he's busy every night of the week. From what he told me, the hardest part is finding good help."

"I expect he will do quite well." Vincent touched the menu in front of him. "Are you ready?"

"Come on, Dad. You know I always get the same thing."

They ordered, and their waiter disappeared into the kitchen as another arrived to fill their drinks. Joey nodded his appreciation. "Thanks, Luka."

The server dipped his head and went off. Joey always made it a point to remember the name of a man bringing him drinks. Joey lifted his wine glass, moving it around to indicate the room. "What do you think of the place?"

"The food smells delicious," Vincent said. "I am glad you chose a new restaurant for us tonight. Food is meant to be enjoyed slowly, and with family."

Joey set his glass down, picked it back up, then smoothed the tablecloth. "What's on your mind, Dad?"

Lines of mirth appeared around Vincent's eyes. "Perhaps I wish to have a meal with my son, nothing more."

"Then I'm glad you invited me," Joey said. "But I know you better than that. Something's on your mind."

"You know me well. As did your mother, God rest her soul." Vincent crossed himself. "*Amore mio.*"

Joey nodded and waited. No one hurried Vincent Morello, not even his son. Besides, he liked sitting with his old man and chatting. Vincent rarely had the time to do it these days.

Vincent's back was to the wall, his eyes covering the room as he spoke. "When I was your age, a restaurant such as this would not have survived."

"The old crew had no interest in Mediterranean meatballs?"

"Heresy," Vincent said. "We must adapt. Those who resist will be lost in the rising tide."

"Wait until you try the baba ghanoush," Joey said. "It's so good you'll cheer for the Turkish soccer team."

"Heathens." Vincent crossed himself again. "There is only one football team – *gli Azzurri*. The Blues. Now and forever."

Joey winked. "To Italy."

Their food arrived, yet Joey knew better than to dig in. His father was the slowest eater on the planet. He meant it when he said food was to be enjoyed slowly. Which also meant it often got cold, but if that was the price of an evening with the old man, so be it. "I think diversity in the neighborhood can be a good thing. We can't just be Italians on one side and Albanians on the other, always fighting. Like you said, the world's changing. Lines are blurring."

"I have seen changes I could never imagine," Vincent said. "Families no longer at war, instead working together for a profitable future. Sixty years ago, I would have said such a thing was impossible. Now I am the one with his hand on the rudder, guiding the ship. The authorities would tear us down if they could, but do you know why we survive?"

Joey did. He did not say so.

"We work together." Vincent pointed at Joey for emphasis. "But always be wary of our partners. The other families do not tolerate me simply because of my strength. They accept my leadership because we all benefit, each of us profiting without spilling blood in the streets. It is a fragile peace, and when I am gone, it will take a strong man to maintain it. One who can anticipate the future."

Joey would have laughed if it weren't true. Talk about pressure. "You're not going anywhere for a long time," he said. "I pay your doctor for updates. He's not cheap."

"Perhaps." Vincent took a bite, chewing without haste. "Only one man knows when I will be called to St. Peter's gates. You must be ready. Our peace is built by force and kept by strength. You will need both."

"I learned from the best."

"The path I took will not work for you." He raised a hand. "Look at what our neighborhood has become. Ahmed opens a restaurant serving international cuisine. And it *succeeds*. Decades ago, this would never be. Now?" Vincent lifted a shoulder. "It is the way of the world. Pay attention, my son. Be cautious with who gets close. Protect everything we've built."

All of Joey's life had been spent at Vincent's knee, learning and getting ready for his place in this world. His mother's death years ago had only strengthened the bond between the Morello men. In truth, Joey had no idea if his mother had even *wanted* him to take over for Vincent. He assumed so, but Vincent never had said as much, and there was no way in the world Joey would ask.

"I can't trust only Italians," Joey said.

Vincent's face was a blank mask. "It is wiser to put faith in those who are most like you. They understand your history. There are requirements to being part of our family."

Maybe that's because you never gave anyone else a chance. "What about Fred Fox?" Joey asked. "He was an American married to a Pakistani. About as far from Italian as it gets, and he was one of your closest associates."

"Fred Fox saved my life without knowing my name. I rewarded him the only way I could: with my trust. Our partnership worked for decades." Vincent crossed his hands on the table. "You also gained a lifelong colleague from the relationship."

"Harry's not Italian either," Joey said.

"He is a true friend. Perhaps when you are my age you will realize how rare that is." Vincent speared another bite of his meal. "Harry Fox is an exception."

Vincent chewed his food. Joey frowned. "You think I'm too trusting."

"I think you are young, and young men are impetuous. Young men also lack experience. You are learning, Joseph. There is much you will not know until life forces you to experience it."

Joey had let his attention wander. As he got older, Vincent Morello was more prone to long-winded chats, to sharing most every thought with his son. Joey treasured the time. Even so, several glasses of wine and a full stomach made it hard to focus. Vincent's words were cold water in his face. "What are you getting at? This is your city, not mine.

You run the families. Nobody's taking your place for a long time."

"I hope you are right," Vincent said. "When this time comes, we cannot afford any sign of weakness. The family heads must see you as the continuation of my power in all ways. I do not worry, for you will be a fine leader."

"Thanks, Dad."

"Your mother would be proud of you," Vincent said. He looked past Joey's shoulder, not to the wall behind him or the swinging kitchen door to one side, but into the past. To a time before Vincent Morello had ruled organized crime in New York. "You were the happiest child. Even then your independence was obvious, that of a child who would grow to be a decisive, focused man. One who does not look to others for his success." Vincent dabbed his lips with a cloth napkin and placed a hand over Joey's. "It has all turned out well."

Joey sat rooted to his chair. His father had never spoken like this before. Vincent planned continuously, but now he spoke about a future without himself in it. Vincent Morello was a rock. He *was* the Morello family.

"Thanks, Dad." His brevity matched Vincent's eloquence. "I love you."

"I love you too, son." Vincent's hand tightened on Joey's. "Now we have much to plan for. A task I will find more tolerable after dessert."

"The baklava is to die for."

Closing time was calling, diners heading toward the door, as Joey ordered for them both. He stole a glance at his father as he sipped his wine. Never had Vincent spoken so openly about the future, about Joey's future. Vincent didn't speak idly, or without purpose. What was he getting at?

His phone vibrated. Harry Fox was calling. "It's Harry," Joey told Vincent, his finger poised over the screen. "Last time I heard from him he was in England."

Vincent motioned for him to take the call. Business never stopped, not even for a family meal. Joey nodded to the bodyguards deep in their meals as he slipped out a side door. "Harry, is everything okay?"

Harry's voice sounded faint, distant. "Better than okay," Harry said. "We know the Romans brought Boudica's artifact – whatever it is – to the Isle of Wight."

"Sara was correct about the tin isle," Joey said.

"The next step is at a set of stone monuments," Harry said. "They date to Boudica and Nero's era. Quintus didn't destroy Boudica's weapon, and he's telling us where to look."

Voices sounded from the front of the restaurant. Joey looked up as a line of people came outside and headed into the night. "Remember the first rule of breaking the law."

"Don't get caught," Harry said.

Harry had learned from the best, so Joey didn't worry about him. "Where's Tony?"

"Meeting us in Oxfordshire. He's renting a car in London."

"Keep him nearby, and keep your eyes open," he offered. "Watch everyone."

Harry didn't miss a thing. "I trust those two women."

"Am I really that obvious?"

"It's coming from a good place. And yes."

"Let's talk when you get back. Safe and sound."

"With a new relic in hand," Harry said. "I have a good feeling about this."

"Your father said that sometimes. He was usually right." Another group walked out of the front door and headed off. He should get back to his father. "Keep me in the loop, Harry."

"I won't forget what you *didn't* say either. I appreciate the concern."

"I need guys like you," Joey said.

"We're good, Joey. I'll be in touch."

Joey clicked off. Leaves rustled as the breeze picked up. A list of names took shape in his mind as he headed for the side door. Men he could fully trust in his life. It was a short list. Three of his crew would have been near the top, but they had been killed not six months earlier when a group of men had ambushed Joey not far from here. Three of the attackers had died. One had got away.

Joey hadn't yet figured out who had ordered the hit, but he would. Anyone dumb enough to go after Joey Morello would make another mistake, and when they did, Joey would be waiting.

He walked inside to find his father's bodyguards still at their tables, eating like someone else was paying. Vincent had baklava in front of him. The place had really cleared out; nobody was left within several tables on either side of their group. Their waiter was headed back to the kitchen, pushing through the swinging doors. He stopped on the other side and turned to peer at Joey through the porthole. Another face appeared in the adjacent window. Joey nodded at the men, who turned away. That waiter was a good guy, and Joey planned to leave a nice tip.

Joey still held his phone, and when he tried to slide it into a pocket the thing slipped out of his grasp. He moved to grab it and missed, managing to knock it clear back to the side door. *Nice move.* With hands like that it was no wonder he'd been a pitcher. Retrieving the phone, it was only when he turned back around that he saw it. A red light blinking underneath his table. The table where his father was sitting. *What the hell?*

The light stopped blinking. A shout formed in his throat. His father started to look over at him when the table exploded in a ball of fire, knocking Joey off his feet and turning his world to black.

Chapter 16

New York City

Ice clinked in a crystal glass, then crackled as vodka splashed over it. Liquid swirled, disappeared, and when the martini glass settled back onto the table there was a brilliant red lipstick stain on the rim.

"To what do I owe the pleasure, Stefan?"

Stefan looked out the window, forcing himself to not glance at his watch. He'd been in this apartment dozens of times. Never had his mind been so far from where he stood. "Not much moves in this city without you knowing. I need to make money for Altin. I need information on where to look for my next payday."

Legend had it Rose Leroux hadn't been conned in decades. Partly because the last man to do it was still at the bottom of the Hudson. In truth — and Stefan never doubted anything he heard about Rose — it was because she had seen it all. Every sharp edge and dark corner in life's closets. No one knew the exact path Rose had traveled to becoming the city's biggest fence, but all agreed it was best left in the past. Rose Leroux exerted more influence over the black-market trade of stolen goods in New York than any other single person. That was why Stefan was here. At least, that was what he claimed.

"Relics of Christianity are in demand at the moment," Rose said. "I know of several sellers offering items from the Middle East with ties to Roman times. Statues, pottery…" She shook her head. "One fool even contacted me about a piece of the True Cross."

"You doubt his story?"

"Enough pieces of the True Cross have been found to fill an entire forest. If you are selling worthless trinkets, do it elsewhere. I do not deal with such trifles."

Rose handled only the best merchandise. Stefan took a drink from his soda. While he often told Altin Cana his own rare alcohol consumption was out of respect to Altin's Islamic faith, in truth that was an expedient answer. Stefan enjoyed a drink at the right time. Just not with Rose. He needed his wits to deal with her. "What other Christian artifacts have you heard about recently?"

"Several." Rose stared at him over the rim of her martini glass. "The most interesting of them, though, is not yet available. One of your competitors is on the hunt as we speak."

Stefan held her gaze long enough to realize he should come clean. "Harry Fox."

She gave an almost imperceptible nod. "Vincent Morello's acquisitions expert. The man who seems always to be one step ahead of you." She did not say it unkindly. "Understandable, given his father's expertise and Vincent's deep pockets. You face a hard road to overtake him."

"Harry Fox is not as impressive as everyone believes."

"Then why are you asking about what you already know?" Rose waved a hand. "Come now, Stefan. I've known you long enough. You know he's in Europe right now, along with a German professor."

Stefan did, courtesy of Tony Cervelli. "I only hear rumors. Nothing certain."

"As do I, except my sources are always correct." A helicopter buzzed through the sky outside of Rose's window. She took her time lighting a cigarette, a ritual Stefan never failed to dislike. Rose Leroux was the only person he'd ever seen use a cigarette holder. It reminded him of Cruella de Vil. "Harry Fox is after a Roman artifact." A stream of smoke issued from her mouth. "Is it tied to Christianity? One might assume so."

Stefan knew bits and pieces of what she meant. Last year Harry had recovered a weapon of some sort, one tied to first-century Rome. Rumor had it the piece was only part of the haul uncovered, though Stefan's inquiries into exactly what Harry had found had gone nowhere. All he knew for certain was Harry Fox had wasted little time filling his father's role as Vincent Morello's antiquities hunter, and in little over a year Harry had managed to become part of Vincent's inner circle.

"What else do you know about it?" he asked, trying to keep his voice neutral. Harry Fox had gotten lucky. His father had paved the way for Harry's success. Stefan had never had that advantage. Everything he accomplished was earned. "Is Harry close? How big a prize is it?"

"He is getting closer, and Vincent Morello does not chase small paydays." Ash fell from the tip of Rose's cigarette. "That's all I have."

You aren't as clever as you think, Rose. Their relationship went back years. People talked to Rose. They trusted her. Which was exactly why Stefan had come to see her tonight. He turned and coughed into a hand, sneaking a glance at his watch.

"Have you eaten?" Rose asked.

Nobody could go from cold-hearted businesswoman to motherly lady quite like Rose Leroux. "I ate before I came," Stefan said. "What other artifacts can you tell me about? I'm willing to pay for the right lead."

That got her attention. Rose mentioned an Egyptian artifact Stefan hadn't yet heard about, though he hardly paid attention. He had no interest in dying of thirst in the desert. Time seemed to slow, his eyes moving from Rose to the window and back, as though news would appear clutched by a messenger bird. Rose didn't seem to notice, pouring another martini as she spoke, a thin line of smoke trailing from her cigarette.

She hadn't finished pouring when her phone dinged on the table. A moment later, Stefan's buzzed in his pocket. He ignored it. Another ding sounded on Rose's phone. She glanced at it. A third and fourth note sounded. Rose set her drink down. "Does Altin know you are here?" she asked. "Nobody else would dare to be so impatient with me."

"He does," Stefan said. An important detail. "He hasn't tried to call me."

Stefan didn't look at his phone. He watched Rose as she read the text message. Her face told the story. Frustration at the device gave way to confusion, chased quickly by disbelief. "This must be a mistake." She tapped at the phone, then placed it to her ear. "Yes, I saw it. It cannot be true." The cigarette holder slipped from her lips. Rose lifted a manicured hand to her mouth. "Who else was there?"

If Stefan believed in luck, he would have crossed his fingers.

"He is alive?"

Stefan bit his lip. *Damn. Joey must have survived.*

"Call me as soon as you know more. A storm is coming."

He waited until she clicked off. "What is it?"

"An attack." Rose looked at her phone as though through sheer force of will she could make it offer different news. "A murder."

Rose moved to light another cigarette. For the first time Stefan could recall, she didn't use the holder. The flame shook so badly it took her two attempts.

"Someone attacked the Morellos," she said. "Vincent is dead."

"Joey survived." Stefan whispered it to himself without thinking as he stared at the polished marble floor. The main target had been Vincent, though his men had been under orders to get Joey if possible.

"What did you say?"

Stefan looked up. Rose's eyes bored holes through him. "What?"

"Just now. You said *Joey survived.* How do you know that?"

Damn. "I got a message." Stefan pulled out his phone.

"You did not. You never took out your phone." Heels clicked as Rose stepped toward him. "You never read a message, and I said nothing." Her eyes narrowed. "How do you know Joey survived?"

He said nothing. Which told her everything.

"You were involved." Her words were so soft that he nearly missed them. "You know Joey survived because you knew they would be attacked." She ignored his protestations. "You are a fool." Rose wrung her hands together, diamonds sparkling on her wrists and fingers. "You had Vincent Morello killed." She aimed her cigarette at him. "You have no idea what you've done."

"I have no idea what you're talking about."

Those few words sparked something inside her. Rose turned on him. The icy queen who fenced everything in New York became an inferno. "Vincent Morello kept your world aligned. He kept *my* world aligned. You and that wretched Altin Cana just destroyed the only reason we have all survived." Faster than should have been possible she was in his face, a manicured fingernail stabbing his chest. "Murdering Vincent Morello will be the death of you. What do you think Joey Morello will do now? He will avenge his father's death. Killing Vincent Morello does not clear Altin Cana's path to the throne. It sends both of you to the grave."

"Altin will not be happy if he hears you accuse him of this."

Rose glared at him. "Do you think I'm mad? If I say anything, Joey may think I was involved merely because you were here." She turned away, hands now on her hips, talking through the obvious. "Joey will think we used each other for an alibi. No matter that Vincent's death does not benefit me at all. Quite the reverse. No, he may think I was involved, even if only to provide you cover." She spun around as realization dawned. "Which is exactly why you are here tonight, is it not? To use me as your alibi."

Stefan was, if anything, practical. Rose wasn't going to sell him out. Why keep up the lie? "You and I are in this together now. We both keep quiet, and Joey Morello doesn't look at me as a suspect."

"You're mad. Who tried to kill Joey earlier this year? Everyone suspects it was Altin. Were you involved with that?" Rose waved a hand at him. "I don't want to know. But this, Stefan. Do you truly believe the only reason Altin Cana is not in charge of the families is Vincent? You cannot be so stupid."

"Altin Cana wants to be the head man in New York. The man who gives orders. That only happens if Vincent is gone."

"Vincent Morello ran this city through *respect*, not fear. Vincent built trust with the other families, turning them from rivals into partners. The other dons followed Vincent because he showed them a better way. There is more profit in cooperation. Vincent saw that, and he changed the rules. And with Vincent dead, another will take his place. Perhaps Joey, perhaps someone else. Regardless, it will be a man who thinks like Vincent." Her eyes were daggers. "Not Altin Cana."

"This is also about me." Stefan pointed to his chest. "About making my place in the world. When Altin gains power, so do I."

"You want to replace him – perhaps you will one day. But then what? Do you think no one else will have the same ambition? Then the question will not be if someone comes for you, only when."

"I am not afraid."

"Which proves you are a fool." Rose leaned heavily on the bar, as though a great weight that had been on her shoulders had finally settled. "I had much greater hopes for you."

Stefan blinked. "What are you talking about?"

Rose picked up her drink and drained it, then set the glass carefully back on the table. "I knew your mother." She looked at Stefan, then away. "When she first came to the city."

"You did?" Stefan took a moment to collect himself. "How?"

"I know everyone," was all Rose said. "Your mother went through unimaginable horrors to bring you here from Kosovo and escape the war. Her parents were killed by a bomb." Rose lifted an eyebrow. "You were an infant. She was left alone with no family and no way to get out. The only way for her to escape and save you was to make a deal with the devil."

Stefan knew his mother had brought him to America from the war-torn Balkans, two ethnic Albanians running from certain death at the hands of Yugoslavian troops. But he had never been told how they had made their way to America. After his mother died, Stefan had lived as a ward of the state for the rest of his childhood. Then he'd met Altin Cana. An Albanian. A visionary. A man who gave him the first real chance of his life.

Rose may have been looking at Stefan as she spoke, but her mind was far in the past. "Your mother agreed to smuggle drugs into America in exchange for passage. Her deal got you into America, but your mother's debt was not paid. She was forced to continue smuggling drugs for the thugs who brought you here until another gang got involved. There was a fight, and your mother was in the wrong place." Despite everything she'd said, Rose came over and put a hand on Stefan's shoulder. "She died from a stray bullet in a gang shooting."

Stefan blinked. All these years, and today Rose tells him about his mother's death. Why now? "You and I have known each other for years. Why tell me now? Why not before today?"

"There are things better left unknown. I have said enough."

Stefan kept still, fingers digging into his palms. This wasn't in his plans. Not now. He'd deal with it the same way he handled so many issues, the only way he knew how. He buried it for later.

"I have to go," he said. "I assume we have an understanding – we were both here, and neither of us had anything to do with a bomb." Rose didn't respond. "When Altin is the new leader of the families, I will not forget who helped me put him there."

"You will only get yourself killed," Rose said.

"Altin will run this city and I will be his top man. Joey Morello and Harry Fox will be put in their places. You and I will have business soon. I have an opportunity in England, an artifact I will need your help to move."

He turned and walked out. Everyone had underestimated him for too long, and now look what had happened. Stefan had toppled Vincent from his throne. The first one to fall, but only the start. Now it was time to bring down Harry Fox.

Rose Leroux stayed on her feet until the door clicked shut behind

Stefan. The boy was a fool. After everything she'd done, more than he could imagine, this was how he repaid her? Using her as an alibi for murder? Without her, Stefan would have been a lost child destroyed by a dysfunctional foster system. Instead, he had been given an opportunity. Not the one his mother had dreamed of for her son, of course, but a chance. Stefan had chosen the life, and through it all Rose had kept him safe, helped him find his way in the underworld until he could stand on his own. Now he'd upended it all.

Her nail beat a staccato rhythm on the stone counter. Vincent Morello was dead. Joey was the likely choice to replace his father, at least for now. She knew Vincent had started laying the groundwork for Joey's ascension. Vincent would already have leveraged influence and bought alliances to ensure Joey moved to the top when he died.

Which gave Rose little choice. Eventually it would come out that Altin and Stefan were tied to Vincent's death, and the Cana family would pay. Rose could protect Stefan only if she had information. That meant keeping her sources open, sources within the Morello family.

Except Stefan had gone a bridge too far. He had killed a good man for no reason other than his own ambition. That alone wasn't enough for Rose to rid herself of him. But killing Vincent and using Rose as his alibi? That was. She couldn't tolerate that kind of betrayal, even though that betrayal was at the hands of a man she'd long ago sworn to protect. A man whose mother Rose had nearly died with.

"I'm sorry, Stefan." Rose picked up her phone and tapped out two messages. One to Harry Fox. The other to a man who could tell her of the dangers Harry could soon face. She would use her contacts to shield herself from the coming fallout. Protecting Harry kept her close to Joey, which in turn might give her a final chance to honor that promise to a dead friend. It was the last time. After this, Stefan was on his own.

Chapter 17

Bethlehem, Pennsylvania

Pete Brody zipped the small travel bag and threw it over his shoulder. He surveyed the storage room. What else might he need? Given he had no idea where the trip would lead, he'd packed lightly. Anything he needed overseas could be provided by his follow Druids, legal or not. For now, he had the Transportation Security Administration screenings to navigate.

Pete had a standing offer to use the private jet of a member of his own congregation, a woman whose outdoor clothing line had started in a garage and ended up on the New York Stock Exchange. Would it be easier to use a private plane? Yes, but he didn't need the image that came with it. No, he'd fly commercial, out of the limelight and away from critical eyes. This mission was worth it.

"Hello, sir." Stan Cobb had materialized outside the door.

"Something wrong?" Pete asked. He stepped out and locked the storage room, a room that required a finger and retinal scan to open. It was the kind of security Pete needed for various possessions used to create a millions-strong following from nothing. Possessions better left in the dark. "Is the helicopter ready?"

"Yes, sir." Stan walked beside him as they exited Pete's private quarters and headed into the C.O.D. complex and toward the helipad. "You have a visitor."

Pete stopped. "Now? Send them away. My flight leaves in a few hours and my men are in the air headed to London. I don't have any time."

"I did not expect him, sir."

"Him who?"

"Your father is in your office."

An icy wind seemed to fill the hallway. His father? Impossible. Pete had spent the last decade making sure the man stayed out of his life. The only time Pete ever saw him was on television, inevitably after another report of Pete's growing influence in the quasi-religious world of Druids. Pete's success was a bitter pill for one of America's best-known pastors, a man whose face regularly graced religious magazines and the occasional Page Six article.

Fire and brimstone were the two words that came to mind when Pete thought of his father, though it seemed the great preacher had tempered his incendiary rhetoric in an effort to draw new members. He would say it was a necessary adjustment, a way to spread God's true word from his pulpit in the ostentatious Grace Baptist Church in Atlanta. Funny how his father's tune had changed when the offering plates stopped overflowing.

"You let him into my office?" Pete asked.

"Not as such."

"He forced his way in."

"More of a barge, sir."

"He thinks the world rolls out a red carpet under his feet. Even if he's the only one who can see it." Pete pulled his shoulders back. He was on the verge of a discovery to expose the charlatans, the snake-oil salesmen, the *opportunists* like his father who built personal fortunes on the backs of desperate people. What Pete had in store would send shockwaves through Grace Baptist and all the other fraudulent churches, shockwaves that would bring their walls tumbling down.

"You know what, Stan? I'm glad he's here. There are some things he needs to know." Pete flashed a thumbs-up, tossed his bag at Stan's chest, and strode toward his office. His father thought merely showing up would intimidate Pete. Maybe a decade ago, but that version of Pete was long gone. Now it was a fair fight, one Pete realized was overdue.

"You should have told me you were coming." Pete marched through his open office door, never stopping as he spoke. "I would have invited your favorite journalists. I know you can't resist a photo op, after all."

Kenneth Brody was not a tall man. He stood behind Pete's desk looking over the C.O.D. campus. When he turned and stepped to one side, Pete couldn't see much of him above his desk chair. Ken seemed to realize this and moved to one side.

"It's good to see you, son." He tilted his head, indicating the view behind him. "The Lord's light shines on you."

"The Lord has nothing to do with this," Pete said. "Human kindness does. Do you know what we do here? It's not my personal fiefdom, paid for by others."

"The Celtic Order of Druids are well known for their benevolence." Ken frowned, as though the words tasted off. "Free childcare for members in need. After-school programs. Hot meals for anyone, no questions asked. College tuition scholarships, career-change retraining programs, even a pediatric medical clinic. Quite the operation."

"Don't forget fundraising for green initiatives across the board. Political, social – it doesn't matter. And my favorite, the research lab where students are working on ways to save the planet. All sponsored by our organization."

Ken smiled, showing a set of dazzling teeth, though the smile never quite reached his eyes. "How noble."

"And one more thing," Pete said. "We pay taxes on all of it, because we're not a scam."

"Some would call you short-sighted, but who am I to judge?"

Pete bit his lip. Now that Ken Brody no longer intimidated his son physically, he used different weapons. No more raised voices and threats of damnation. Biting words were his preferred course.

"One day the bill will come due for what you've done," Pete said. "And no one will be there to help pay it for you."

"Peter, it almost sounds as though you're unhappy to see me." Ken spread his arms. "Your own father."

Pete walked around his desk, stopping inches from Ken. It pleased him beyond measure to see the man flinch. "Sit in the visitor's chair," Pete said. "This is my desk."

Ken recovered quickly. "How hospitable."

"Why are you here?" Pete asked his father's back. "Money? I hear your congregation is shrinking. Hard to afford three-thousand-dollar suits on a budget. Or a second Rolex? Those aren't cheap."

Ken actually glanced at his suit jacket for an instant. A gold watch protruded from the edge of his sleeve. He moved that hand out of sight as he walked to the front of Pete's desk. He did not sit down.

"You can't see the forest for the trees," Ken said. "I do the Lord's work. One must dress for the work to be done."

"You fleece people every day."

Ken laid his hands on the back of a chair. The gold watch peeked out. "I didn't come here to argue." He sighed. "I want to talk. A real talk, like we used to have."

The only thing we ever talked about was your church. "I have a flight to catch. What do you want to talk about?"

"You." Ken Brody had made a fortune telling people what he thought they wanted to hear. He'd done it with so many different stories and promises, yet every single one rode on the back of his intensity. When Ken Brody wanted to, he could make you *believe.* Pete nearly stepped back. It had been a long time since that fire had been aimed toward him.

"I want to help you," Ken said. "You've done great things. So many people given safety and shelter, offered wisdom and guidance. You have a gift, son. One that can change the world. But only if we work together. Ten years ago, you left our home, striking out on your own for reasons I didn't understand, but that doesn't matter now. You have forged your own path. Just as I once did."

"I left your home because of your demented worldview. Your

religion allows people to abdicate responsibility for their actions by turning to you for salvation. For you and your followers, there is no higher cause. Only your greed and thirst for attention."

Ken went on as though Pete hadn't said a word. "You left, and now I see it's my fault."

Apologies weren't in Ken's vocabulary unless there was profit to be made. "You're not listening. You never do."

Ken stopped waving his hands around. "I am, son. I know you left because of a misunderstanding. Which I'm here to fix."

"I left because I finally got a chance to experience the true scope of what your religion does."

A dark cloud flashed across Ken's face for an instant. "Don't bring up that nonsense about the Catholics. You're wrong."

"You mean Brazilians, not Catholics. Brazil, one of the most faithful Catholic nations in the world. I saw exactly what blind faith does."

Years ago, when Pete still lived with his father, Ken Brody had decided his son should expand his horizons on a charitable mission. While other college students partied in Cancun, Pete had traveled to Brazil with others in his father's church to build houses in the *favelas* of Rio de Janeiro. A week in some of the world's poorest slums was intended to show him how blessed he was, and a chance to bolster his résumé for a future role in the church hierarchy. Ken Brody's plans included his son, and this mission trip was a step on that journey. Little did Ken realize where it would lead.

"The people in Rio were faithful," Pete said. "They listened to their priests, prayed, and donated what little they had to the church. What did you promise in return? Eternal salvation."

Ken had heard it before. "Those people were happy and fulfilled. They lived in God's embrace."

"Tell that to the children born in Rio with a life expectancy of forty-eight. Children who die during asthma attacks because they have no medicine. Or the infants whose limbs are cut off because of untreated infections. Untreated because they don't have any doctors. What does the church do to help them? They tell them to pray."

"Those are rare cases that don't—"

Pete smacked the desk. "I'm not finished. Your religion created an entire society that *accepts* that five men should have more money than fifty percent of the population. Extravagant wealth at the top, abject poverty for the rest. You preach that God rewards the faithful. That's garbage. Faith has nothing to do with it. Those people are sold false hope while church and business leaders plunder Brazil's wealth. The rich praise their God's generosity, and the rest think they can be like those rich people if only they work harder and pray a lot."

It all poured out, everything he'd seen.

"Don't say it's not true, because I heard the sermons, saw the Ferraris drive past crippled beggars on their way to church, saw the overflowing offering plates, while I had to build a crutch for an orphaned five-year-old because he had no one to buy it for him. You know what he was using? A broom handle with a shoe taped on top of it."

Ken's lips were a thin line. Like any bully suddenly confronted, Ken didn't know what to say.

"Those people sell the only marketable skill they have: their labor. They work in soul-crushing factory jobs under conditions that are illegal here. And what happens to them and their families if they can't get one of those jobs? They're doomed."

Ken found his voice. "We are imperfect creatures, but we strive to improve every day. The church is a vehicle for betterment. For everyone."

"I'll tell you where that vehicle leads." Pete slowly circled the desk. "Do you remember the family I built a house for? Of course not. You never met them. You never even asked their names. The dos Santos family. Five children living in a *favela* with their parents. Two bedrooms. No reliable running water. The electricity went out every day. And no sewers. Those kids played in streets with raw sewage running down the middle of them."

Pete kept moving, edging closer to his father. Ken's false smile had vanished.

"The sewage contained bacteria, which the children occasionally swallowed. Most of them were lucky. Stomach cramps, vomiting, nothing major. One little boy wasn't so lucky. One of the dos Santos sons contracted cholera from the sewage. Remember how I said these people didn't have access to doctors? Guess what untreated cholera does? It kills you. That's what happened to Thiago Emiliano dos Santos. He died from untreated cholera."

Ken blinked, twisting his hands.

"He was three years old. And do you know the worst part?" Pete gritted his teeth. "With no access to doctors, the family went to their priest. They relied on the church, and this priest told them to pray. By the time anyone with medical training found out about the child, he was dead. I saw pictures of his funeral. The church sent a bishop. He wore a gold cross that could have paid for an entire block of new homes in the *favela*." Pete was inches from his father now. "That's what your church stands for. And I'm going to destroy it."

Ken stepped back, his hands up. "You need to think clearly. You have a chance, Peter. To expand your reach. All you need to do is open your eyes, make a course correction, and rejoin the fold."

Rejoin the fold? Pete's eyes narrowed. "You want me to join you. Be a part of Grace Baptist." He shook his head. "You don't want my help. You need it. You're *afraid* of us."

"Not afraid. Thinking ahead." Ken reached out as though to take Pete's hand. "An alliance. Your energy, your new angle – think about what it could do with the power of Grace Baptist behind it. Father and son. Together we can show that religion isn't irrelevant. We can change things, Peter."

Pete couldn't speak. He had nothing to say. His father still thought this was about showing him the error of his ways. It was pathetic.

Ken took the silence as consideration. "What do you say?" He touched Pete's arm. "Are you with me?"

The touch jolted Pete back to life. "You aren't listening." He stepped out of reach. "I'm not going to partner with you. I'm going to *eliminate* you." Pete pointed toward the door. "Get out of my office. When you hear my voice again, it will be me telling the world your religion is finished."

Ken wasn't just afraid of him and his Druids, Pete realized. He was scared to death. The gifted orator who had terrorized Pete all through his childhood gave his son one long, final look and left without a word.

Pete stood by the desk, staring at the open door. He had always known this day of reckoning would come, but he had wondered if he could really push back and stand up to the man who'd molded him. Turns out he could.

Stan appeared in the door. "Your father is gone, sir."

Pete nodded and headed for the door, his steps lighter than they had been in years. "I need my phone."

Stan handed it over, carrying Pete's bag as they walked toward the helipad. Pete dialed a number with the country prefix *44*. The code for England. His SAS man answered on the first ring.

"Hello, sir."

"I'm headed to the airport," Pete said. "What's the situation?"

"They left Wight and are driving north."

"Any idea where they're going?"

"Not yet," the SAS man said. "I'm maintaining distance. I suggest sending someone to the ruins they visited. Something there caught their attention."

"I'll have someone check it out. Anything else?"

"Their group is smaller. One of the women left." The SAS man described her.

"Jane White." Pete stopped at the exterior door leading to the helipad. "It would take something major to pull her away. Unless they're investigating two possible leads."

"Do you want me to follow her or the other two?"

Pete considered. "Stay with Harry Fox and Dr. Hamed."

"Understood."

"I'll call you when we land," Pete said, and clicked off.

He pushed the door open, wind from the chopper blades whipping across his body. Two questions ran through his head as he ducked beneath them and climbed on board:

What had Harry Fox found in Wight, and why had his group split up?

Chapter 18

Oxfordshire

Oxfordshire is a three-hour drive north from the Isle of Wight docks. Three hours of flat green land dotted with small villages, tidy farms and the occasional larger town. The dark clouds that had doused Wight earlier had given way to a very non-English blue sky, though Harry had learned the hard way not to predict the weather around here. The day's last few hours of sunlight warmed his arm as they drove. More than once he turned without thinking to look for Jane's car behind them. It was nowhere to be found.

"I hope this guy Parker is right," Harry said as Sara took the Oxfordshire exit. A lonely cow munching grass looked up as their tires chirped. He was not impressed. "Jane's local knowledge would have helped us."

"Jane said he's usually right."

Sara twisted the wheel and stepped on the gas, pressing Parker against the door. He'd become accustomed to it and leaned to compensate. They went from smooth pavement to cobblestones, entering another town where the average structure was hundreds of years old. Sturdy stone buildings pushed in on the narrow streets. A pair of construction cranes rose above everything in the distance, though what they could possibly be doing was beyond Harry. Perhaps lifting one of the boulders that seemed to comprise most of the structures in England.

"Parker's an interesting guy," Sara continued. "Jane hasn't told me much about him, though her lack of sharing speaks volumes."

"They have a thing?"

"Yes and no. Jane isn't the kind of woman to be easily swept off her feet. Despite this, Parker seems to have done the impossible. Jane likes him. Which is a challenge given how they met."

"How's that?"

"Jane knew Parker's fiancé. Her name was Erika."

"Was? She died?"

"Killed by a car bomb meant for Parker. He was seriously injured and ended up in Scotland for a time dealing with it."

"A car bomb? Only a certain kind of enemy blows up your car." The kind Harry knew all about. "Who is Parker?"

"A banker, believe it or not. A successful one. Jane doesn't know much about what happened with the bombing. She did say Parker suspects the person who bombed him has ties to the British government."

"Sounds like he made a connection with Jane."

"They bonded over a shared adventure," Sara said. "Not unlike ours. Jane uncovered information during a cultural dig in her town. An old letter found on a skeleton hidden behind a castle wall."

"You can't leave me hanging on that."

"Others wanted what they were searching for. They survived and eventually uncovered lost property belonging to the Scottish government. She never told me precisely what it was."

Harry caught Sara's eye in the mirror. "I'd like to know what sort of *property* they found."

"As would I." Sara pointed out of his window. "I took a class at the university in this town."

Gothic structures stretched as far as Harry could see. Pointed spires and crenellated walls lorded over everything, instilling a darkness even in the afternoon sunlight. Harry wouldn't have blinked if knights on horseback had trotted into sight, lances held high, ready for battle.

"Nice buildings," Harry said. "Lifts the spirit."

"It does have a sense of foreboding," Sara said. "Good preparation for the true nature of academia."

"Soul-crushing boredom?"

"I was thinking more of cutthroat politics."

Harry studied a particularly imposing structure. "Is that the dungeon?"

"The dungeon is across campus."

A black bird perched atop one spire took flight, gliding down toward the cars below before alighting on a streetlamp as they passed.

"Nice of Jane to let us use her car," Harry said.

"I told her you would cover any damage I cause."

"If we find the Celtic artifact, it's a deal."

"Are you doubting our quest?"

"My dad always cautioned me about getting ahead of myself. Focus too much on the finish line, and chances are you'll stumble on the way." Harry's phone vibrated with a text message, and he pulled it out and glanced at the screen. "Tony will be at the site in an hour."

She hit the gas and fifteen minutes later the site appeared. Oxford had vanished, the medieval urban city replaced with well-marked green fields and rows of leafy trees, with barely a car or person to be seen. There were two parking areas alongside the road, but only one contained a vehicle. Sara and Harry got out as an older couple were walking toward the parked car. The couple waved as they passed. "They're leaving," Harry said. "I think we have the place to ourselves."

He got out as the couple got into their car and motored away. No one else was in sight. "Good timing," Harry said.

Sara grabbed his bicep and pulled. "It's going to be dark soon."

"Don't you want to make a plan before we start wandering around?"

"We have no idea how long it will be until someone else arrives." Sara pointed to the field beside them. "There are three sets of stones. One is called The King's Men." She twisted to point across the road. "There's one over there, which is the King Stone. And a third one that way." Sara indicated an area several hundred yards away, further off the road on the side where they'd parked. "Those are the Whispering Knights."

"They've been here at least thirty-five hundred years," Harry said. "Since before Nero's time."

"The King's Men is actually a circle of around seventy stones," Sara said. "All that remains of the original hundred. I say we start elsewhere."

Harry and Sara had talked their approach through at length. Nothing in the writings from Dagda's subterranean grotto pointed to a specific location among the Rollright Stones, so Harry expected Quintus's approach regarding the next marker to be more subtle. A familiar engraving, perhaps. Or a phrase tied to him or Nero. The shrine at Wight had been well hidden, yet Quintus hadn't called out where to go to locate Queen Boudica's *terrible power*. Perhaps Quintus had had the foresight to see a time when Rome no longer ruled on Wight. Or maybe he had wanted to keep the path concealed from even his closest comrades. Perhaps a bit of both.

"First, let's look for anything tied to the grotto," Sara said. "An image, a phrase, even a single word. We'll start with the King Stone because it has writing on it. Faded, but still a place to start."

They crossed the empty road, Harry following her over a walking bridge spanning a steep hollow. Two other paths had been mowed into the flowing grasses, taking visitors on a more circular route around the hollow. She stopped at a waist-high metal fence surrounding the stone, raising a hand against the setting sun.

"Watch your footing. And be careful hopping this fence." She pointed to wicked spikes atop each post. "Those will hurt."

Harry vaulted over the fence without speaking. "Need a hand?" he asked, turning to offer one.

Sara took a step back and then mirrored his own leap. "Find another damsel to patronize."

Wildflowers brushed his legs as Harry approached the stone. Over ten feet high, the twisted rock had been weathered by time so it resembled a gnarled tree trunk, lopsided and pitted with small holes. If Harry and Sara stood on either side, they might have been able to touch hands around it, but barely. Brute strength had put this here.

"There's writing here," Sara said as they both pulled out flashlights. "It's Brittonic. Jane sent me a translation of it." She pulled out her phone. "Scholars have different interpretations of the message."

"Not the individual words."

"Right. Context gets lost over time."

"We'll go with Jane's interpretation." She'd found the *rodland rix* reference buried in Quintus's message. No reason to lose faith in her now.

"Agreed." Sara played her light across the stone. Tiny mineral specks flashed in the gloom. Letters ran across the rock, some washed away, others still distinct. Harry squinted, tilted his head. He couldn't read a single word.

"What's it say?" he asked.

"According to Jane, great deeds about people we can't identify. The prevailing theory is this rock was initially a memorial. Human remains have been found all over this area."

Harry glanced at the ground with distrust. As a rule, he tried not to irritate spirits. Not that he believed in that sort of thing.

"The King Stone name is not about an actual king," Sara said. "It appeared over time. There are no references to royalty on here, not even regional rulers who would have controlled this land in the Dark Ages."

"Why does the stone look so funny? Like part of a DNA strand."

"Most people say it resembles a seal balancing a ball on its nose, but I like your interpretation. It's actually from souvenir hunters stealing bits of it over time. Like the Colosseum in Rome." She indicated the spike-topped fence around them. "Hence the need for this."

"Lot of good it does out here in the middle of nowhere."

"Indeed. Let's keep moving. Jane's translation suggests this stone's purpose changed over time. Different tribes or groups left their own inscriptions on the stone."

"Any Latin or Roman references?"

Sara shook her head. "It's all Brittonic. Nothing ties to the Romans. The people who wrote on here were local chieftains, not Roman generals."

"Then why are we starting with this one? Sounds like a terrible choice."

"Which is what I thought at first. Read this."

She handed him her phone. Jane's short translation was on-screen.

"That's it?" Harry read the text, his heart dropping a bit with each line.

Great leader of the fields, fallen in age as called by the spirits.
A wise and honorable leader whose lands touch each horizon.
We beseech the gods to send us rain and sun.

It went on like that, random strings of text one after another. "It's like medieval wishes for good fortune," Harry said.

Sara's face was darker than the sky overhead. "It's possible to have too much history in one place. It can make deciphering anything impossible." She took her phone back. "Let's move on."

Headlights flashed in the distance. A car crested the gently-sloping road, washing the site with brilliance like sun parting the clouds at midday. Harry dropped to one knee. Sara didn't, so he grabbed her by the waist and pulled her down.

"Why are you hiding?" she hissed.

"Wouldn't you rather see who it is before revealing our position?" He pointed to the waving fields of grass around them. "This keeps us out of sight. Maybe the car goes by and we're fine. Maybe it stops. Then we stay still until we know who it is."

They kept low until the car briefly dipped out of sight, both of them using that chance to hop back over the fence. He didn't want to be trapped inside the fenced area if this person stopped for a visit. The car slowed on approach, pulling off into the same parking area they'd used and rolling to a stop by their Range Rover.

Harry's phone vibrated. He pulled it out.

"Put that down," Sara whispered. "Your light will give us away."

"I hope so." He brushed off her arm and stood. "That's Tony."

"*Tony?*" Sara was on him in a second. "You nearly give me a heart attack because you forgot he was coming?"

Harry pressed a button and put the phone to his ear. "It's me. Kill your lights and look toward the fence."

Tony stepped out of the car as Harry flicked his flashlight on and crossed the bridge, Sara right behind him. She was muttering things he couldn't and didn't want to hear. Tony watched them approach, hands in his pockets, his face tight.

"You okay, Tony?" Harry stuck out a hand.

"I'm fine." Tony shook it, then nodded to Sara. "Dr. Hamed."

"Call me Sara."

"Glad you made it," Harry said. "Listen up, because we have to move fast." He brought Tony up to speed, skipping most of the details about Wight. "Which brings us here. We checked the first monument. There are two more."

"What if we strike out on those?"

Sara jumped in. "Then we reassess. The light's running out, so let's move."

A thin orange line was all that separated the night sky from fields stretching into the distance. Harry looked up at a moon waiting to take center stage. "Did you let Joey know you got here?" Harry asked.

"No." Tony held up his phone. "I got a prepaid when I landed. I still have to load a new SIM card into my own phone, but I didn't want to miss connecting with you before I got here."

"Smart." He reached up and clapped a hand on Tony's shoulder. "Let's not keep Sara waiting. She runs a tight ship."

Tony dipped his head, the hard set to his mouth never fading as he followed Harry and Sara alongside the roadway. The King's Men monument was behind them, that circle of stones Jane deemed too old and pillaged to be a viable target. Which left the grouping called the Whispering Knights, situated a hundred yards down the mowed pathway they now walked, then another fifty yards into the field beside them. Thank goodness for the walkway, or else they'd be moving through waist-high grass with no idea what was underfoot.

"What do you think of England?" Harry asked.

"A lot different from Brooklyn," Tony said. "Where can I get good Italian food around here?"

"My guess would be a long way off. Might be faster to hop on a plane for Rome."

A crack in the pensive gaze. "That would be something. Never been there."

"Never been to the motherland?" Harry winked as he said it.

"I'm a Brooklyn kid all the way. My accented Italian wouldn't pass muster in the old country. Plus, the flights have to be crazy expensive."

"Help me find the end of Nero and Aristotle's path and you'll have enough money to fly your family there first class."

"My mother would love that."

Sara piped up from in front. "If you go, be sure to add a side trip to Pompeii. It's the most incredible site I've ever visited."

"She's right," Harry said. "When we get back, I'll remind Vincent to add round-trip tickets for everyone to your cut of what we find. He takes care of his people." Harry tapped himself on the chest. "Look at me. A half-Pakistani guy working alongside the Italian mob."

"Not something you see every day."

"It began with my father, but after he died Vincent gave me a chance. I proved myself. I was loyal, and I made him money. Now he trusts me, which is worth more than any amount of money."

Harry grinned when he said it, yet Tony's face went pale. "Don't worry," Harry said. "It sounds like a lot, but it's no pressure."

As they reached the rocks, Sara turned to them and clicked her fingers. "Get over here and out of sight," she said, then looked at Harry. "You're the one who warned me about vehicles coming past."

"We are," Harry said. He moved to Sara's side, looking at the group of rocks in front of them. Where they stood, the stones shielded them from any passing cars. "This fence has spikes on top of it as well. Careful."

They went over one at a time. The metal barrier was identical to the first; tall grass inside the enclosure waved in a soft breeze as they pushed through it. Unlike the first monument, the Whispering Knights consisted of five vertical stones and a horizontal one on the ground. Harry nudged it with his toe. "Looks like this one may have been on top of the others and it fell."

"That's exactly what happened," Sara said. "This is an ancient burial chamber. There likely were other support stones to hold the capstone," she indicated the horizontal stone, "but they're gone now."

"That Whispering Knight would have made a loud noise when it fell," Harry quipped.

"Very funny," Sara said.

"What did you call this?" Tony asked, and Harry repeated the name. "That's a weird name."

"And Mr. Cervelli thinks more critically than Mr. Fox." Sara tapped Tony's arm. "Well done. According to legend these stones used to be a king and his army. They offended the wrong witch, who turned them to stone."

"Neat story," Tony said.

"Any witches have long since hopped their brooms for more active pastures. Fortunately for us the people who raised these stones wrote on them. I suggested checking the other monument first, given it's a single stone and it had more writing."

"More?" Harry asked.

"Focus on the little this large monument tells us." Sara led them to the largest stone. "Again, the writing is a version of Brittonic, but Jane was able to translate most of it." Sara read aloud from memory as she traced letters even more faded than the others.

Let the King be strong, the mighty warrior who brings peace with strength. The Crown from above, the strength and true power of Britannia beneath. Guardian of all lands and people, his memory shall live eternal.

Her words floated away on the breeze.

"That doesn't even make sense," Harry said.

"It did to them."

Tony had been standing behind them, and when Harry looked back, he saw that Tony was watching the road. "Don't worry, Tony. We'll see someone's headlights coming long before they see us."

"Right," Tony said. He peered over Harry's shoulder at the rocks. "Not much to go on." He leaned closer, squinting. "What's at the bottom."

Sara aimed her light to where he pointed. "I'm not certain."

"Jane didn't mention it?" Harry asked. Sara shook her head, so Harry bent down to get a better look. "These don't look like words," he said as he touched the irregular lines. No, not irregular. Worn. "It may be a drawing of some kind. A child's drawing, but still. And here, beside it. That could be another one."

"You think that's a drawing?" Sara asked. She knelt beside him, one hand on her chin. "Perhaps."

There were two sets of lines, parts of them so faded they were scarcely visible. The one on the right was a vertical straight line, wider at the top. Beside it, so close they touched, was a shape that was rounded at the top and flat at the bottom. His flashlight played over it. Was that a line connecting the two?

"This one on the left looks like a bird," Tony said. "With big claws."

A bird? Harry moved his light around. With a bit of imagination, the crude triangles and circles morphed into a bird-like drawing, like one of those pictures that revealed a hidden image if you looked at it long enough. It could be a bird. A bird with a fearsome beak and sharp talons. "These could be wings." He traced the lines running away from what might have been a body, one on each side. "This looks familiar." A thought buzzed at the back of his head. "What does this text say again?"

Sara repeated Jane's translation. She only made it halfway.

"Stop. Say that line again. After *The Crown from above.*"

"*The strength and true power.* It's just like what we read in the grotto."

"How long do you think these inscriptions have been here?" Harry asked.

"Up to several thousand years. These pre-date Nero."

Tony piped up. "General Quintus couldn't have written this message then."

"No," Harry said. "He couldn't have. But he could have known the message was here and used the same phrase in the grotto."

"It's possible Quintus knew of these monuments when he created the Dagda shrine on Wight."

"I know it's only a few common words. But there's more."

"What do you mean?" Tony asked.

"The image." A cloud briefly covered the moon as he pointed. "Look at this carving. It does look like a bird. With big talons. You know what has serious talons? An eagle."

"The Roman Legion standard," Sara said.

"The second image has two parts." The cloud moved on, moonlight bringing the carving into view. "One side is rounded on top and flat on the bottom. If you use your imagination, it looks an awful lot like a man wearing a robe."

"I guess so," Tony said. "What about the line coming out of the robe?"

"That could be an outstretched arm. Holding something?"

Tony wasn't as sure. "Maybe. But what's he holding? It could be anything."

"This line is thin and straight until the very top, where it gets bigger. Almost like a staff with something on top."

"Dagda," Sara said.

"What?" Tony asked.

"It's Dagda," she said. "The hood, the robe, a staff. And look where they carved it. Below the text."

"These images could have been added," Harry said. "If Quintus knew about this memorial, he could have made the grotto first and carved these images after. I think this is the next location Quintus chose to hide Queen Boudica's *terrible power.*"

Sara wasn't buying it. "Anything Quintus hid here would have been found long ago."

Harry shook his head. "Give Quintus credit. He hid it where no one would look."

"I'm listening."

"It's right here in front of us." Harry aimed his light at the inscribed text and read aloud. "*True power of Britannia beneath.*"

"*Beneath,*" Sara said. "Literally, as in beneath these stones?"

"This one stone." Harry touched the one with writing on it. "You could move it without upsetting all the others."

Harry looked to Tony. The kid again had his eyes on the road, peering intently into the distance. "Take it easy," Harry said. "We'll see anyone coming."

Tony started. "Sorry. Just nervous."

Harry turned to Sara. "What do you think?"

"I think my relationship with you cannot be entirely healthy given I'm considering desecrating a national treasure." Sara pushed at the stone to no avail. "Perhaps we can knock it over gently."

"Sounds like you agree with me."

"In the context of this mad chase, what you say is logical." She pushed the rock again, then her teeth flashed. "That means I do."

A yellow glow caught Harry's eye. Tony had his phone out. "Is it working now?" Harry asked.

Tony fumbled the phone and nearly dropped it. "What? No, not yet." He tapped the screen and shoved it back in his pocket.

"Help me push this rock over. Gently," he quickly added, with an eye to Sara. "Let me think about how to do this."

The five stones formed a rough circle. Another laid horizontal on the ground. Breaking their targeted stone in half was the last thing he wanted. Lucky for him, it stuck out a bit from the main circle. "If we can get a grip on the back of it," Harry said, "we should be able to push it forward so it falls toward the grass. We see if there's anything under it, then lift it back up."

Tony finally seemed to be paying attention. "Harry, that stone probably weighs a thousand pounds. If we tip it, there's no way the three of us can lift it back into position."

Harry gave a practice shove on the rock, which didn't move. He pushed again, harder. Nothing. "I may have overestimated myself." So tipping it over was out. "New plan. We tilt it so Sara can look below."

"You expect me to reach under a thousand-pound rock while you two hold it?" Sara crossed her arms, glaring at Harry. "Not happening."

"You're the smallest person here."

"No chance."

"Tony and I can tilt and hold this rock enough for you to see underneath. Right, Tony?"

Again, the kid had his eyes down the road. "Right."

"I'm not getting under that rock."

"You're telling me you don't want to see what's beneath it?"

Her mouth tightened. "If you drop this rock on me and I survive, you'll wish I hadn't."

"We won't drop it." Harry grabbed one side of the rock, motioning for Tony to do the same. "Find a grip." The rock had plenty of crags and crevices for handholds. "Ready?" Harry asked. He couldn't see Tony around the stone.

"Ready," Tony said.

"Try to rock it." Teeth gritted, he pulled. Tiny pebbles broke loose from where the stone rested against the others. "It moved."

"It's bigger at the top." Sara pointed out the curvature. "It will be easier to move once it starts rocking."

"Then watch out. This thing could—"

"Get *down*," Sara suddenly hissed. She shoved his shoulders, pushing him to the ground. The world vanished as the tall grass swallowed them. "I see headlights."

"How close?"

"Several hundred meters down the road. They couldn't have seen us."

Rising to one knee, Harry poked his head just above the grass. A pair of headlights approached slowly. A hundred yards away and closing.

"He's slowing down." Sara popped her head up beside his. "Let's circle around when he gets out. He won't see us coming from behind."

Harry shushed her. "Take it easy. The car hasn't stopped yet."

Sara quieted and watched as the car rolled closer, its headlights reflecting off their pair of parked cars alongside the road. Harry's chest tightened as the vehicle slowed further. His legs tensed. If that guy stopped, he'd never see them from the road – not unless they had to jump up and over the fence now penning them in. Harry grabbed Sara's arm, ready to push her behind him. Where had Tony hidden? Nobody would stop out here at this time of night.

They watched as the car slowed near their own parked cars as though the driver were inspecting them, then kept moving along the road, closer to their location. An orange dot glowed in the driver's-side window as it passed. Was the driver looking their way? The car passed, and a long breath later the only thing left of it were the red taillights growing smaller in the distance.

Harry and Sara got to their feet again.

"Tony," Harry called out, and Tony materialized from behind the stone. "Grab hold and keep pulling. This rock is moving one way or another."

Rather than resuming his position beside the stone, Tony pointed at Harry's chest. "What's that?"

Harry looked down. "An amulet." He shoved it back into his shirt. "My good-luck charm."

"I have one too." Tony reached under his own shirt and pulled out a necklace. A tiny little man dangled from it. "Saint Francis. My mother gave it to me. For protection."

For a reason he couldn't quite voice, Harry pulled his amulet back out. He never shared this story. "This is from my father. You could say it does the same thing."

"It's nice," Tony said. "Real nice. It must work, too. You're always successful in the field."

"My dad taught me well. He was good at finding these kinds of things." Harry indicated the stone. "Sort of like he's still watching out for me, you know?"

Tony's gaze unfocused for an instant. "Yeah, I do." His eyes hardened. "That's what family does." He reached over and grabbed Harry by the bicep, startling him. "Let's get this rock off the ground."

"You got it," Harry said. Damn, the kid was strong. He quashed the urge to rub his bicep. The kid was *really* strong.

Harry latched onto the stone again and pulled. Tony grunted as he followed suit, the pair of them making primitive noises as they tugged and twisted. Harry's feet slipped, he regrouped, then when the stone had nearly scraped his fingers raw, Sara called out from where she lay on the ground.

"Keep pulling. I can see beneath it."

"Rock it," Harry called between gritted teeth. "Let it down, then pull back hard. On my count." On three they abruptly reversed course, pushing at the rock to shift its weight before pulling back again.

"Hold it," she called.

Except the rock had plans of its own. Harry and Tony held it for a beat. Then, in a slow, sickening tilt, it went too far. One instant they had it under control. The next, gravity took over.

"Move!" Harry shouted and kicked at Sara.

She screamed, he kicked again, and the rock slipped from his grasp before crashing to the ground. Harry had the presence of mind to jump clear. The last thing he saw before falling into the grass was Tony diving the other way.

His molars rattled when he hit the ground. "Sara." Jumping up, he shouted her name. Was her arm pinned? Had the rock crushed her?

"Stop shouting."

Harry was on his knees. Sara lay in the grass mere feet away. "It didn't crush you." His voice was weak with relief. She yelped as he ripped her off the ground, arms going round her in a bear hug. "It didn't crush you."

"No, but you are." Her words were muffled. She didn't sound happy, but didn't push him away, either. "I'm okay."

"I lost my grip," he said, the words coming in a rush. "We rocked it too far and I just lost it."

"I can see that," Sara said. "I'm fine. Will you let me go, please?"

"Sorry." He released her as Tony bounded around the fallen stone.

"Are you okay?" he said breathlessly. Sara assured him she was. "Thank God." Tony hugged her, less fervently. "I'm so sorry."

"That is the last time I – oh my." Sara pushed them both away. "Look."

Moonlight played over the toppled rock. Underneath, the loamy earth was dark as night where the huge stone had been standing. Harry peered closer. Metal glowed dully in the dirt.

"It's a box," he said.

Sara fell to her knees. "Bronze. Look at the patina." The flat box turned a dark shade of green under her light. "Beautiful. And look here." Her voice was almost giddy. "There are engravings on it."

Harry peered over her shoulder, his chest tightening. "Another eagle."

"It's a Roman piece." Sara pushed several baseball-sized chunks of the fallen stone aside to get a better view of the box. Harry crowded closer, Tony on the other side. Sara elbowed them away. "Space, please."

"You sure you want to be in front of it when it opens?" Harry asked.

"You think it's booby-trapped?"

"I've learned to be careful."

"The hinge is on the back side," Sara said. "Chances are if a trap exists, it's set to fire toward the front side, away from the hinges. Where most anyone opening it would be." She turned the box around so the hinges faced her. "Care to open it?" she asked Harry.

"Not by hand." He grabbed a shard of fallen stone lying between a pair of bigger fragments. "Watch out." He slipped the shard between the box's lid and body; its hinges creaked as they moved a millimeter. "Here goes nothing."

Teeth gritted, he lifted the lid, turning aside as he did. Tony did the same, yet Sara never moved. The lid squealed, then stuck. Silence. Nothing else. Sara leaned forward with her flashlight, then gasped audibly.

"Look inside."

Harry leaned over. The air in his lungs went cold. "That's gold."

Dull yellow ingots flashed inside the bronze box. "There's something under the gold," Harry said. "What is it?"

"Leather." Sara twisted the box around. "No, not leather. Papyrus. It's a scroll. Here." She placed the gold ingots in Tony's hand. "Do not drop those."

Each ingot was the size of a battery. The metal was worth thousands of dollars, yes, but there wasn't nearly enough gold here to make it worth secreting under this massive rock. "The scroll is the real prize," he said.

"Glad you're keeping up." Sara lifted the scroll. "This is definitely papyrus."

"Scraped animal skin," Harry said to Tony.

"I know what papyrus is."

"Both of you be quiet." Sara turned the scroll in her hands. "This is the proper shape and size for Roman-era scrolls."

"Are you going to open it?" Harry asked.

"We should wait for better conditions," Sara said. "The moisture in the air could damage this."

"You have to be joking."

She didn't bother putting up a fight. "Shine your light on it." Sara put her own flashlight away, grabbing hold of the leather strip that bound the scroll and then unrolled it carefully. "I see writing."

Snick.

"Drop it."

A strange voice filled the air, right after a sound Harry knew too well. A revolver being cocked.

"Now."

Harry turned to find the barrel of a pistol aimed between his eyes.

Chapter 19

Oxfordshire

Clouds covered the moon. The pistol vanished from view for an instant, then glinted again in the faint light.

"Hands up, and drop the tube." The man holding the pistol pointed it at Sara now.

Harry peered into the night at the intruder. *I know that voice.*

Two other men, both of them beefy, approached out of the darkness on the other side of the fence and climbed it to join the first man. A memory ran screaming to the front of Harry's mind as he noted the tattoos on the gunman's forearm. A skinny guy with tats, and two toughs along with him. The same trio who had accosted him outside his apartment.

"Said I'd be seeing you, Fox." The tattooed leader laughed. "You should have given me those Greek documents. Now get up. All of you."

They stood, hands in the air. "You're not with Charles," Harry said. "He'd never be this stupid."

"You were lying about not having his papers."

"No idea what you're talking about."

"Save it."

Sara spoke over Harry's shoulder. "This is a Brittonic site. It has nothing to do with Greek artifacts."

"Shut her up or I will." Tattoos stared at Harry as he said it. "All of you back up."

175

They all stepped backward. Harry stumbled on one of the chunks of rock from the toppled stone. The two beefy men were focused on Tony, their biggest captive. Tattoos kept his attention on Harry, and he was the only one holding a gun. A six-shot revolver. That told Harry these guys didn't have great connections outside of America. Firearms were harder to come by in the United Kingdom, but a revolver? These guys were outside their comfort zone.

Harry needed to control the situation and put these guys off balance. He played his only card. He started talking.

"You want the documents? Get Charles on the phone and I'll tell him where they are."

"What?" Sara grabbed his arm. "You will not."

Tattoos spoke to his friends in a language Harry didn't recognize. Hard consonants littered each word. The beefy pair made noises that could have been laughter. Tattoos turned back to Harry. "You had your chance. Tell me where the documents are, then tell me what you're doing here." He barked at his men again, and one of them pulled out a flashlight. It took only a second for them to spot the bronze box.

"What the hell?" the tattooed man asked. "That box was underneath it." Lines creased his forehead. "How?" He rattled the pistol, as though Harry had forgotten about it. "Lie and I shoot your knee out."

Harry spoke quickly. "I had the documents, but I lost them."

Tattoos looked up from the box. "You had the papers in your place earlier?" he asked. Harry nodded. "Too bad you didn't give them to me then. Now, what's in the box?"

"Gold. A lot of it." Greed was a powerful motivator. Maybe strong enough to throw these goons off the scent.

"Where is it?"

Harry pointed at Tony. "He has it."

Tattoos aimed the gun at Tony. "Bring it here."

Tony did as ordered, displaying the ingots for inspection.

"That's all?" Tattoos asked. Harry nodded. "What else is in there?"

"Historical papers," Sara said. "You keep the gold. Just don't destroy the rest of it."

"You think I'm a fool?" Tattoos sneered. "The papers are worth more than the gold."

"The paper is written in a dead language. No one can read it."

Tattoos chewed on that one. Harry tried to keep still as he used his foot to pull two of the baseball-sized stones closer.

"I bet you can read it." Tattoos turned the gun on Sara. "You're some kind of professor."

Harry's chest went cold. Charles had no idea Harry worked with Sara Hamed. How did this thug know Sara's background?

"I can't read it without help."

Tattoos waved a hand at her. "Two sand-caters like you and Fox can't read it? You're lying. Doesn't matter. Tony will tell us the truth."

Harry's heart stopped beating. *Tony.* This guy knew Tony's name.

Then Tattoos lowered his gun and touched Tony's shoulder. "Isn't that right?"

Tony's head dropped.

Harry sputtered for a second, head spinning, then stared at Tony. "You sold us out?" An emptiness filled him when Tony didn't deny it. "I trusted you. Brought you with me."

Tony finally met his eyes. Even in the moonlight, Harry saw the pain. "I'm sorry, Harry. They threatened my family."

"Threatened your family?" A rage Harry didn't know he could muster took hold. "Why didn't you tell me? Vincent would have helped us."

Tattoos snorted. "Not now."

Harry was too angry to notice. "You're part of the Morellos," he went on. "They're like family. They helped me when my father died. They'd help you. But you didn't ask." The scowl on his face appeared to physically wound Tony. "Instead, you sold us out."

Tattoos may have said something else, waving his gun again, but Harry couldn't look away. Tony, a man he'd trusted with his life, was a traitor. In Harry's world there was nothing worse. No matter what, you stuck with your friends. Lose those bonds and you were nothing.

"You're right." Tony was facing away from Tattoos, talking directly to Harry.

Harry cocked his head. "What?"

"I'm sorry," Tony whispered. "Take the leader."

Harry blinked, and Tony Cervelli came alive. Tattoos never saw Tony's arm flash out and smack his gun away. A gunshot split the air as the tattooed man stumbled back, and Tony landed a solid punch to the nearest larger man's chin. The big guy went down. Harry scooped up a baseball-sized rock and let it fly. The second big man went down, the rock cracking off his head with a sickening *thunk*. He bounced off one of the standing stones before falling into the tall grass.

The first goon was back up and wrestling with Tony, who used his long arms to get a grip on the guy's neck. Harry turned and found Tattoos had recovered his footing and was digging in the tall grass, searching for the gun. Harry ran at him, closing the gap as Tattoos found his pistol and lifted it. Tattoos took aim at the struggling pair, the gun barking an instant before Harry slammed into him and they went tumbling in the thick grass. Someone cried out.

Harry fought like a kid from Brooklyn. Eye gouges, groin kicks, the dirtier the better. Metal flashed as the gun barrel swiped across Harry's face, clipping his chin and knocking him off the tattooed man. Harry grabbed for the man's wrist as he fell and the gun went off again. Another shout of pain filled the air.

Harry twisted, the gun came free, then a lightning-fast kick knocked the wind from Harry's gut. Tattoos was trying to stand. Harry whipped his boot out, missed, and got a foot to the knee in return. He rolled away and found the pistol in the grass. He grabbed it as Tattoos flew at him, snarling. Harry pulled the trigger. The muzzle flash lit up the night. Tattoos kept coming and Harry fired again.

Tattoos dropped heavily into the grass beside Harry. He didn't move as Harry scrambled away, pistol in hand. Two shots left. Where were

Sara and Tony? What had happened to the first goon?

Harry jumped up, finger on the trigger. Sara stood by the Whispering Knights. Both hands covered her mouth as she stared at the ground.

"He's dead." Her voice was muffled.

"Who's dead?" Harry kicked Tattoos; he didn't budge. Nobody with that much of their neck missing would. "Are you hurt?"

She didn't respond. Harry darted to her side and stopped as realization hit him. *They're all dead.* One of the big men had been the first hit when his boss fired wildly. The second thug had suffered a much different fate. The rock Harry threw had knocked him backwards to the ground – directly on top of an upright shard left from them tipping over the stone. The spear like flake of rock protruded through his chest.

"Where's Tony?"

Sara moved aside. "Here."

Tony lay at her feet with a small bullet hole above one eyebrow. Harry didn't have to lean over to know a much bigger hole was on the back of his head.

"The second shot hit him," Harry said.

"He came back," Sara said. Both hands still covered her mouth. "He tried to save us." She turned to Harry, latching onto his shoulder for support as tears muffled her words.

Harry gripped her arm with one hand, scanning their surroundings as he did. He kept the pistol in his free hand. "He sold us out. That's how these guys found us here. It's how they found me in Brooklyn. They had Tony on the inside. We have to go," he said. "Frisk the guy who got impaled. I'll check the others and Tony."

He knelt by the tattooed man, checking his pockets to find a cell phone and a set of keys before going to Tony and the thug who'd been shot. Sara hadn't moved. "What are you doing?" Harry asked her, standing up to face her.

"Tony's dead." She wiped away tears. "He tried to help us, and now he's dead. Because of what we're doing."

"His choices got him killed. Not us."

"He didn't ask for any of this."

"No, but he caused it. He should have told me someone threatened his family. I could have taken care of it. Then these goons wouldn't have shown up at my house, wouldn't have followed us here with a gun, and Tony wouldn't have gotten shot. None of this would have happened if Tony had made the right choice."

Her eyes narrowed. "What do you mean, 'taken care of it'? You sound like some kind of gangster." She moved toward him, her eyes not moving from his. "You tell me you acquire information and artifacts for a living. For whom? You never say. All I know is you work with the New York police, you have connections to incredible information, and you seem to have an endless supply of money to run around the globe." Sara stepped forward again until their noses almost touched. "What exactly do you do, Harry Fox? I don't know anyone whose job involves so much destruction." She indicated the carnage around them. "Or so many dead bodies."

Harry bit his lip. Of all the times for her to start asking questions. "I'm employed by a private citizen, a very wealthy one. I'm not always after artifacts. Information can be even more valuable, and when there's a chance artifacts are involved, I use them to follow a trail." His arms went wide. "I'm not one of the bad guys."

He was surprised to find his jaw was clenched. Sara Hamed stirred emotions in him like no one else. She must have felt it too, for she stood there, her head tilted, studying his face. Harry took his opportunity. "We have to clean this site and leave. You want to find out what Quintus left for us?" He nodded to the bronze box. "Then help me. We can't find anything in a police station."

To his surprise, she didn't argue. "Perhaps I don't know as much about you as I should," she said, her voice softer now. "And you'd better tuck those out of sight." She pointed to his amulet, and then the pistol.

"Right." He tucked the pistol into his waistband, and the amulet disappeared beneath his shirt, but not before it triggered a memory. Harry filed that for later.

He checked Tony's pockets, removing his cell phone and wallet. From the other two bodies he retrieved sets of keys and cash. "Three sets of keys, three cell phones, and cash," Harry said, half to himself. "No identification on the three of them. Maybe we'll find more in their cars."

Sara stepped over a pair of bodies and knelt in front of the hole they'd uncovered beneath the fallen stone. "I need space and light to inspect this scroll," she told him, all business again. "The box itself is incredible." She held the artifact in front of her. "Two thousand years underground and it still looks amazing."

It dazzled in the abundant moonlight. The sky was now a sea of midnight blue pierced by stars. Beautiful as it was, it also left them visible to any passing cars.

"I'll find us a quiet place to do that," Harry said. He headed for the fence and prepared to climb up and return to their car.

Sara stayed put. "We're leaving Tony here?" she asked.

Tony was dead. Did that bother Harry? Yes, more than he'd let on. "We can't take his body."

"He deserves better than to be left behind."

"I'll take care of getting him home. We won't convince the British authorities this was self-defense, Sara. We have to keep going. Do you want to throw away everything we've discovered so far?"

She hesitated for a beat, then slowly followed him over to the fence. He clambered to the top of it, reached down and took the box from Sara, then dropped to the ground. She climbed over and joined him, and they both headed to their car. They had made it to the parking area when Harry stopped, staring in dismay.

"Shit."

Sara stopped, her head twisting around. "What?"

Harry pointed at their car. "Look what they did."

All four tires on the car were flattened, the sidewall on each one punctured.

"We can't fix them," he said. His hand went to a pocket. "Each of those guys had a set of keys. So where are the cars?"

No other vehicles were in sight. "They could be far down the road," Sara said. "Why didn't we hear them approach?"

"We should have seen the lights. Unless they drove without any on, which is crazy. One wrong turn on these hilly roads and you're in in ditch." Another thought slipped into his head. "Each of them had keys. Why would they have three cars?"

"Because they didn't drive cars." She pointed in the direction they'd come from. "Fifty meters ahead."

"Motorcycles?" He looked at Sara and then back at the row of bikes. "You up for it?"

"As if we have another choice." She hurried over, and Harry followed her, keys jingling in his pocket.

They had used a stolen motorcycle to get out of a sticky situation near Cairo. Harry had never suspected Sara knew how to ride a bike until she'd kicked him off one such machine and deftly driven it past numerous security guards. That was the last time he'd underestimated her.

"These are electric," Sara said when they reached the bikes. "Did you ever ride one? They're practically silent."

Harry had not. "No wonder we didn't hear them. Keep the lights off and they'd be invisible. Smart." He gave her a set of keys, which fired up the second bike she tried. Harry started one of the others, the engine scarcely purring when it came alive. "We passed a hotel in the last town," he said. "Big and anonymous. The kind of place we can lie low for a night."

"Won't that be the first place authorities will look?"

"Yes, but we won't stay long. Get some sleep, figure out what's inside the box, then move on." He straddled the bike, throttled the engine and held on as the machine took off. His phone vibrated in his pocket. Three quick rings, all in a row. A unique ringer that told him Joey Morello was calling. He'd get back to his boss later.

Sara kept pace as they crested a rise before flicking on their headlights. The countryside was a dark blur as they rode faster than necessary back to Oxford. A generic chain hotel they'd passed was still open, the bright sign a welcoming beacon. Sara and Harry parked their bikes on the far side, beside a row of hedges so they weren't visible from the road.

"Get us a room," Harry said. He gave her a handful of cash.

"They'll ask for my identification."

"Use it. We won't be here long." Sara cradled the bronze box as she walked inside. Harry grabbed his phone, checking the screen to find two missed calls. No text messages. Interesting. The second missed call made his eyebrows rise. What did Rose Leroux want? He dialed Joey first. The phone rang and rang, which was odd. Joey normally had his phone with him, and if he didn't, one of his bodyguards did. The voicemail was ready to pick up when Joey answered.

"He's dead, Harry."

Ice spiked Harry's gut. "Who's dead?"

"My father."

Chapter 20

Southwest of London

The London skyline was an hour in the rearview mirror when Pete Brody's phone rang. The other two men in the sport utility vehicle fell silent when he answered.

"Yes?"

"We have a complication."

It was his SAS man, a sympathetic Druid Stan Cobb had found, a man with the skills to track Harry Fox. His name was Wayne Lineker, and from what Pete knew about him, he was exactly who they needed.

"I'm listening," Pete said.

"The two targets left Wight and traveled to the Rollright Stones. That's where I am now. Another man joined them here."

"Any idea who he is?"

"No. He doesn't have identification."

Pete sat up in his seat. "Are you with him now?"

"What's left of him. I have a question." An unmistakable hardness crept into Wayne's voice. "Is there anything you didn't tell me about Harry Fox?"

"Stan gave you all we know. Why?"

"The intelligence report said he collects artifacts for a New York crime boss. Educated. Intelligent. Nothing to suggest he is a violent man."

"Correct," Pete said. "We didn't find anything like that."

"I'm looking at four corpses. None of them is Harry Fox."

Retired Captain Wayne Lineker, who had served in Afghanistan and Iraq, was not easily disturbed by violence. Pete had read his file. Wayne had entered both wars with a desire to make the world a better place by serving his country. Somewhere on the desert battlefields Wayne had had a change of heart. Pete assumed it tied to the oil field fires Saddam's men had set to stop invading forces. Forty-eight Iraqi civilians burned to death in the blaze, many of them children. Wayne's unit had been the first on the scene. After that, Wayne no longer fought for Britain. Instead, he had fought to protect the land, to stop men from ravaging nature for their own political gain, collateral damage be damned. It hadn't taken long for people in Pete's orbit to take notice of a man with his talents, skills that were quite useful to Pete Brody.

"Three of the dead I don't know. The fourth is the man who met Fox here at the Rollright Stones – he's dead too. Fox and the woman traveling with him arrived in one car. It's now sitting beside the road with four slashed tires. I think these dead men didn't want Fox to leave."

"So now they're on foot," Pete said. "You should be able to find them."

"Not quite. These three dead men all came on motorcycles. Harry's dead friend came in a car, which is still here, and so is one motorcycle. The other two motorcycles are gone. I found tracks heading toward Oxford."

"Harry and the woman drove motorcycles back into town?"

"I think so," Wayne said. "Electric bikes."

"Think you can find them?"

"I'm SAS. I can find them. If you and your men come help, we find them a lot faster."

"How far to Oxford?" Pete asked the two men up front.

"An hour."

Pete relayed this to Wayne. "Start searching now. I don't have any other leads on their location besides you."

"I'll check the local hotels first. That's where I would go." Wayne paused, perhaps studying the dark countryside. "Hopefully they need to get cleaned up before heading on. There's a lot of blood here. Three of the men died from gunshot wounds. One was impaled on a sharp stone."

"A sharp stone?"

"Looks like Harry and his companion knocked over one of the stones. The stone broke apart when it fell, and some of the fragments are quite sharp. I think something was removed from under the stone after it fell. I found blue-green flecks in the dirt. Metallic."

"Start searching in Oxford," Pete said. "I'll call when we get there."

He clicked off and leaned toward the front seats. "Go faster," Pete said. "We're running out of time."

Chapter 21

Oxford

Harry sat on a hotel room bed. He stared ahead, not really seeing the generic prints on the walls or hearing the traffic passing outside. His world had changed. The two most important men in his life were gone, both murdered by unknown assailants. No matter how strong he imagined himself to be, Harry was not prepared for this.

Sara lay on the bed, having collapsed in a heap minutes after Harry bolted the door behind them. "The aftereffects of adrenaline," he'd told her. "Don't try to analyze the scroll now. You'll miss things. Your body needs rest. I'll wake you in a few hours. Then we keep moving."

For once, she'd listened to him and merely snapped a few photos of the scroll before falling asleep.

Harry, too, had closed his eyes, though sleep proved elusive. The conversation with Joey replayed in his mind. A bomb had exploded at Sanna while Vincent and Joey were there for dinner. Joey had been on the phone with Harry just moments earlier, a call that had saved his life. If not for that, Joey would be dead alongside Vincent.

Headlights of a passing car turned the window's curtains translucent, and Harry held his breath. As though someone were coming after them now. The men who'd chased them were dead. Even so, he had covered their stolen motorcycles with a blanket from inside the hotel room.

His thoughts turned back to Vincent Morello. Vincent was dead. The thought was almost too much to take in. Vincent, gone. Right now, Joey needed support, needed Harry to do his part. Which was to unravel the mystery of the scroll.

Harry got out of bed, moving with care so as not to disturb Sara. He opened his bag and slipped the knuckledusters he'd carried from home into his pocket. Not that he wanted to use them. His father had always said a smart man outwits his opponents. That meant being prepared, and with no chance of sleeping any time soon, Harry figured he might as well reconnoiter the area for trouble. It beat staring at the ceiling.

Harry slid out into the hallway, a sliver of light falling on Sara's closed eyes before he locked the door behind him. Their ground-floor room was at the building's rear, close to a back exit to the parking lot where they'd hidden their motorcycles. He passed a window looking out over the well-lit parking lot. Nobody prowled the asphalt, no cars sat idling in the lot.

An attendant manned the front desk. Hair cut as though his barber was in training, the young man clicked madly at a keyboard, eyes glued to the screen. Either he cared more about room assignments than anyone should, or the kid was playing video games. Harry kept close to the wall as he moved silently along the carpet, alert for any other guests. No one else seemed to be around, and the kid didn't move when Harry stopped in front of him. Harry leaned an elbow on the counter. No response. Harry cleared his throat.

The kid didn't look up. "How may I help you?" Flashing lights reflected in the young man's eyes.

He probably made criminal wages working the graveyard shift. An opportunity.

"I need a favor."

A couple of clicks, then the flashing lights stopped. The kid pulled an earbud from one ear and finally met Harry's gaze. "Yes?"

Harry pulled a fifty-pound note from his pocket. "I'm here on personal business, and I need to make sure no one knows I'm here."

The kid looked at the money, then at Harry. "I see."

"I'm hoping you'll help keep my privacy. Have you seen anyone who looks out of place?"

The kid at least had the decency to pause before responding. "No, sir."

"Good. Anyone asking odd questions, maybe telling you they were looking for someone?" Again, the kid said no. "If anyone does, would you let me know?" Harry slid the fifty pounds across the counter.

The note vanished. "Of course, sir."

"Good man. This stays between us, right?"

"Yes, sir."

An engine rumbled faintly outside. Harry turned and looked through the entrance, out over the main road fronting the hotel. No cars passed.

"Thanks," he told the kid. "I'll swing back later to see if anyone caught your eye."

"Understood, sir."

Back to his video game before Harry had even turned away. Not the best sentry, but the best available. The thin extra layer of protection would have to do; they needed only a few more hours in this place. Harry went through the front doors and outside. A chill had come in with the stars overhead, and he put his hands in his pockets. Across the road was an office building fronted by a fountain. Cars lined the sidewalks on either side, all of them empty. Harry poked his head around the corner of the hotel, looking up and down in either direction. One man stood outside a parked car down the block, too far away to make out clearly. An orange dot flickered when he tossed a cigarette to the pavement before hurrying out of sight. He never looked up.

Nothing doing out front. Now for the rear, and then maybe his mind would settle enough to get a few hours' sleep. He still couldn't process Vincent's death. The New York he'd return to would be far different from the one he'd left. Joey Morello now had the weight of the world on his shoulders. He needed Harry's help, and Harry had his own burden – fixing things with Sara.

Who could help him right his world? The only person Harry could count on for that help was the one he wanted least to ask. Agent Nora Doyle had tried to recruit him when they'd first met, to use him as a way inside black-market antiquities deals. He had declined, even as they became reluctant allies in Iran, teaming with Sara on a journey that forged the sort of trust only dodging bullets and falling boulders can. Nora Doyle had vouched for Harry once. Now he had to enlist her again to show Sara he wasn't a mobster. He needed to transform himself in order to make that happen, go from being a pure treasure hunter to a person Sara could trust. Maybe he couldn't go totally straight, but he had a plan to get close to legit – to become a sort of modern-day privateer who helped himself and the authorities. If he was smart, he could work with Nora to improve Joey's position while also getting Sara to trust him.

He warmed to the idea while crossing the parking lot. It could work: offering Nora information in exchange for her cooperation in not arresting him. Work with her on one end, keep doing what he did now on the other. That way he could finally be honest with Sara, tell her what he did and have it be legit – or at least as close to legit as he'd ever get. Without that, Sara would never accept a man like him. The way she'd looked at him tonight as they stood amid the carnage had made that clear, and he didn't blame her. She'd worked her whole life to become a tenured professor of Egyptology in Germany, no mean feat for an Egyptian woman.

Tempered hope rose in his chest as he passed through a dark area of the parking lot and approached the charging station where he'd plugged in their motorcycles. He was lost in thought, which was why he didn't notice that the motorcycles were now in plain view until he was on top of them. He stopped short. *That's not right. I tossed a blanket over them.* The blanket lay beside the exposed bikes.

The breeze had died entirely. Harry leaned over and sniffed the air. Cigarette smoke? He stood up, a sixth sense telling him to turn, that something was seriously wrong. Harry dropped low, which was why the man who stepped out from around the hotel didn't see him. A man who glanced toward the bikes, his gaze lingering on them for a long moment before he turned back and headed around the rear of the building. Back toward the rear exit, the one near Harry's room.

Harry watched this unfold from between the spokes of a motorcycle tire. The guy could be a hotel guest. Or Harry's overactive imagination could be putting him on edge, the toll of their deadly evening. But then again, his gut instinct might be correct – that this guy didn't belong here, and he was looking for Harry.

What had Fred Fox always said? *I can't afford to believe in coincidences.* Harry moved quickly back to the front entrance. If this guy was looking for him, chances were he'd checked at the front desk first. Maybe those fifty pounds would pay off.

He ducked through the front doors to find his front desk attendant had vanished. Harry knocked on the counter. Where was that kid? He leaned over the counter. A man's shoe was lying on the floor. Harry leaned farther forward and saw that the shoe was still attached to a foot and a leg, and when he propped himself up to get a better look, he realized it was the kid's leg. The guy was lying flat on the ground, face down. He wasn't moving.

Harry ran around the counter and knelt beside the prone kid, checking for a pulse. Strong and steady, same as the kid's breathing. Harry grabbed the kid's shoulder and shook hard. "Hey, buddy. Wake up."

The kid's eyelids fluttered. "You okay?" Harry asked.

"What happened?" The kid tried to get up, making it to one elbow before his face clenched up. "Damn, that hurts." Harry helped lift him to a sitting position as the kid grabbed the back of his head. "That guy whacked me."

Harry froze. "Who?"

"Some guy who asked about you." Fear flashed on the kid's face. "I didn't tell him, I swear." He rubbed his head and then stared at his hand, checking for blood.

"What did he look like?" Harry grabbed the kid's shirt and lifted him up. "Where did he go?"

The kid started talking. "He didn't look like you. A white guy,

British. He came in, said he was looking for a man that looked like you." The kid gestured at Harry's face. "Egyptian, whatever you are."

"I'm from Brooklyn," Harry said.

"I turned to the rear monitor to act like I was checking for you. He must have come around the desk and hit me." The kid's gaze went over Harry's shoulder. "Uh-oh."

"What?"

"My keycard is gone. I keep it on that hook. Next to the list of room assignments."

"I don't see a list," Harry said, turning and following the kid's gaze.

"It's gone too."

Harry didn't see the kid hit the floor when he dropped him. The assailant knew what room he and Sara were in. He raced down the hall and skidded to a stop at the corner of the corridor that led to their room. The knuckledusters slipped around his fingers. He leaned around the corner slowly, his chest tight.

The hall was empty. Harry moved silently toward their door. A quick glance into an alcove where the ice machine hummed found it vacant. A few more steps and he could finally see their room door.

It was ajar.

Barely open, as though the lock hadn't caught when someone had tried to close it. Or perhaps it had been left open because the person coming in didn't want it to make noise when it shut. Had Sara woken up and headed out, looking for him? That was one reason the door might be open.

But no. He craned his neck and saw that Sara was still in bed, out cold. She wasn't roaming the halls searching for him.

Harry crept closer to the door, barely breathing, listening carefully. *There.* The floor creaked, as though someone was walking lightly inside the room. Harry nudged the door open far enough to see a shadow sliding across the carpet, backlit by the partially open window blinds. Only a sliver of light fell through, a sliver that now lit an intruder moving in the room.

The figure stopped near the bed with his back to the door. *He was going for Sara.*

He didn't stop to think. Silent as a cat, Harry stepped in, took a breath and charged. The intruder whirled towards the sound of Harry's footsteps an instant before Harry smashed into the man with a lowered shoulder and sent him sprawling. Harry bounced off and rolled to one side, catching a glimpse of the intruder's face as he fell. Something dark and metallic flashed in the intruder's hand. Harry hit the ground and rolled, two whooshes of air sounding inside the room. *Pfft. Pfft.*

"Sara, wake up!" Harry shouted in the darkness. She shouted, rolling off the bed on the far side and out of sight.

The guy had a suppressor on his gun. Harry spun, rose, and kicked the intruder's legs out from under him. The man fell, his gun arm pointed at Harry, and another shot buzzed out. Harry was on his feet in a second. His foot slammed on the guy's arm. The intruder grunted, letting go of the gun before twisting away and out of reach. Harry kicked the gun as hard as he could.

"Harry, are you hurt?" Sara's panicked voice filled the air.

"Run!" Harry shouted, aiming a kick at the fallen man.

She rose from her crouch on the opposite side of the bed. "What?"

"Get out of here!" That was all he had time to say before a fist like iron smashed into his gut. He twisted so he fell back instead of down. The knee strike that would have cracked his chin missed. Harry caught himself with one hand and lashed a foot out at the intruder's other knee. A cry sounded as the knee buckled. He fell back toward the gun Harry had booted away, and which was now lying in the light falling through the window.

"Harry, where are you?" Sara called.

"Down here." He stood, reached over the bed and grabbed her arm. "Come on – let's get out of here!"

Sara jerked her arm free. "The scroll!" she shouted. Sara dropped down, reached under the bed and came out with the bronze box.

That was the last Harry saw before the intruder barreled into him.

The room spun. Harry tried to twist as he fell, but the guy had him in a bear hug and crushed him to the floor. A head butt rattled his brain, the dark room going fuzzy for an instant. Harry rolled over, brought his knee up and jammed it into the man's groin. The intruder yelped and rolled off him, but it wasn't enough. The intruder lifted an elbow and aimed it at Harry's face.

Thunk. The man fell like a stone. He bounced off Harry's forearms and rolled back, away from the window. Sara stood above them, the bronze box in both hands, lid flapping open as she watched the man roll and readied her box for another blow.

"Move," Harry yelled as he ran and launched himself at the window. For the briefest second, he wondered if this would work. Glass shattered, cool air rushed down his shirt, and the hard ground came up to meet him. He rolled, getting to his feet. He turned as more glass crunched and Sara dove through the hole he'd created and landed on her shoulder, tucking and rolling until she rose to her feet. She ran toward their bikes as Harry dug in his pocket for a key.

"Jump on." He leapt astride the bike, firing the engine as Sara threw her leg over the seat behind him. He twisted the throttle and they whizzed out of the parking lot.

"Stop," Sara shouted. "We left the scroll."

He looked over his shoulder. Sara held up the bronze box. It was empty. "Where is it?"

"It fell out when I hit him," she said. "I have to get it."

Sparks bounced off the pavement at Harry's feet. The intruder was leaning out of their hotel room window, taking aim for a second shot.

Harry punched it. Wind whistled in his ears as muzzle flash glittered in his handlebar mirror. "Do you have your phone?" he shouted over a shoulder. "You took pictures of it."

"That's not good enough. We need the scroll."

"Too late now." He blew through a stop sign and drove deeper into Oxford. To where, he had no idea. Streetlights buzzed past overhead as they sped away from an unknown enemy. An enemy trying to kill them to get the secrets hidden in the scroll. Unraveling its secrets first was the only way for Harry and Sara to win this race, and win they must: Harry had no intention of finding out what happened to the loser.

Chapter 22

Oxford

Twenty minutes later Harry finally stopped in front of an all-night takeaway near the Oxford campus. Even at this hour, a slow stream of people walked in and out of the restaurant, and several bicycles were propped outside the front door as deliverymen waited for orders. A row of benches offered resting spots along the sidewalk. Harry parked their bike in a shadow, then led Sara to an equally hidden bench. He could feel her shaking as she leaned against him.

"This will do for now." Harry eyed the brick wall to their backs, ten feet tall and topped with a spiked metal fence.

"We need the scroll," Sara said again. She pulled her wind-swept hair up and secured it behind her head. One of the bicycle deliverymen cast a long eye her way. She scowled. He suddenly found the ground interesting. "I only have some pictures."

"Which will have to do," Harry said. "You start looking at them. I'll get coffee."

He fidgeted in line at the takeaway store, anxious to get back to Sara. As expected, she was completely fine on the bench when he returned.

"Here you go," he said, handing her a paper cup.

She set the phone down and sipped her drink. "Believe me when I tell you half of what I learn from a scroll isn't written on it. There could be other markings my camera didn't capture. Without examining the material, I can't say with any certainty where it came from."

"Work with what you have," he said. "Don't worry about what you don't. My father used to say that."

"Fred Fox gave Ben Franklin a go in the quotes arena." A hint of a smile crossed her face. "Unfortunately, whoever was after us has the scroll, and if I miss anything from these pictures, they likely won't miss it. Their entire team died at the Stones, yet they still found us here."

"I don't think that gunman at the hotel was with those other three from the Stones."

"Why not?"

"A couple of reasons. Those three men were working through Tony. He was the reason they found us. How would anyone else know where we went without Tony?" Harry fell silent as two women strolled past, both wearing backpacks. "That, and the fact the guy at our hotel had a suppressed handgun. The three men at Rollright had one pistol between them, and it was a revolver. Getting a suppressed semiautomatic in England?" Harry shook his head. "That takes serious juice. A kind the Stones team didn't have."

He looked over to find her peering at him. "What?" he asked.

"How do you know what sort of *juice* it takes to acquire a semiautomatic in England?"

Harry shrugged. "Gun laws are strict here. You can't just pick them up from your local dealer."

"I don't have a local gun dealer. Do you?"

"I'm not a big fan of guns," Harry said. "The last thing I want is to be around more of them."

"Yet you know quite a bit about them." Sara crossed her arms. "I wanted to ask you this before I flew over, but I talked myself out of it. You've told me very little about yourself. Given that I've nearly died with you more than once, I don't even know what you do. And Joey, the man I met in Brooklyn. He looks like a gangster."

Harry bristled slightly. "Joey Morello is my closest friend."

"Which doesn't answer my question. Joey and his father employ you to, what – collect artifacts?"

"I manage part of the Morello portfolio." Weak, even to Harry's ears.

"That could mean anything. And your connection with the D.A.'s anti-trafficking team." She pointed at his chest. "Do you work for them?"

Harry laughed, because it was both absurd and close to the truth. "I'm too honest for that sort of job."

"If someone asked me what I did, I could clearly say I'm a tenured Egyptologist at the University of Trier. I lecture, conduct research, and occasionally work at dig sites." Now her gaze returned to him. "Your turn."

Stars dimmed by the city lights faintly lit the sky. Cool air snuck down his shirt collar. Inside Harry's head, warring thoughts raged. On one side, the desire to tell her everything loomed large. He was tired of hiding things from her, worrying she'd figure it all out anyway and then want nothing more to do with him. Maybe that was the best-case scenario, he thought grimly. Harry could stop hiding who he was, throw open the doors and let her in.

On the other side, he could stall and stick with his plan, officially working with Nora Doyle and the Manhattan D.A.'s office. This had, of course, been a ludicrous idea not even twenty-four hours ago in a world where Vincent Morello was alive and well. But now Vincent was gone and Joey had the weight of Vincent's legacy on his shoulders. Joey needed Harry, and that came first. The best way to help Joey was shoring up their power in any possible way. Finding Queen Boudica's mysterious relic and gaining support in the D.A.'s office seemed a pretty good way to do that.

Harry took a sip of his coffee and made the decision. "I used to work for Joey's father," he began. "Now I work for Joey."

"Why the change to Joey?"

"Because his father was murdered yesterday."

Sara's hand flew to her mouth. "What?"

"He died in an explosion in New York. Joey and the police are trying to find out more right now." That was the truth. "Now Joey will run his father's entire business. Which includes what I do." He took a breath. "Buying, selling and locating artifacts is my role."

"And that can be quite opaque when it comes to legality."

"Every artifact I deal with has legitimate provenance." Mostly. "I didn't ask for this line of work. I inherited it." She raised an eyebrow. "My father did the exact same work for the Morellos. He taught me the business. When he died, it became my job."

"That sounds like a long story."

"Yes and no. Too long to go through now. I promise I'll tell you everything when this is all over."

"If we survive." Sara leaned back on the bench. "That's the problem, Harry. I search for artifacts in my job, but it has never resulted in anyone getting injured, much less killed. Which seems to happen regularly for you."

He couldn't argue there, so he stayed quiet.

"You're a fascinating man. I've never met anyone like you. You have adventures and quests – and they are truly quests – and each one is the thrill of a lifetime. Other scholars would love to experience even one of them." Sara looked down at her phone. "But I'm not sure I do. It's dangerous. Too dangerous for me."

"It's not always like this." A lie, through and through. "You're not so uninteresting yourself, you know."

"That is beside the point. You live an endlessly dangerous life." Sara tapped a button on her phone, bringing up images of the scroll. "I can't do this. It's simply not who I am."

"You're giving up?"

"No," she said sharply. "We'll see this through, then I'm finished." She paused "One more thing. I told you I learned more about your amulet."

Harry sat forward. "Yes, you did. What is it?"

"It's about the double-headed eagle necklace you purchased in Brooklyn before I arrived. It was something Tony said at the Stones that jogged my memory. He wanted to visit Italy, remember? I said he shouldn't miss Pompeii."

"What does a volcanic island have to do with Cleopatra's necklace?"

"I told you earlier the necklace you purchased looked familiar. Now I remember why. I saw a necklace like it in a beautiful mural preserved in the ruins of Pompeii."

"Did Cleopatra ever visit Pompeii?"

"Not that I know of."

"Then it makes no sense. It can't be the same necklace." He studied her face, finding only certainty. "Can it?"

"The Pompeii mural was copied from another painting that was in the Temple of Caesar. That mural was destroyed after Antony and Cleopatra lost the War of Actium against Octavian. The Pompeii copy is the only one that survived from antiquity. That mural is where I believe we should look to find answers as to what the necklace signifies."

Harry stood quickly. "If Cleopatra wanted to leave a clue, she'd be hard pressed to do better than paint it in full sight in the Temple of Caesar. She never suspected she and Antony would lose the war and die so soon," he said. "The woman certainly didn't think she'd ever lose."

"She had little reason to," Sara said. "History bent to her will, not the other way round. Until the end, that is."

He sat down. "Thank you. I appreciate it."

She looked at him with an expression he couldn't decipher. "You don't have to thank me." She sighed, then returned to her phone. "I may have figured out one part of the scroll."

The page had turned on his amulet search for now. Harry touched the golden piece around his neck – for luck or comfort, he wasn't sure. "What is it? I can't translate Latin as well as you."

"This scroll is different from the other markers we found. The message is much clearer."

"How so?"

"The message from Nero cloaked General Quintus's destination by obliquely referring to metal that was produced there. On the Isle of Wight, the homage to Dagda hid the real message, which pointed us to the Rollright Stones. Quintus hid this scroll beneath the stones, which we found only after interpreting an inscription on the stone." She looked at him. "What's my point? All of these were obscured, messages hidden inside other messages. This is straightforward except for one part. Listen."

Sara began reading aloud.

The path of Dagda and the Keltoi must be respected, for at the end lies the terrifying power of Queen Boudica. I cannot allow this gift from the gods to be lost, so I must betray my Emperor. Death is the reward for such acts. Given this, I must believe those who read this follow the one true faith, that of the Keltoi.

You visited the shrine of Dagda below the tin isle. You discovered the truth beneath the rodland rix. You, fellow believer, have proven yourself worthy. Now venture to the high castle of the Dumnonii. Kneel at the pillar of Dagda, then peer down from the northern edge to the white wrath of Nuada. Hold fast to your faith. Leap to his embrace when he slumbers most. Nuada will reveal himself. Nuada holds the terrible, magnificent gift from Dagda.

Do not pair the powers to make it greater. Two will bring the wrath of Dagda, destroying those who tempt his gift.

"Dagda again," Harry said. "What's the Dumnonii, and who is Nuada?"

"Focus on the opening paragraph. This confirms that the *terrifying power* Nero tasked him to get rid of still exists. He also confirms that the path he laid out is the one we followed, and this tells us there's one more stop on the journey. Another check that whoever's following his trail worships Dagda and the Keltoi."

"What's the warning about not pairing powers?"

"I don't know. I hope it becomes clear once we find this next location. I'd rather not deal with Dagda's wrath."

"Agreed." He looked up as the nearest streetlight went dark, their murky bench becoming even gloomier. "Are the Dumnonii part of Celtic lore?"

Sara shook her head. "No. The Dumnonii were a British tribe who lived in various parts of Britannia over time. In Quintus's time they occupied what is now Cornwall."

Harry's grasp of English geography could have stood a refresh. "Where's that?"

"The southwest corner of England."

"Only people knowledgeable about Britannia's geography and cultural makeup would understand him."

"Exactly. He's using the local knowledge to hide his path from other Romans."

The nearby streetlight flickered back to life. Sara's eyes lit up. "Quintus points to a *high castle* where the tribe lived. What would have constituted a castle in Britannia is much different from the castles we see today."

Harry might not have known exactly where Cornwall was, but he had a firm grasp on England's legends, stories born centuries ago and shaped by each passing generation. One of England's most legendary figures had ties to a castle near Cornwall. A man whose sword Harry had once discovered.

"There's a castle near there where King Arthur was supposedly conceived."

The Sara he knew from before she had grown wary of him came alive now. "A bit of sorcery was involved, if I recall."

"Tintagel Castle," Harry said. "Legend has it Merlin disguised Uther Pendragon, Arthur's father, as another man, the man who owned the castle. Uther got up to some chicanery with that man's wife, which produced Arthur. Tintagel Castle is in ruins now," he said. "Popular ruins, which lots of people visit. There are also graveyards there, and archaeologists don't usually dig where people are buried. That's a positive."

"Which means it is more likely that anything left by Quintus is still there," Sara said. She touched his arm. "Have you ever been to the site?" Harry said he hadn't. "Neither have I. I know it's on a cliffside over the ocean."

"A lot of ground to search," Harry said. "Good thing Quintus told us to focus on the northern edge. What did he say about the *pillar of Dagda?*"

"To kneel there, then *peer down from the northern edge to the white wrath of Nuada*. First, we find this pillar." She looked at her hand and seemed surprised it was still resting on his arm. "Have you heard of any pillars associated with Celtic myth?" Sara tugged on her hair as she spoke. "I have not."

"Me neither."

Sara stood from the bench. "Then we will just have to find it when we get there."

Harry grabbed her hand, hauled himself off the bench, and a minute later they buzzed out of Oxford into the night, on a path for Tintagel Castle. Sara wrapped her arms around his midsection the entire ride, a journey through seemingly endless fields of black with only the occasional town breaking through the darkness. Urged on by a sense of unease, Harry spotted the ocean less than three hours after leaving Oxford. Whitecaps frothed in the moonlight below rocky cliffs, the castle seeming to hover above the water, perched on a hilltop.

Bridges and walkways connected various high points of the area. Harry parked at the base of one prominent ridge, the earth running steeply up to an imposing stone structure thrown into shadow by the moonlight. The wind whistled through each crag and crevice. Harry nearly tumbled off the bike, his entire body stiff from the ride. Sara hopped off with ease, while Harry groaned softly and stretched every muscle he could.

"Where to start?" Sara asked herself.

Harry's phone vibrated. *Rose Leroux?* He glanced at Sara and touched a finger to his lips. "Evening, Rose." It was late the previous night back in New York. "Have you spoken to Joey?"

"Yes. It's tragic, but that's a different matter." Rose was a chameleon, impossible to read, though right now she had one focus. "We need to talk about your safety."

"I'm listening."

"Where are you?"

His training said to hold back. His gut told him this was real. "England. Searching for an artifact." Worry spiked in his chest. "Did Charles tell you to call me?"

"Charles not holding onto his merchandise is his problem, not mine. He'll be lucky if he avoids jail after that fiasco."

Rose always knew everything. "How is Joey?"

"About as you would expect. But as I said, that's a different matter. I'm calling about you, Harry. You are not safe."

"What do you know?"

"I suspect you have no idea who you're actually dealing with, and he is a very powerful man. Tell me what's happened."

He walked a few steps away so Sara couldn't hear him. "You're right. I'm not safe. Here's why."

Recounting his adventure in very general terms, he gave specifics on the three men who had accosted him in Brooklyn before reappearing at the Rollright Stones. Rose merely listened until he recounted Tony's betrayal and death.

"Be gentle with Tony's memory," she said. "He did what he felt he must. Even if you don't understand." Harry didn't, but he kept his mouth shut. "The coming days will decide if Joey replaces his father or if there is a war. Do not tell anyone else what Tony did. If there's any chance a Morello rival co-opted Tony Cervelli, admitting it makes Joey appear weak."

Harry agreed, then told Rose about the man who'd attacked them at the hotel in Oxford and his suspicions this man wasn't allied with the others. "It's not just the gun. This guy was much more organized." Harry thought for a second. "Lethal. The guy knew how to fight. He wasn't a gangster."

"You are correct."

"I am?"

"Unfortunately, yes." Rose paused, and Harry heard the sounds of her lighting another cigarette. He could practically see it sliding into a long-stemmed holder. "Certain information came to my attention during the course of a transaction."

Harry knew better than to ask what sale she'd brokered. "How does that relate to me?"

"The man who retained Charles to purchase the Greek letters was involved, and he is the reason you're in danger now. This adversary is far worse."

"Worse than another family trying to kill me?"

"These are religious fanatics."

"The path we're on isn't religious. It's pagan."

"What makes you believe there are no modern pagans?"

"What does that mean?"

"The documents you used in your search were written in Roman times." He had no idea how she knew that, but Harry confirmed it. "The path to your relic is hidden, at least in part, because the men who created it couldn't openly share their beliefs. Beliefs about what? Their religion."

An alarm bell dinged softly in his head. "You can't possibly have figured all this out from documents you've never seen."

"I have one other piece of information. The name of the man chasing you."

"Who is it?"

"Peter Brody. He is the Grand Archdruid Pete to millions of devotees."

Harry reached one hand out toward the motorcycle. "Grand *what?*" That got Sara's attention, and she came closer. "Hold on," Harry said to Rose. "I'm putting you on speaker. There's someone else here who needs to hear this."

Rose's voice rang out a moment later. "Professor Hamed?"

Sara visibly jumped. "Yes?"

"Hello," Rose said. "I am calling to help Harry in a time of danger. His and your safety is my top concern."

"How do you know my name?"

Harry took that one. "Rose knows everything. We can trust her."

"A dangerous man is chasing you," Rose said. "Much more deadly than those who blackmailed poor Tony Cervelli. The man following your path is Pete Brody. He leads the Celtic Order of Druids, a well-funded and rapidly growing organization. He desperately wants whatever you are chasing. It does not bode well for the two of you."

"Why not?" Sara asked.

"Pete Brody sent the man to your hotel," Rose said. "I suspect it was merely an initial salvo. Pete needs to find the end of this path before you do. Killing you would not give him pause."

"I thought Druids were peaceful," Sara said. "They protect the earth, strive to live in harmony with nature."

"Seemingly devout faith can mask true intention," Rose said. "Ten years ago, Pete Brody was the son of a conservative megachurch pastor. Now he's openly warring with other organized religions and has millions of followers. Pete Brody is ruthless."

"How do you know this?" Sara asked.

"I learned of his involvement during a business transaction. That is all I can say, though Harry will assure you I do not exaggerate."

"She's saved my life before," Harry said. "And my father's as well."

"What sort of transaction?" Sara asked.

"The private kind," Rose said. "Focus on your safety. The best way to do this is to complete your search at once. As long as you are following the trail, Pete Brody is following you."

Sara hesitated for a breath. "Thank you."

"We're on it," Harry said. "One more thing." Sara had already turned and headed for the ruins, flashlight in hand. "Tell me about Joey."

"This is the challenge Vincent was preparing his son for," Rose said.

"I cannot predict whether the other families will accept Joey in his place."

"The Canas won't."

"That's expected," Rose said. "They never allied themselves with Vincent."

"What are you going to do?"

Another long inhale of smoke on the other end. "I am not a kingmaker," Rose finally said. "But I am a practical woman. The wisest choice for everyone is to have Joey continue his father's legacy of relative peace and cooperation. It will be a profitable outcome for me, and the one I hope for. If I can help Joey, I will."

"Joey will be grateful."

"People will be hurt before this is over. That much is certain. Joey needs to be strong. He needs people around him that he can rely on. You know this, as much as you know the best way to support him is to succeed in your search." The sharp click of high heels on marble flooring ticked in Harry's ear. "Be alert, Harry. Joey is not the only one counting on you."

She clicked off. Harry stared at his phone for a moment. *Who else is counting on me?* Sara, but was Rose as well? Rose didn't rely on anyone other than herself, yet now it sounded like her future was in some way tied to him.

Sara called out from ahead. "You coming?"

"Right now." Harry pulled out a flashlight and hurried to her side, burying the unease in his gut, locking it away. He'd deal with that later. Once they survived tonight. "Find anything?" he asked.

"Steps." She aimed her light at the ground. Weather-beaten stone steps had been carved into the hillside. "These should take us toward the edge of the island. The northern edge. Let's hope there's a pillar there." She walked off without another word.

Harry followed, and they began ascending the incline toward jagged rocks that formed a long wall across the hilltop's southern side. The north side required no such fortification, as the ground fell away on a sharp cliff, the water lapping softly a hundred feet below.

The stone steps curved gently as they walked. Halfway up, the slope steepened and the stairs straightened out. The first defensive tower they passed stood no taller than two men, clearly a sentry's outpost well below the main castle. Harry looked up to find the sky had darkened, the moonlight filtered through a blanket of misty gauze. A second outpost stood closer to the top. Sara barely glanced at it as she passed, striding with purpose until it seemed she would vault over the summit and launch into parts unknown.

"Hurry." Sara jogged the last few steps to crest the hill. "Only one road leads into this place. We have no escape route."

A potential trap Harry had already recognized. "Makes it easier to see anyone trailing us. They will be visible a mile away."

"Still no reason to waste time. This Druid zealot likely has reinforcements beyond the man we bested in Oxford."

Sara didn't move when Harry stopped beside her. They stared up at the castle before them. Sharp rocks had been stacked, the piles like broken teeth, a crenellated jawline fronting an open courtyard. Imposing, frightening even, yet eerily quiet. The imposing structure told him the true story of Tintagel lay within its dark walls, a danger hidden for thousands of years. Harry marched toward the battlements and a curved doorway. "This castle isn't as big as I thought. It's – oh."

His words trailed off as he entered the doorway. He'd walked into a courtyard surrounded by the ragged stone walls to find this was merely a foregate, an initial fortification protecting the true castle, which waited across a vast emptiness with nothing but rocks below. If attackers managed to breach the advance gate, they then faced the challenge of a hundred-foot bridge only wide enough for two people abreast. He turned to Sara. "I didn't realize the castle was on the far side of a gorge. This bridge is a deathtrap."

"It's a trap, yes. But we'll only die on it if we stand here and keep talking."

He walked over to the bridge. The surf was loud below them. One wrong step and it was a long way down to the narrow beach below. "This can't be safe to cross." He stuck a foot out and tested the first board he touched. It held.

"The authorities would block it off if it weren't passable," she assured him.

"Wonderful. A bunch of retired postmen deciding whether this thing is going to fall or not."

"Do you see any other way to the cliff part of the island?" Sara asked. "The *north* side?"

He grumbled, but she had a point. "This is another one-way trap. We're stuck if anyone shows up."

"Not necessarily." Sara pointed below them. "We can always jump off and swim." Then, without hesitation, she walked onto the bridge. She did, however, put both hands along the waist-high walls running on either side of the ancient structure. She did not look back.

Harry started moving now too. Wind whipped his hair, clouds scudded across the moon, and Harry did his very best to think of anything but the emptiness beneath him as he moved at speed across the bridge. It felt like forever, though in truth it was no more than thirty seconds before he reached solid ground. Harry was never more grateful for a slippery path. The air had a sharp tang of salt when he opened his mouth.

The ruins of the Brittonic castle stood before them. Some stone walls were collapsed; others were still standing, and the rest were somewhere in between. The walls that stood were twice his height and stretched a hundred feet in either direction. The square enclosure roughly mirrored the hilltop geography. "Which way now?" he asked.

"Ahead and left. That bridge took us a bit away from the cliff."

He followed her to the far wall of the enclosure. A doorway opened to the empty hillside, with the ocean just ahead. "Through here," she said. "There's a path. I suspect this used to lead to another building."

Sara was right. Foundation ruins and not much else were all that was left of the structure. "I imagine this was a church," she said, "which doubled as a storehouse. Enclosed space was at a premium here."

"Not much left." Harry walked the perimeter, flashlight leading the way so he didn't trip on any rocks. Wind whipped up the cliffside, which was closer than he liked. Halfway around the ruins, he stopped. "Sara, look here."

"What is that? It looks like a tombstone."

"Out here? They wouldn't waste the space burying bodies."

"Agreed." The stone undulated under her light as Sara approached. "This is taller than I realized. Too large for a Brittonic grave marker."

"That's a lot of weathering," Harry said, looking closer. "Hold on. Are those—"

"—*letters*." Sara knelt in front of the stone. "Or images, rather."

Harry glanced over his shoulder. On this part of the hill several standing walls shielded them from the mainland. Nobody looking at or approaching Tintagel could see their flashlights. "Can you read it?"

"These aren't letters," she said. "Harry, they're carvings."

"Of what?"

"Hard to say. This close to the shoreline they are exposed to all manner of weather, not to mention all the salt water." She touched her chin. "What do they look like to you?"

"I see three shapes in a row." He reached out to touch the stone. "Numerals? No, they look like bent lowercase *l*'s." Sara didn't move beside him. Almost as though she weren't breathing. "You okay?" he asked.

"These aren't letters or numbers. I'm certain. These are images."

"How can you be so sure?" Harry turned his head this way and that. Still looked like a row of rough *l*'s to him, the top of each angled to the left.

"You can read this inscription. I know you can, because this is the third time we've seen it."

Third time? He rubbed his eyes, rolled his neck, and looked again. "Staffs," he said finally. "Those are broken staffs."

"*Dagda's* broken staffs." Sara pointed at the left-most one. "Three of them. What do you think that represents?" She didn't give him a chance to answer. "The three times we've crossed Dagda's path. First, the grotto. Second, the Rollright Stones. And third, right here."

Keen excitement rose in his gut. Harry pushed it back down. "Are you sure?"

When she looked at him, her face mirrored the bright moon. "There are times when you need to have faith. Right now, have faith in me. If these engravings represent each time we've encountered Dagda, then this is a marker from Quintus."

His father had advised caution in the field. *Look for evidence.* Fred Fox had also told his son this profession occasionally required a leap of faith. "It's possible," he said. "Quintus pointed us here. If this stone has been here since his time, it's at least possible."

"This castle has stood since Rome ruled Britannia." Sara pointed behind them. "Look at the castle walls. The same composition and aged coloring as this marker."

His father had also advised listening to the evidence. "Okay, I'll buy it. This is the next marker and those engravings are of Dagda's staff. What else did the scroll say?"

Sara took out her phone.

"Kneel at the pillar of Dagda, then peer down from the northern edge to the white wrath of Nuada. Hold fast to your faith. Leap to his embrace when he slumbers most. Nuada will reveal himself."

She touched the stone. "This must be the pillar. We're both kneeling."

"You have to kneel to read the stone," Harry said. "Now *peer down.*" He pointed to the ground, or rather to where it vanished over the cliff mere feet away. "Think that's what he means?"

Sara stood, Harry joining her, each taking a firm grip on the stone marker. Leaning forward, they looked over the edge of the cliff. Salty air blew cold and steady. The water frothed below in the moonlight. "Who's Nuada?" Harry asked.

"A Druidic sea deity."

"One of Dagda's buddies."

"In Celtic mythology there's no one overarching leader, like God or Allah. Nuada was a one-armed lord of the oceans. He controlled wind and water, creating the tides and storms."

Far below, the ocean lapped almost gently at the vertical cliff wall. Harry hesitated. "That can't be it."

"The surf is white," Sara said.

"No way."

"The sea is fairly obvious."

"No." It was crazy. Quintus was a soldier, not a sailor. Soldiers hated the ocean. Didn't they? "How in the world would we climb down there? One slip and you're sliding down the cliff. Which, by the way, looks like a cheese grater."

Sara was quiet. Harry kept shining his flashlight down, for all the good it did. The beam hardly seemed to touch the water below. "Do you think there's a beach down there?"

"No. This side of the island doesn't have a beach. Boats could pull up to the cliff if they were allowed."

"*Allowed?*"

"This entire island is a protected historic site. No boats are allowed near it. And there is no exploration beyond guided tours."

"Nobody's explored around here," Harry said. "No scuba divers, no fisherman. This place is pretty much undisturbed." His mood lifted.

"At least that's one good note."

Her face gave him pause. Mainly because she didn't take her eyes off his. "What?" Harry asked. "Did I say something?"

"No. You figured it out. I had the same conclusion." She turned her light to the cliff, leaning out far enough that Harry grabbed her arm. "One false step and you slide down this cliff. Chances are it kills you. Quintus wouldn't have expected his followers to climb down this wall. It's not as though they had climbing gear of any sort."

"You don't climb. You *leap*." Harry swallowed, his throat dry. "The scroll said *leap to his embrace*. Quintus is telling us to jump into Nuada's arms. Into the sea." He frowned. "That's a hundred feet down. Can you even survive that kind of fall?"

"Yes."

"How do you know?"

"I know a man who served in the Egyptian navy. He was taught how to jump into the water from aircraft carriers in an emergency. The jumps were at a hundred feet. He said the key is going feet first, arms over your head."

"You're joking."

"I am not. He also said to be sure the water is deep enough."

"How deep do you think it is here?"

"There's no beach on this side. You need around twenty feet. That's what he said."

"Twenty feet deep isn't that much." He stood back and rubbed his head. "What am I saying? There could be boulders under the surface."

"There aren't any disturbances in the waves," Sara said, as though telling him about her lunch. "I can't see where any rock has sheared off the side of the cliff. It looks intact."

"You do realize I'll die if you're wrong."

"I'm not telling you what to do," she said. "If you want to get a boat in the morning and sneak over here, I will help you. I only hope the men chasing us don't decipher the scroll."

"What about another way down?" Harry nodded over his shoulder. "From the other side. We get down to the beach and work our way around in a canoe. Or even swim."

"Perhaps *you* can. That's too far for me to swim."

He was a city guy. Oceans were meant for looking at from the boardwalk. "What about a boat? We row around, see what we can find."

"If you can find a boat, then yes."

"That could work," he said. "Or there might be another way down. A cave or tunnel."

"Starting from where?"

"From whatever's down there. What am I supposed to do, jump and then tread water? There has to be a reason I'm jumping, something down there where Quintus could hide the *terrible power*. He wouldn't have just tossed it into the sea."

"There is a cave on the far part of the island," Sara said. "It's well explored, so that isn't where Quintus went. But what if there's another cave, one we can't see?"

Harry blinked. *That's it.* "When he *slumbers most*. That's what the scroll said – to jump when Nuada is slumbering. When does the sea slumber? At *low tide*. Quintus wants us to jump at low tide. That could be so we can reach an underground opening."

"A place you can't see or reach at high tide." Sara grabbed his hand and stepped back from the edge. "An entrance below the waterline could have remained hidden since Quintus was here."

"Especially if no one has been able to explore this area with modern technology."

The wind carried their words away, back toward the castle walls. Sara led him into the lee of the wall. "You may be correct about another exit. Quintus needed a way to get in and out of any hidden cave or tunnel. Perhaps he even created an escape route."

The enormity of what she *didn't* say hit him. "What if he didn't and there's no other way out? Then I'm stuck down there and my only option is to swim for it."

"Yes." She frowned. "But if we find a boat, I can get you." Her face lit up. "That's how we do it. We need a boat."

Phew. At least she wasn't pushing for him to jump. "We buy a canoe and radios in town and come back tomorrow night." Her face had gone pale, so he cracked a smile. "That guy chasing us won't figure out what the scroll means. Know why not? He doesn't have you."

Snick. Harry spun around.

"Don't move." A handgun barrel was inches from his face. "I assure you, it's loaded."

Chapter 23

Tintagel Castle

The *snick* had been the slide racking on a semiautomatic pistol. A pistol now in Harry's face.

"Move back."

The gunman had a British accent. Harry slowly stepped back, hands in his pockets. The gunman stayed in the shadows. The pistol never wavered as Sara moved back beside him. "Stop," the gunman told them. "That's far enough."

The gunman stood beneath an arched doorway in the castle wall. Now a second man stepped around him. His eyes reflected the moonlight.

"Harry Fox," the new man said. He studied Harry closely. Harry stared back. The longer it went on the more Harry got an odd feeling about the man. Odd in the sense that this man looked composed on the surface, but underneath it all he was definitely wound tight. Too tight. "Nice work on finding this place, Harry." The man looked to Sara. "You must be Dr. Hamed?"

Sara gasped.

"Who are you?" Harry asked, but thanks to Rose, he already knew. Pete Brody.

"You took something of mine. I want it back." Pete laughed, short and sharp. "Although I'm not so worried about it now. You uncovered the path I intended to find. And led me here."

Sara recovered quickly. "How do you know my name?" she asked. "We have no idea who you are, and you sound like a crazy person."

Harry didn't bother saying it was not a good idea to tell a crazy person they were just that.

In a sudden movement, Pete grabbed Sara's arm and pulled her toward him. She yelled, Harry went to grab her, and suddenly the pistol was in his face again.

"Easy," Pete said. He whistled. Two more men darted from the shadows to grab Sara's arms and Pete stepped back. "I know you're a smart lady, Dr. Hamed. I need you to promise me one thing." He pointed at Harry. "Promise me you'll be honest tonight. Do it, or he gets a bullet in the foot. Won't be swimming much if that happens."

"Okay," she spat out. "I will."

Pete Brody snapped his fingers. The men let her go. "Thank you, Sara. My name is Pete, and we're all working together tonight to figure out why the letters from Aristotle and Nero lead here."

"You paid Charles to get them," Harry said. "Those were your artifacts."

"They're still mine," Pete said. "I'll pay you for them even though you stole them from me. Give them back and we won't hurt you." He shrugged. "Melodramatic, I know, but I must have them."

"You want to talk?" Harry asked. "Tell your goon to get his gun out of my face."

The goon lowered his weapon. Harry didn't have a chance to blink before the guy's fist smashed into his nose. Harry's legs wobbled; he held on for a beat, then collapsed onto his backside.

"Call me a goon again and I'll shoot you."

It didn't sound threatening, not in a posh British accent. Harry knew better. This was the guy from the hotel. And he could punch like a prizefighter.

"Enough," Pete said. "I heard you say something is hidden over the cliff." He pointed to where the ground vanished. "Might be a cave, with the entrance underwater even at low tide. It's possible there's a second way out that you don't know about."

Sara glowered at Pete. He shrugged. "We were on the other side of the wall," Pete said. "I heard you."

"How did you get so close?" she asked, sounding genuinely puzzled.

"Same way as before. Electric motorcycles with the lights off. Hard to believe how quiet they are, isn't it? I saw your flashlights bobbing around up here."

Sara cursed, and Pete actually smiled. He turned to Harry. "It's time to jump into the water and see if your theory is correct. My money says you are."

Harry had heard enough. "So we die in the water and you don't have to shoot us?"

"Shoot you? I don't want to kill you. I'm here for the power that Queen Boudica used against the Romans."

Now it was Harry's turn to be puzzled. "Why? You followed us across an ocean. You must be rich already. Why do you want this artifact so badly?"

"Many reasons."

"Maybe we can make a deal."

"I had a deal," Pete said. "With Charles. He was too scared to get my documents back from you, so I had to do it myself. There's no deal here."

"You're the one with guns," Sara said. "We just want to get out of here alive."

"You will if you cooperate." Pete aimed a finger at Harry's chest. "I know you're connected. After this ends, you go your way, I'll go mine. That's our deal. You help me, give me the documents, and you go home. I'll pay you for the documents. Same as I paid Charles."

"Harry bought the documents," Sara said. "He owns them."

"I suspect he did pay for them," Pete said. "But for the same reason I'm paying you. I don't want to piss off his boss."

Sara looked at Harry, her face making it clear that Pete had just confirmed her worst suspicions. A man holding *them* at gunpoint was nervous about Harry's boss. Vincent and Joey Morello must be truly bad guys. Which made Harry no better.

Pete flashed a thumbs-up with each hand. "We're good? Excellent." He turned to Harry. "Better get jumping, Harry. Otherwise, she goes first."

"She's with me," Harry said. "Hurt her and it's the same as hurting me."

"I don't believe that," Pete said. "I think you two don't really know each other all that well. If you do, well, someone's been lying."

A silence heavy enough to crush hopes and dreams stood between them. Sara glared at each man in turn. Pete looked a bit too satisfied with himself, and Harry's mind churned to no effect. He couldn't try to rush the gunman. The guy was too far away and way too good for that. The other two were also likely armed. He and Sara had nowhere to run, and Harry believed what Pete said. He would toss Sara over the edge without a second thought.

Harry looked at Sara and she averted her gaze, her anger causing physical pain in his chest. The gaping hole in his gut hadn't found bottom when an idea flared. A tiny spark, but it was his best option. His last chance to make everything right. For now.

"Fine."

Pete tilted his head. "What?"

"I said fine." Harry looked at the cliff. "I'll jump."

"Glad to hear it." Pete turned to the British guy. "You think there are rocks down there?"

The Brit gave Harry and Sara a wide berth as he circled to the cliff's edge. He didn't seem the least bit afraid as he leaned over. "The water's calm. No disturbances that look like rocks." He leaned farther. "The cliff is sheer." Now he stepped back, walking around until he had Harry and Sara between him and the cliff. "The lady was right. You don't need more than twenty feet. Go feet first, arms over your head, and you'll survive."

"You're not the one jumping."

"I am if you die."

"What if there's no cave down there, no entrance?"

"Then keep looking," Pete said. "Until you can't any more. After that, swim around to the beach. We'll regroup and expand the search."

"He'll be exhausted," Sara said. "He could drown."

"You'd be surprised what you can do," the Brit said. "He'll make it."

"Enough." Pete reached into his pocket and pulled out a serious-looking flashlight. "You'll need this." Harry snatched it out of the air. "Signal if you find anything. Three flashes." Pete pointed at the ocean. "Time to go."

The ground seemed to have taken hold of Harry's feet. Stars winked overhead, the heavy taste of salt coated his tongue, and the soft breeze died. Harry blinked, his eyes like sandpaper.

"Now," Pete said. "Or she goes first. I really don't want to do that."

"Sure you don't," Harry muttered as he stepped to the cliff's edge faster than he wanted. "Stay alert," he whispered to Sara as he passed. "I'll find it, I promise."

Sara's arms were folded tight across her chest. "I believe you," she said.

He wanted to tell her it was a lie, that he wasn't a criminal. That he had never meant for any of this to happen. He wanted to say all that. Except nothing he said now would change her mind. No, he'd have to follow the plan, nurture his spark of an idea, and that plan started with him jumping. He had to find Dagda's broken staff.

Harry called over his shoulder to the British gunman. "How far out should I jump?"

"Get well away from the rock," the Brit said. "A couple of steps back, then go for it. Jump up, not just out. Jump straight out and you might go horizontal. Stay vertical."

"What happens if I don't go down feet first?"

"Then it's my turn and I try not to hit your body floating down there."

"Thanks." Harry turned away from the guy, who had kept his gun up through it all. Smart move, because Harry had taken a few steps closer as they were talking in case the guy dropped his guard. The thought of jumping off this ledge suddenly made rushing the Brit more appealing. Would he get shot? Maybe. But at least he wouldn't end up lifeless, floating on the water. The Brit didn't cooperate, though, keeping his gun on Harry.

Harry grabbed hold of the stone marker and leaned over. The cliff wall actually seemed to slope in on the way down, the bottom not easily visible unless he leaned way out. Minimal waves, nothing sticking out of the water. He leaned back and almost laughed. *What the hell do I know? That water could be four feet deep and I'd have no idea.*

Except you brought Sara here; you got her caught up in this. You let this happen.

Sara had come to Brooklyn to uncover the truth behind his amulet, and now they were on the English coast and in way over their heads. Or, based on the past, in their usual spot. The only path out led forward. One day he'd be smarter than this. Perhaps tomorrow.

He knelt, running his hands over the grass and dirt. Hard-packed ground, grass not slippery, and near the edge it was stone. Sturdy enough for a good leap. He stood, facing the cliff edge, and walked backwards. Four steps ought to do it. Enough to avoid being a smear down the cliff. Standing ready, he noticed that every sound was more acute, from the ocean to the wind down to the rustle of grass beneath his shoes. His hands shook slightly; his breath came short and fast. He watched himself run, leap out, the water racing up to meet him. *Feet down, arms tight, hold your breath at the bottom.*

He charged. Four steps passed in a blink before he flew out and up, the darkness below a void with no bottom, the horizon ahead of him not moving. An instant after going airborne his stomach shot up into his throat. Time slowed, as though this was outer space and gravity didn't command here. He seemed to float, arms fluttering while stars flashed in front of him, the moon nearly full and so close he could reach out and touch it.

Harry barely had time to pull his arms up and point his feet before impact. He exploded into the water, the bone-chilling cold shocking him like an electric surge. The world turned to black. Harry fought the reflex to breathe, letting himself plunge into the void. Water churned, the bubbles clouding his vision for what seemed an eternity until he finally stopped. He never hit bottom.

The frigid water. The utter darkness. The need to breathe. Panic threatened to steal the last bit of air from him. Then he realized his eyes were closed. He opened them. Murky light wavered above when he looked up. Arms and legs kicked as he focused on that, pushing everything away. Kick and pull, again and again. The light got brighter.

He surfaced and shot out of the water. Air sweeter than anything filled his lungs. Like a bobber he plunged back down, got a mouthful of salty water, and nearly hacked up his guts. Wiping away blurry tears, he treaded water and took stock. He was alive, and in this instant that was all he could think about. No rocks had smashed him to bits. The sharp cliffs hadn't cut him and the sea hadn't claimed him.

All he could see was sky and stars, the moon and the sea. He'd turned around in the water and found the cliff behind him, stretching to the sky. At the very top, which didn't look nearly as imposing now that he'd jumped it, two bits of light hovered on the edge.

Sara's voice cut through the night. "Harry?" Not frantic, not yet. "Harry?" He splashed around, trying to disturb the water and help her locate him. It worked. "I see him! Harry, can you hear me?"

"Yes," he shouted back. "Hang on."

As though she had other options. He kept treading, arms and legs moving to keep his head above water. Where to go? The cliff face looked impenetrable. The water lapped at the rocks, and that was where he headed. It was low tide, the time when Quintus had told them to leap.

Water splashed as he swam to where rock met sea. Under the sun it would have inspired awe, striations in the rock creating this testament to nature's majestic beauty. Sparkling silver-gray stone topped with lush greenery changed in the darkness. Now it was forbidding, ominous, and above all *sharp*. He swam until he nearly lost sight of Sara's light. He stopped, pulled out his own flashlight and hit the switch as a signal.

"Are you okay?" Sara called down.

"Yeah," he said. "I'm going under."

He flicked the light off, jammed it in his pocket and swam on. The lightweight hiking pants he'd worn weighed practically nothing, and they had enough pockets for him to carry the flashlight, his phone, and the knuckledusters. They'd helped him escape more than a few jams. Never from a salt water bath a hundred feet below the bad guys, though.

The cliff came up on him fast. One second, he was swimming for it; the next, his hand barked off rocks. He shouted a few choice words as salt water stung his scrapes. He took hold of an outcropping and looked down. The water was impenetrable. He couldn't see his feet below him. He flicked his flashlight on underwater and his feet immediately came into view, tinged greenish-blue with nothing but dark water below. A flashlight beamed down from directly above on the clifftop, which meant he was right below the marker. If Quintus wanted his followers to dive, this was the place. Several deep breaths, and he dove.

The water became far colder as he descended. Using the cliff to help fight his natural buoyancy, Harry pulled himself deeper, inverting himself, kicking and descending into the gloom. Shadows played at the edges of his vision as bubbles flew upward with each stroke. The cliffside remained solid as he descended. Every foot down intensified the pressure in his ears, now filled with a crackling noise that took on an echo-like resonance. The surface had faded, nothing more than a dark shadow above him now. He kicked on.

A jagged outcropping nearly sliced his forehead open when it appeared out of nowhere. His lungs ached. One glance below this rock before he needed to go up for air. Harry grabbed the rock and pulled. The bottom came into view, ten feet below. It may as well have been a hundred for all the chance he had of reaching it. He couldn't go another foot, lungs empty and body aching. Twisting, he grabbed the outcropping to turn and fire himself to the surface and found himself staring into an opening in the cliffside. Right beneath the rock he held, which in truth was a lip covering the cave entrance. And cave it was, the opening stretching down to the seafloor ten feet below. You could drive a Humvee through it. He aimed his light inside. There was no end in sight.

He could swim inside. Just as Sara had predicted, and what Quintus had intended. The sheer improbability made his mouth drop open, which promptly filled with seawater and nearly made him gasp. His empty lungs caught fire and he pulled himself frantically to the surface, kicking and cursing all the while. Up and up, his eyes blurry with stinging salt water before he surfaced and gulped a great lungful of air.

"There he is." Sara's voice came down from above. "Harry, can you hear me?" He shouted that he could. Now Pete Brody called down. "Did you find anything?"

He didn't have to think about this. "Not yet," he yelled. "I'm going back down."

He grabbed the cliff, filled his lungs and went back under. Knowing the cave was there made this dive easier. Harry clutched the flashlight in his mouth and pulled with both hands. He made it to the outcropping in short order and pulled himself under. The cave was no more than twenty feet down, and when he slipped under the lip and went in, Harry started counting down from twenty. Any longer than that and he risked not being able to get back to the surface.

Harry kept to one side as he pulled himself along. The roof seemed to rise as he went. Ten seconds passed with nothing but dark water ahead. Fifteen seconds; still nothing. The clock in Harry's head hit nineteen when wavy ripples appeared above him. What was that? Another kick, knowing he was pushing his luck, and all became clear. Literally, because the ripples had been the water's surface. Harry pulled himself one more time and surfaced. He held onto the rocks and took a tentative breath.

The air was dank and warm, heavy with the weight of tons of rock above it. One breath, then two. His arms tingled in the sudden warmth while he played the flashlight around, feet kicking slowly as he treaded water.

He'd surfaced in a cavern. A *big* cavern. The hole he'd swum through was a tunnel, and the sea floor had followed his path upward until it broke the surface ahead of him, a stone floor rising gently from the water. The ceiling shot up and outward, rising at least twenty feet overhead and stretching out on either side. It was an open area that was also completely empty. As he swam to the shoreline, his feet found bottom and Harry was able to walk out of the water and onto wet stone covered in algae. One careful step at a time, he walked until the ground leveled out. His eyes were blurred from the swim, so he rubbed them with vigor until his vision cleared. Harry aimed the light ahead.

Three carved giants stood in front of him, each ten feet tall and etched out of the cave wall. A hooded man knelt in front of another standing one, while a third stood at the rear. The standing man held a massive spear and looked down on the hooded man, one hand outstretched toward him. The third stood behind and watched them both.

The standing figure had a trim beard that seemed to shine under Harry's flashlight; water dripping down the walls reflecting light back at him. The kneeling man clasped a rod in both hands. Harry blinked, stepping closer. No, not a rod. A *staff*. Curved at the top.

Dagda. He knelt in front of the one who stood. The god Dagda, whom General Quintus had truly worshipped, the one who'd gifted Queen Boudica a terrible weapon to use against the Roman invaders. The deity who had stood first in line for Quintus, yet here he knelt, acknowledging another god's greatness. And an imposing god it was. No man was that big or carried a spear so large. With the corona around his head, it seemed as though the sun were rising behind him. That, or his hair was actually made of flame. The third carved man who stood behind Dagda held a massive sword at his side. Oddly, the sword arm wasn't attached to his body, instead seeming to float beside it.

The walls to either side of the figures were solid, the tunnel curving left ahead of Harry and leading deeper into the cliffside, a natural opening that stretched farther than his flashlight could penetrate. Notches had been cut into the walls at regular intervals, with stone torch holders extending from each. Any wooden torches had long since rotted to dust.

Three torch holders were above the head of each carved man as well, to provide light when Quintus or his followers worshipped here. For this must have been a place of worship, holy ground where the Romans who followed the ancient gods could pray in safety. Holy ground, but what else? Quintus wouldn't have sent his followers here without reason. He had laid this path to keep a secret safe. The secret of Queen Boudica's power. So where was it?

Harry moved deeper into the cavern. Stone walls perspired in the light as he walked, walls no man had seen for two thousand years. Twenty yards on, the tunnel began narrowing until two people would have been hard pressed to stretch their arms out on either side. Harry came to a wall. A solid wall through which there was no exit. His stomach dropped. *There must be more.*

He reached out to touch the wall and stumbled to one knee. It wasn't a dead end. The wall looked flat from a few feet away but was actually a doorway, carved so that it gave the appearance of there being no way ahead. The illusion was astonishing. Harry stepped through the doorway to find steps had been carved into the rock, wide enough for a single person to ascend and no more. The steps led up to a landing, then turned and continued out of sight.

He turned and looked back the way he'd come. Darkness had followed him in, the stone seeming to absorb his light. These steps went up, so that was where he'd go. He had an idea where they might lead. If he was correct, it changed everything. The stairs led to a second landing before turning back on themselves and then proceeding up.

The way was steep and narrow; he climbed carefully past a half-dozen more landings, each with a torch holder carved into the wall for light.

Harry turned a corner and stumbled over several fallen stones hidden in the shadows cast by his flashlight. He put an arm out and caught himself, kicking more stones in the process. Damn, it was dark in here. In stumbling he'd dropped his flashlight, and he bent down to retrieve it. The feeling of abject emptiness turned his stomach cold. Not an emptiness inside of him. One in front of him. He stood very still with one arm on the wall for support. Only with the most cautious of movements did he reach out to retrieve his light. He locked his fingers around it, leaned back to gain balance, then aimed the beam forward. Scattered stones at his feet rustled and rolled when he kicked one.

A hole with no bottom yawned in front of him. The fallen stones were all that remained of a wall that must have blocked it off at one time, the mortar crumbled ages ago. He'd tripped over stones that had fallen onto the stairs. A single level of the wall remained in place, just high enough to trip anyone who took a wrong step on this landing. In one direction lay safety, the proper way up. In the other, a chasm you'd never get out of. Harry kicked a stone over the edge. He counted to five before a distant splash sounded.

He kicked another loose rock over the edge. Then another, until only one larger stone remained, about the size of a cantaloupe. That one he put in the middle of the landing. His plan now had two parts.

Onward he moved until he hit the tenth landing. There he paused as fresh, cool air slipped down his neck from above. He flicked off the flashlight and found a faint glow coloring the wall, so weak he'd nearly missed it. The white glowing light coming from a nearly full moon.

Harry took the last set of steps in silence. These steps ended not in a landing, but a ceiling. A stone ceiling with a single crack running down the center of it. That was where the faint moonlight slipped in. He crept to the ceiling and put an ear against it. Wind whistled through the stone, then he heard it. A voice. *Pete Brody.*

Harry was beneath the castle ruins. One of the fallen structures lay atop the stone steps, a secret passageway to a holy Celtic grotto hidden far beneath the ground. Judging from how loud the voices were, Harry was close to the wall where they'd been ambushed. He couldn't make out what Pete was saying – they were standing near the cliff edge waiting for Harry. Sara could be running out of time.

Harry worked his way back down the staircase to the open cavern. Several fallen rocks he'd spotted earlier lay against the walls. He gathered them, taking those that were roundest and roughly the size of a baseball, then put them where they'd be of most use. It only took a minute of working in the shadows before his welcoming present for that British guy was ready.

He took one last look at the carvings. Now he noticed that the torch holders above each carved man glinted. He looked closer, realizing they weren't merely carvings, but actual pieces of art with Latin writing etched into the stone. Each letter of the writing was painted gold. No, not painted. The letters were *made* of gold, solid gold embedded in the stonework.

Water splashed behind him. Harry whirled, his light playing across the pool from which he'd emerged. Ripples ran across the surface. Nothing stirred in the cavern. Probably the tide.

He pushed it out of his mind and hurried back to the top landing, where he put an ear to the ceiling. Intermittent voices sounded. Putting a shoulder to the stone above him, he squared his feet and tried to stand, using his legs to press himself against the rock above. For once his average height proved useful, giving him the chance to squeeze into the narrow opening right below the stone and push. He'd half expected the rock to be stuck tight, time locking it in place. Then he'd have to shout, hoping the others could hear him and somehow rip it out from above.

The last thing he expected happened – the stone shot up as though propelled by explosives. He pushed, the rock held for a breath, and before he realized it, he was sprawled beside a wall at ground level, the one Pete Brody had hidden behind before ambushing them. The flagstones clattered like gongs as they rolled away, the racket drawing Sara over to where he had burst from the ground, their enemies on her tail.

"Harry?" Sara stopped when he stood and looked at her. "How in the world did you get here?"

He swiped moss from his forehead. "There's a cavern under the island. A staircase leads back up here."

Pete pushed her aside and stood next to the new opening. "A cave and a hidden entrance. General Quintus was brilliant. He hid everything right beneath his feet." Pete looked up at Harry. "What's down there?"

"Come see," Harry said. "I'm not sure what to make of it."

Pete made no move to descend. "You go first," he said to Harry. "Then you." Pete pointed to one of his two colleagues. "Dr. Hamed follows me. Understood?"

Harry didn't argue. "What about the British guy?" The real muscle behind Pete was nowhere to be seen.

Pete looked to his other two men. "Make sure Wayne stays down by the bikes."

Harry's ears perked up. The British man was Wayne. And he wasn't here.

"Tell him to call us if anyone shows up." Pete turned to Harry, giving him a view of the pistol he held. "What did you see?"

"Hard to describe," Harry said. "Let's go." He turned and led them down the stairs, forcing everyone else to hurry behind him. When someone had a gun at your back, you took every possible chance to gain control. Forcing Pete and his goons to hurry would knock them off balance. "The steps are slippery," Harry called over his shoulder at the first landing.

Down, down they went, zigzagging from one landing to the next, descending into the ground, the only light coming from their flashlights.

Pete called out when they were nearly to the deep hole. "How far down is it?"

"Not much farther," Harry said.

He picked up the pace, forcing the man behind him to hurry. They turned another corner, the one before where he'd left the single stone, and Harry moved even faster. Footsteps came rapid fire as the man behind him worked to keep up. Harry covered his flashlight so the beam narrowed. The guy didn't notice as he hurried along. Harry slowed without warning, waiting for the man to come around to the landing where he'd run directly into Harry. Unless Harry dodged to one side.

The man didn't disappoint. As he hurried around the corner, Harry quick-stepped to one side, pressed his back to the wall and shouted, "Watch out!"

The guy looked down, tried to avoid the single rock and failed. He stumbled, arms flailing as he took one final misstep. Harry shouldered the man toward the dark hole. The guy never knew what happened. He never even cried out. One grunt, as though he'd smacked his head on the stone, and that was it. The *splash* of a body hitting the water below came at the same time Pete Brody rounded the corner. Harry had his back pressed to the wall, his light on the hole, breath coming in ragged gasps.

"He fell," Harry said. "I tripped on the stone, and he fell over me. I didn't know this hole was here."

The hole was set back a few feet from the walkway. Plausible, yes, but would Pete buy it? Harry blinked, and the semiautomatic pistol was aimed at his chest again.

"What happened?" Pete demanded.

"I tripped on the stone and he fell over me. The guy was right on my back."

"You didn't see this hole before?"

"How would I? It's way back off the steps. You think I wanted to poke around while you had Sara?"

By now the other man and Sara stood behind Pete. The guy had grabbed Sara, who glared at him but didn't try to get away.

"Where'd he go?" the remaining man asked, looking around uneasily.

"He fell down that hole." Pete pointed. The man aimed his flashlight, then loosed a string of curses. Pete said nothing as he turned his pale gaze on Harry again. "Is there anything else you didn't see on your way up I should know about?" Harry said there wasn't. "That man was a friend of mine. Now he's a martyr. Try anything tonight and you'll join him down there. Now move."

Harry took the remaining stairs at a more sedate pace. No one spoke until they made it to the bottom; Harry kept moving until he made it to the cavern's open area. He stayed to the far side, away from the carvings, casting his flashlight on the water's surface. "That's where I came in."

Pete pushed past him. "Where's the opening?" he asked. Harry described how he had dived down under the lip on the cliff and pulled himself through. As Harry hoped, everyone kept their eyes ahead and on the water. Everyone except Sara. She shrugged off the hand of the man holding her, walked to Harry's side and slipped her hand over his arm. A second later her foot slipped on a puddle of water.

Harry grabbed her. "You okay?" he asked. He stared at the ceiling above her. How'd the puddle get here? Water must have dripped from the ceiling. He hadn't walked over here before.

"I'm fine," Sara said. "What is this place?"

"Stay beside me," he whispered. "No matter what." She nodded as Harry turned his flashlight away from the pool of water and spoke louder. "You'll want to see these."

The carvings lit up as though spotlights had burst on. "Carvings of Celtic deities," Harry said. "I think the hooded man is Dagda. I don't know the other two."

"Those are Druidic entities," Pete said breathlessly. He sounded for all the world like an energized schoolchild describing a favorite book. "The one standing in front of Dagda is Lugh. He controls the sun. You can see it behind his head, and he's known for carrying a spear." Pete traced the beam of his flashlight over the corona around Lugh's head and then the massive spear. "The third figure is Nuada." Pete pointed to the one standing behind Dagda. "You can tell by the sword he carries, and how his arm is detached from his body."

"Why is it detached?" Sara asked.

"Legend says Nuada lost his arm in battle. Eventually some believe it was replaced or regenerated."

Pete turned around to face them. At that moment he didn't look like a tyrant, like the sort of man who would hold others at gunpoint. Eyes wide, he seemed to come *alive*, energy emanating from every pore. In short, he looked like a man who inspired others by the thousands, the kind of man who made you believe. To Harry, he looked utterly terrifying.

"Druidic beliefs are like America," Pete said. "A melting pot, evolving over time as our understanding of ourselves and our world evolves. It's a metaphor for human existence. The true belief system in which our every fault, stumble, experience and triumph guides us to greater knowledge. To a place where we live in harmony with all creatures." He paused, and the next words out of Pete's mouth sent a chill up Harry's spine. "A place without the tragedy of false belief."

Harry glanced at Sara. She'd picked up on it too.

"I've heard of Lugh and Nuada," Sara said quickly. "They were supernatural, the same as Dagda. But why would Dagda kneel to Lugh while Nuada looks on? That's not how I understand their relationship."

"I think you know the answer," Pete said.

Sara's mouth formed a hard line. "I'm not following."

"Yes, you are." Pete walked to stand in front of her. Taller by a head, he looked down, his face tilted to one side. "I'm in charge here, Dr. Hamed. Our deal can change at any moment. Now, be honest."

Harry and Sara stood farthest from the carvings. Everyone else was between them. The cave wall to Harry's back was mere feet away and shrouded in darkness. Exactly what he needed if his plan were to succeed.

"Hold on," he said. Pete's words had struck a chord with him. "Let me try."

Pete looked puzzled. "Try what?"

"To answer your question."

Pete shrugged. "I'm listening."

Sara already knew the answer. Harry could tell from the set of her shoulders and the look on her face. He had an idea of it, but even if he was wrong, they needed time. He needed Pete to keep talking and the other man to keep listening.

"These deities are more or less equals," Harry said. "Based on that, Dagda wouldn't bow down to either of these two. Quintus knew this. These carvings serve a purpose. They weren't done at random."

"Agreed," Pete said. "And that purpose was…?"

"To deliver part of a message. Dagda is kneeling, showing deference to Lugh. Nuada is standing behind them." Harry glanced at Sara. Her face revealed nothing. "These carvings are part of what Quintus is telling us. It's the second part of a message you already have."

"It is," Pete said. He quoted the scroll Harry and Sara had left in Oxford. *"Nuada holds the terrible, magnificent gift from Dagda."*

"Nuada is separated from the other two," Harry said. "Dagda's *terrible power* is somehow tied to the sun. That's Lugh's domain. Dagda gave this power to Queen Boudica, but it relies on Lugh in some way. Nuada is standing back, almost waiting, as though he's overseeing it all."

"Holding the gift," Pete said. "The question is where?"

Sara couldn't stay quiet any longer. "Look at these torch holders." She walked past Pete as though he wasn't there. "They're different from the others we passed." She pointed to the torch holder above each deity. "Those are gold letters inscribed in the stone."

"Latin," Pete said.

Sara glanced at Harry. "What does it say?" she asked Pete.

"You tell me, Dr. Hamed." Pete looked at Harry. Not quite at him, but through him. "I assume you read Latin better than I do."

Harry felt a twist of unease in his gut. The guy was up to something. He was too calm, too relaxed for a man who nearly had the prize in his grasp. A prize he'd crossed an ocean and killed to get. This was wrong.

"They aren't letters," Sara said. "They're numbers. Written in word form. The numbers go in descending order."

"*Tres.*" Pete pointed at Lugh. "*Duo. Unus.*" Down the line he went, to Dagda and then Nuada. "Three, two, one."

"An educated man knows the Bible," Sara said. "I assumed you could read Latin."

"Thank my father for that," he said. The bitterness in his voice made Harry take note. "Forced study as a child. Be grateful he wasn't your father."

Now Harry was totally lost. This guy was the definition of a zealot, yet he talked about religion like it was pure evil? Whatever personal demons were in Pete's head had him glaring at the ground now, lost in some dark reverie. Harry stepped closer to his hidden rock pile.

Pete shook his head as though to clear it, never looking up, pistol still in hand. "Enough of the past," he said. "Dr. Hamed, what do you think the numbers mean?"

"I'm not sure. It could be tied to their belief system, a hierarchy of sorts. Or it could be something else entirely." She crossed her arms. "You seem to know a lot about this era. What do you think?"

"The numbers don't connect to any structure I know," Pete said. "Nuada, Dagda and Lugh are equal in stature, controlling different components of the physical world. They balance each other, so ranking them is pointless. Quintus knew they stood shoulder to shoulder, never as master and follower." Pete reached into his pocket. "I think the answer is here." He pulled out the scroll.

"Be careful with that," Sara said.

"We both know this is the key. The answer is here." Pete held it out. "Quintus told me exactly where to look."

Quintus told me. This guy really thought whatever had been left behind was for him. Zealot didn't begin to cover it.

"It's in the final line. '*Two will bring the wrath of Dagda.*' Quintus labeled the torch holders so I would know who has the broken staff."

"I'm not following you," Sara said. "There are three numbers up there. One above each deity."

Pete turned and pointed to them with one hand; his gun hand dropped to his side. "The word *two* is above Dagda. That's not what we want. Quintus is clear about it."

Harry edged closer to the rocks. They were now by his foot. All he had to do was bend over and grab one. That, and be sure he didn't miss.

Pete was still turned, looking closely at the carvings. "I'd say *one* is the place to look, but why is there a number three? Three options means we have a problem. That it's not Dagda, but Lugh or Nuada. But neither of them gifted this *terrible power* to the Druids."

Harry bent over and rubbed his knee as though it ached. He quietly grabbed two rocks from the floor and shoved one into each of his back pockets. Both were small enough to fit into his hand. Like baseballs.

"I have the answer." Pete's shadow danced across the walls as he turned around. "Druidic lore teaches us the world must be in harmony. We are all a part of this journey. When humanity doesn't accept that, our missteps compound over time until they spiral out of control. That's the key." Pete aimed a finger at Sara, his gun seemingly forgotten. "It all *adds up*. Like the numbers."

"I still don't follow," Sara said.

Pete came a step closer. Close enough that Harry thought this might work. "Quintus tells me to avoid *two*. Dagda is marked with the number to avoid, but not Lugh or Nuada. They are where we look for the next steps."

"You think the torch holders are the next marker."

"I know they are. I only need one. Quintus would not have left this to chance, so he implemented one final safeguard. His path was for a Druid to follow, a true believer. A man who understands we are but a piece of the total." Pete paused. "Like numbers, we add to the total, good or bad."

He pointed to Lugh. "*Tres*. Three. You get three by adding two and one. Two, which Quintus says to avoid. This is a map only the faithful can read. To find the gift of Dagda, I look to Nuada."

Pete pointed at the sea god. Everyone looked to the towering figure and the golden word above him. Even Sara was caught up in it. Harry reached for the rocks in his pockets. This had gone on long enough.

He peered through the shadows and took aim. Pete's head was a catcher's mitt that Harry fired a rock at, hitting him square and sending him down like a sack of sand. Pete grunted, the gun clattered away, and Harry threw again. This one was low, catching Pete in the back as he twisted on the stone floor. The other acolyte didn't have time to react before Harry ran for the gun, racing to the far corner where it had landed. Shadows flew across the wall. Halfway there Harry bent, reaching for the pistol; now he had the only gun in the cavern. *I can't believe this worked.*

A gunshot boomed, splitting the dank air. Sparks erupted at Harry's feet. He danced away from them, sparks flashed on the floor once more, and Pete's surviving acolyte screamed.

The British man burst out of the water to their backs and into the cavern. His pistol was aimed at Harry's chest. *He dove off the cliff and snuck up behind us.*

"Move and you're dead," Wayne said. "Drop the gun and get back."

Harry stumbled out of the way as Wayne scooped up the fallen pistol and ran to the acolyte's side. The man lay on the stone floor, unmoving. The Brit knelt and put a finger on his partner's neck. He growled, a primordial sound, then stood and moved to where Pete lay sprawled. Wayne kept one eye on Harry as he knelt and shook Pete's shoulder. "Are you injured?"

"What happened?" Pete reached around and gingerly probed the back of his head where Harry's rock had smashed him. "I'm bleeding."

"It's a cut, sir." Wayne glanced down to inspect the wound. "Head wounds are bloody. You'll be all right shortly." Pete moved to get up.

Wayne helped him to a sitting position. "Sit a moment."

Pete did as he was told, turning his head to face Harry. He picked up the rock Harry had whipped at him. "You threw a *rock?* When I have a gun?" Pete actually laughed. "Ballsy. I knew you wouldn't understand."

"You want me to take care of him?" Wayne jerked his chin at Harry. "Won't take a second."

"No need."

Wayne leaned down and spoke in Pete's ear. Pete turned, seeing their fallen comrade. "Are you sure?" Pete asked.

"Ricochet. Caught him in the heart. He's gone."

This time Pete stood and waved off the assistance. "That's the last believer you kill, Harry Fox." He stopped speaking, bent over and grabbed his head, wincing with pain.

"Let me help you," Wayne said.

"Back off." Pete shoved his hand away. "Don't shoot him. We may need another hand."

Wayne handed Pete his gun back. He glowered at Harry, letting him know exactly what he wished Pete would say.

"This is why we're all here." Pete stowed the pistol in his waistband and turned back to Nuada's carving. "The torch holder. It has the answer." He looked over his shoulder. "Dr. Hamed, do you agree? Don't lie or I'll shoot Harry."

"That's where I would look," Sara said at once. "The torch holders are too intricate, too detailed for their purpose. I need to see them up close."

"He'll lift you up." Pete nodded to the Brit. "Get on his shoulders and figure out why Quintus pointed me to it."

Sara wasn't happy about it, but she followed Wayne and obediently climbed on his shoulders. He balanced her with ease as he stood and brought her eye level with the torch holder. Pete made Harry go back to the water's edge.

"Don't jump in the water," Pete said. "I have lots of bullets if you try."

Harry had no intention of doing that. He'd had enough ocean to last him for years. Out of rocks and options, he could only watch as Sara studied the torch holder. She ran a hand over its outline. Her lips moved in silence.

"What?" Pete asked.

"The letters are solid gold," she said. "I could pry them off the wall with the proper tool."

"Are they part of Quintus's message?"

"No. The torch holder itself is a separate piece from the embedded letters."

Pete frowned. "Why would he do that?"

Sara looked down at Wayne. "Stay still." She grabbed the torch holder with both hands. "Hold my legs tightly," she ordered. "Now pull me down. I think the torch holder is a lever."

Wayne wrapped his arms around her thighs and leaned back. Sara pulled hard on the torch holder. Muscles corded in her arms. "Harder," she called out. "I can feel it moving."

"Get over there and help." Pete barked at Harry. Harry ran over and boosted himself up using Wayne's thigh. He grabbed the torch holder and forced it up and down, working in tandem with Sara and putting every ounce he had into it. Finally, it shifted.

"It's moving." Harry's face was inches from Sara's. They stared at each other with gritted teeth; he could see that Sara was stretched to the breaking point. Harry put two feet on the wall and pushed, leaning back until he was almost parallel to the floor. Sara shouted, he kicked again, and the torch holder gave way.

They all collapsed to the floor as dirt showered them, a cloud of heavy dust forming where the torch holder now hung at a sharp angle out from the wall. The sound of rock grinding on rock echoed in the cavern. Harry staggered to his feet. The swirling particles of dust scraped Harry's eyes as he rubbed them, blinking through tears while trying to find his flashlight. He grabbed it, stepped back and ran straight into Pete. The Archdruid pushed him aside.

"Look."

Pete stepped past Sara and the Brit. Sara got to her feet and moved to Harry's side. Wayne had his gun out once more, aiming it in their general direction as Pete stood in front of the wall, his body only a hazy outline in the slowly settling dust cloud. Harry's flashlight reflected on a million tiny bits of silica.

"There's a hole in the wall," Pete said. "A chamber." He handed his flashlight to Wayne. "Hold this. And keep them back."

Wayne waved his gun, Harry and Sara stayed back, and Pete moved to one side so they could all see what had him so awestruck. A piece of wall about the size of a dumbwaiter had pulled away to reveal a hidden chamber.

Harry aimed his light inside it. A pedestal stood just inside the small chamber. Two items lay on top of it, glinting in the darkness. Pete reached in.

"Beautiful." Pete's soft words were nearly lost in the chamber. "It's as though they're alive." He reached into the darkness. "This is *heavy*."

He stepped back and Harry could see something cradled in his hands. Perhaps two feet long, the circular object had a ninety-degree bend in the middle so it resembled the corner of a square, or a bent tube. One end was flat, with the other narrowing to a point. The flashlight beams seemed to disappear into it, the dark material absorbing any light. Iridescent red sparks flashed inside the black object, like buried rubies shining through smoke clouds.

Harry had never seen anything like it. "What are those red things inside it?" he asked.

Sara stepped over and stood beside Pete. "Let me hold it."

"There are two," Pete said. "Pull the other one out, Dr. Hamed."

Sara reached in and lifted out the second object, grunting at its weight. This one was also circular and shaped like a tube. Or at least it had been at some point before it had cracked in half. The pointed end was missing from this artifact. "It's only half as big."

"I've never seen rock like this," Pete said. "It feels strange. Smooth, but not man-made. It's too clean."

"It's too *perfect*." Sara looked up. "I've studied thousands of relics made of every sort of material you can imagine. I've only seen this sort of material in one other place."

"Where?" Pete asked.

Sara didn't answer him. "It had an incredible coloring to it," she said. "Like this, with tiny specks buried deep inside. Specks that flashed blue under light. Blue specks buried inside a dark, cloudy rock. There's only one problem…"

"Where was it?" Pete asked again.

"In a Mayan tomb. That artifact was small, no bigger than a deck of cards. No one ever identified what material it was made from, because it didn't come from this planet." She looked at Harry. "I think this is from another world."

"A meteorite," Harry said. "That makes sense. This could be what Aristotle saw in Greece. What Boudica eventually possessed. No one had any idea what it was then because no one could possibly have seen anything like it before, nor would they have had the words to describe the concept. It came from outer space."

"No." Pete spoke softly. "This was no accident. This is a gift from Dagda. Meant to save the Druids. To show this world the true path."

Harry's blood got hot. He couldn't stand guys like this – fanatics, so sure of themselves – and right now he couldn't help himself. "If it's so special, why didn't it work for Boudica?" he asked. "She died even with this thing. Which, to be clear, doesn't look like a weapon."

"Simple," Pete said. "This was meant for me. Boudica was one stop on the journey, as was Quintus. Two believers who left this for the one person who could use it, when the world most needed it. Right now."

"These are two rocks," Harry said. "What are you going to do, bash non-believers over the head with them?"

"You can't see the truth." Pete looked at Harry, and something in his eyes made Harry shrink back. "You're not a true believer. Not yet. Only true believers would know the power of what these can do. Today

I will show you exactly how powerful Druids can be. Follow me. It's almost time."

Pete pointed Sara toward the stairs. "You first. Carry the smaller stone, and be careful. If you drop it, I'll shoot you. If you try to run, I'll shoot you." He grabbed her arm, pulling Sara around to face him. Pete looked as though something had taken hold of him, a look that Harry imagined he had while on stage in front of his followers. It was scary as hell. "I want you to see this, Dr. Hamed. You can't imagine what's coming." He glanced at his watch. "It's almost time."

Harry began to walk, and as he passed Wayne, the man reminded Harry he also had a gun and would shoot Harry if he tried anything. Their group moved up the stairs single file, Harry glancing at the hole down which he'd lured one of Pete's men. Pete did not. Up they went until they were out of the tunnel and back inside the ruins of Tintagel Castle. The edge of the horizon had warmed as soft red light colored the sky. The sun would be up soon.

"Out here," Pete said. "We can't have shadows." He led them away from the ruins, toward the marker from which Harry had leapt into the sea. Only when they were close to the edge and well away from any standing walls did Pete stop. He set his strange rock down, ordering Sara to do the same. "I have a story to tell you," he said. "Then I'm going to change the world."

He sounded like a madman. One with a gun. Harry looked everywhere but at Pete. How to get away? They were on a hill, with a cliff to one side and a gunman to the other. There wasn't much choice. It was the cliff or nothing.

"There is a Druidic legend that speaks of ancient Druids and a great weapon they once held," Pete intoned. "This weapon could have made them kings of men. However, these were Druids. They chose to keep this power hidden, for no man should wield such fearsome strength without grave consideration."

He looked to the horizon. "These Druids never used this weapon. They stored it, passing down the knowledge of its existence, and of its terrible power. Eventually this weapon came to Queen Boudica." Pete pointed to the stones at his feet. "That weapon is here today. These stones were the great power my forefathers could have used to rule the world. Instead, they left it for a time when it was most needed."

Sara crossed her arms. "First, these are not weapons," she said flatly. "They are *rocks*. Your story is just that — a story. Second, assuming those rocks are actually dangerous, why don't you stop and think about what actually happened. Boudica lost."

"But that's it, don't you see? She lost. Boudica was victorious in two battles. Then she lost, and I know why." Pete pointed to the sky. "There was an eclipse. The sky turned dark as Boudica unleashed her fury for the third time. The sun was blocked."

Harry could see where this was going. "You think the sun activates the rocks."

"I know it does," Pete said.

"What, is this some kind of death-ray?" Harry almost laughed. "That's crazy."

"Is it?" Pete studied him with the looks of a man slowly losing his grip on reality. "Watch and learn."

"Hold on," Harry said. "What are you going to do, burn the world?"

"I will use this weapon to make people *believe*. These stones will show the world that Druidism is the only way for us, for this planet." A black cloud crossed his face. "The non-believers and the charlatans will come to see how wrong they are. This is why these gifts have been delivered to me across two thousand years. To save us all." He paused. "If that requires a show of force, so be it."

Harry couldn't get out of there fast enough. Let Pete stick those rocks together. Good luck with that. The only thing he cared about was grabbing Sara and getting off this damn hill without any bullet holes in them. "Sounds good," Harry said. "We'll leave you to it."

Pete's gun appeared in a flash. "You can't miss this. You need to see the rebirth of an idea that will save the world. Then you can be part of the change."

Sure, buddy. Whatever you say. Harry was trying to figure out whether Sara would ever forgive him if he threw her into the sea. He didn't realize that the Brit had moved from behind them until Pete spoke again.

"You have it?" Pete asked.

Harry turned to find Wayne walking back toward them from around the ruined walls. "Right here, sir." He set a slab of dark metal on the ground.

"What's that?" Harry asked.

"Tungsten." Pete picked up the metal object, which was a curved tube cut in half lengthwise. The perfect thing to hold a bent piece of stone if you expected it to get really hot.

Dawn's first ray raced across the ocean, a billion diamonds sparkling as sunlight chased darkness over the water. The night's shadows lifted like a curtain from the hills of Tintagel. Pete jumped about as though electrified. He set the tungsten tube down, placed the whole piece of rock into it. The broken piece remained at his feet. It glowed like a black ruby.

Harry bit his lip, thinking fast. That rock was only half of another one. Which meant there was another half of a rock out there.

"Aim at the water," Pete said.

Wayne followed orders, helping Pete get set up to catch the sun's rays while keeping one eye on Harry and Sara. He never lowered his gun.

"This narrow end must focus the beam," Pete went on, "while the flat top catches the sunlight. Keep hold of me."

"We have two, Archdruid." Wayne nodded at the broken piece. "A backup."

Harry touched Sara's arm as Pete and Wayne made ready. "There are two rocks here." He whispered so only she could hear. "Remember what the scroll said? *Do not pair the gifts to make it greater. Two will bring the wrath of Dagda.*"

"I remember," Sara said.

"I think it's a warning about the rocks. If that thing really is some sort of laser, it's logical to think using two stones would strengthen the effect."

"Don't tell him to do that."

"What if it's a bad idea because it's too powerful?" Harry asked.

"This is all crazy, Harry."

"Maybe. Maybe not. We're about to find out."

Pete cradled the tungsten holder, turning so the rising sun was at his back. "The true gods are ready to speak," he shouted.

"Ready?" Wayne asked.

"Take it off."

A thick cover had been draped over the stone. The Brit pulled it off as Pete shielded the stone with his body so no light hit it.

Sara grabbed Harry's wrist and held it tightly. "This is impossible," she whispered.

Pete Brody squinted into the sunlight. The wide sea stretched in front of him. Birds floated above the nearby cliff. Pete studied the sky a moment longer, then shifted so the flat top of Boudica's rock came into the light.

It all happened at once.

The stone began glowing a deep red that spoke of distant galaxies and eons of time. A flash of blood-red so deep and pure it was incandescent, then the fire was swallowed by the stone, hidden beneath a haze of darkness somehow stronger than the ruby specks that flashed inside the stone, their red fire bursting to life like lightning in a storm cloud. Smoke seemed to swirl inside the stone.

Harry blinked.

Red lightning flared from the stone now, to course in a disjointed line out to sea. The water erupted, spray exploding toward the sky. Thunder roared. Harry saw but didn't hear Pete scream. The black stone in his arms almost seemed to twist, pulsing with a darkness not of this world, the scarlet flashes frantically bursting to life inside it, a flashing beacon of terrible power.

The red beam disappeared. Pete fell to one knee with the single stone still in his grasp. Charged particles of ozone tingled on Harry's tongue and pricked at his skin. Red dots flashed across his vision. Sara clung to him. Change had come, a long-forgotten power that would turn the page once more on what humanity understood.

"It works." Pete sounded distant when he spoke. "It works! A gift from the gods."

"Are you burned?" Wayne hurried up to Pete, checking him for injuries.

"I'm fine," Pete said. He set the stone down and lifted his arms. "The gods protect me. Can you deny my truth when it manifests in front of you?"

"You cannot," Wayne said.

"I can end the scourge of false religion forever." A dark shadow crossed Pete's face. "That will show him who was right."

"That guy has an ax to grind," Harry told Sara. "This isn't good."

"Then do it," Sara said. "Trick him."

Harry watched Pete and Wayne, his mind whirling. He and Sara could destroy Dagda's gift and end this madness. Sure, that rock could be worth a billion dollars, but at what cost? Harry needed to use his head, because today he'd brought knuckledusters to a gun fight.

He stepped toward Pete. "You can do more than that," he said.

Pete looked over at him. "How?" Pete asked.

"The stone. You can make it better." Harry hesitated. "More powerful."

"More than what you just saw?" Pete laughed, and it was not the laughter of a sane man. "Dagda's broken staff is all I need."

Harry pointed at the second rock. "Quintus didn't include the other rock for show. It's here for a reason. Look at it. Both sides are flat. You can stack the second rock on top of the first one and double the power."

Wielding immense power did many things to a man. Clouding his judgment was near the top. "Do you think so?" Pete asked, eyeing the stones speculatively.

"Quintus and Boudica wouldn't have saved it without good reason."

Pete cocked his head. "No, they wouldn't." He stood. "Bring it to me." Wayne helped Pete set the second rock on top of the first. It balanced with ease. "A perfect fit," Pete said.

He walked toward the ruins, circling around Harry and Sara until they stood between him and the sea. He stopped, looked up to the sky, then said something to Wayne that Harry couldn't hear. Wayne moved aside as Pete turned to face Harry and Sara.

"This story cannot be contradicted." Pete aimed the stones at Harry and Sara, angling them to catch the full light. The stones again began to glow.

"Come on!" Harry pulled Sara toward the cliff, legs churning as he dragged her along. He looked back as the surfaces of both stones began swirling, the black tendrils covering tiny bursts of ruby light. "Time to jump!" he shouted.

The edge was too far away; time seemed to stand still as he and Sara stumbled toward the precipice. They wouldn't beat the explosion. Harry's mouth tingled as the air charged around them. He grabbed Sara's arm, using his weight to heave her over the cliff and out of harm's way. She looked back at him, reaching out toward him, as she plummeted over the edge.

The sky turned red. Pete and the British man didn't move as the stones turned to fire, the black clouds inside them bursting as the light pushed through, up and out in a massive explosion. Suddenly Harry was weightless, lifted off his feet and sent sailing over the cliff. Water sparkled beneath him and red light covered the sun as Harry was shot by Dagda's wrath into the glittering blue ocean far below.

Epilogue

Brooklyn
One Week Later

The rising sun had never had much of an effect on Harry Fox, but that was before a terrifying morning atop a cliff in England. Now Harry Fox was a changed man. If the sky was clear and he got up early enough, he took time to watch the first rays of dawn push away the night, bringing a new day. A chance to start all over again. A chance to remind yourself nothing should be taken for granted.

This was one of those days. Harry leaned against his kitchen counter, sipping coffee and forcing himself not to check his phone. He had a lot of yesterdays to make up for. In order to do that, he would need to make an agreement with the enemy. Funny how the world worked. He pulled out his phone. A text message waited. He decided to call her instead.

"Anti-Trafficking Unit. Doyle speaking."

"It's Harry."

"I figured you might call." Nora Doyle took a long breath. "Change your mind?"

"I said I'd sleep on it," Harry said.

"Big decision to make."

Harry fingered the medallion around his neck. "I'm in."

"Good."

"You have to hold up your end."

"I'm on my way."

Harry sipped his coffee and dialed another number. It took her four rings to pick up. "You okay?" he asked.

"I'm fine," Sara said. "Packing my things."

"You want me to pick you up?"

"In that monstrosity of a car? No, thank you. I'll find a cab."

"I'll be here."

He clicked off. Monstrosity? The lime-green paint job was rough, sure, but if Sara ever found out how he'd come to own a 1970 Chevy Chevelle SS 456, she'd never speak to him again. The guy who'd had it before deserved what he got. Harry had just never expected to end up with a dead man's car. He had Joey Morello to thank for that.

Harry poured fresh coffee. That was in the past. Today marked a chance for him to take a new direction. It would impact Joey, he knew. The new Morello leader was desperately in need of people he could trust. So was Nora Doyle, who needed the sort of information only Harry could offer. And Sara, the wild card in all of this.

Harry walked to his front door. The drywall around it had been repaired, and he'd installed a steel-frame door with an unnecessary number of locks, but he couldn't do much about the outside brickwork. He stepped out, eyeing several bullet holes that would never be completely repaired. In truth, he sort of liked them. They gave it character. Harry sat on his front step and waited. The sun warmed his face.

Sara's cab rolled to a stop in front of him minutes later. Her dark hair lung loose around her shoulders as she got out. The cabbie fell over himself running around to get her single bag out of the trunk. She tipped him well. Sara ran a hand through her hair, watching Harry watch her as she walked over, the little roller wheels of her suitcase bumping on the sidewalk. A gold necklace flashed at her throat. She didn't ask him for help with her luggage.

"Come in," Harry said as he held the door.

Sara put her suitcase by the front door and pulled a folder from the front zippered pocket, holding it to her chest. "Have any more coffee?"

Harry indicated one of two cups beside the pot. "Extra strong, the way you like it."

"The way all coffee should be." Sara nodded at the other mug sitting beside hers. "Expecting company?"

Harry grinned. "Patience." He went to the dining room table and sat down. "What's in the folder?"

"My research on Pompeii."

Harry touched his amulet. "About the mural."

"Yes." Sara helped herself to coffee, carried it to the table, and pulled up a chair beside Harry. She seated herself, removed a set of photographs from the folder and spread them across the table. "You can see the mural in each of these. It's a copy of one from the Temple of Caesar."

"The temple mural that was destroyed after Antony and Cleopatra lost the War of Actium against Octavian."

"That's it. Look here." She pointed to a familiar woman in the mural. "Cleopatra. She's wearing the necklace."

A double-headed eagle. Rubies and sapphires. All rendered in exquisite detail. "It has to be the same one. There's no better place for Cleopatra to put the next step on her hidden trail than in plain sight in a temple she believed would stand for thousands of years."

"Say I'm correct. What's the message?" Sara leaned closer to look at the photo from another angle. Her hair brushed his shoulder.

"Hey." Harry touched her knee. "I really appreciate this. There's no one else I can trust to help with this."

She sighed. A passing car outside the window caught her eye. "Harry, I know what happened last week isn't the norm."

"Maybe it's not, but it has to be more fun than lecturing undergrads."

"I didn't say it was no fun. My point is it's not supposed to be *normal*. What most people would call the adventure of a lifetime is your monthly routine." She gave him a fleeting smile, then grew serious again. "It's not only that. You have yet to clearly explain what you do. I do know that sometimes it ends with people dying. Good people like Tony Cervelli."

"Who sold us out."

"To save his family," she said. "But why did Tony have to sell us out to save his family? Why not go to the police? Apparently, that's not an option for the two of you. Do you know what that makes me think?" She leaned across the table. "You don't involve the police because you can't. Only criminals think that way. So, are you a criminal, Harry? Do you steal artifacts for Joey Morello?"

The direct question she'd never asked. She'd finally come out with it. And he was ready to answer. With the truth.

A knock sounded on his door. "Come in," Harry called out. Nora Doyle walked in and closed the door quietly behind her.

Sara stiffened. "Nora?"

"Hello, Sara." Nora sat down at the table and laid a thin folder down in front of her. "Glad to hear you're okay."

Harry jumped in before Sara could respond. "I told Nora everything. About the Greek and Roman manuscripts, the Isle of Wight, Tintagel Castle, all of it."

Sara appraised Harry with an inscrutable look. "You never mentioned Nora was involved with all this."

Nora leaned over the table. "I asked him not to."

This time Harry and Nora studied each other across the table. In the days since he'd returned from England, he'd spoken with three people. The first was Joey Morello, who was solely focused on securing his grip on power. Harry knew the best way for him to help Joey now was the way Joey would never approve. But to Harry's surprise, Joey had listened to Harry's plan and agreed on the spot. Times were changing, and it seemed the Morello enterprise needed to change as well.

Next came Sara, who was still processing how a meteorite had blown them into the sea. They'd managed to get out of the water and leave the area on their motorcycle. Later news reports attributed the explosion to a natural gas build-up under Tintagel Castle. A massive new crater marked where Pete had tried to use Dagda's staff to turn Harry and Sara into charcoal. Now the subterranean Druidic tomb was buried beneath a mountain of rubble, lost to the ages.

Finally, Harry had called Agent Nora Doyle, and a somewhat complicated partnership was born. Nora had been in Iran with Harry and Sara. She knew how Sara felt about Harry's profession, what Sara knew, and – more importantly – what she didn't know. Based on that, Nora Doyle had made a business decision: keep Harry happy and he'd be the best asset she ever had. A little white lie about the timing of their agreement wouldn't hurt anyone.

"Harry hasn't been entirely forthcoming about what he does because he couldn't be," Nora told Sara now. She tapped the folder in front of her. "He's been a part of my team's undercover operations. Hundreds of millions of dollars' worth of stolen antiquities come through New York every year. I'd miss out on a lot more than I already do if I didn't have Harry. He risks his life to protect the world's cultural heritage. That's why he never told you the full story about what he does." She crossed her arms. "Without him I couldn't do my job."

Harry turned to Sara, a twinge of guilt in his stomach. "I had to protect myself, and I had to protect you. I wouldn't last long if anyone found out the truth."

Sara ran a hand through her hair. She pursed her lips. "I'm sorry, Harry. Truly sorry. I started to think you were one of the bad guys."

"What you know now cannot leave this room," Nora said. "Understood?"

"Of course," Sara said.

"Good." She turned to Harry. "Here's your updated contract. Get it back to me by tomorrow. We'll go from there."

"Sounds good." Harry tried to express his thanks without talking, and hoped he succeeded.

"Right, then." Nora stood. "Good seeing you, Sara. Don't be a stranger."

Sara responded with the air of someone whose world had just gone a bit off-kilter. "I won't."

Harry stood quickly. "Let me get the door."

Nora frowned. "I can find my way out. I think you two may have things to sort out." She paused at the door, where Sara couldn't see her, and winked at Harry. "See you soon, Harry."

The door clicked shut behind her. Sunlight fell through an open window, and Sara looked at Harry as though she'd never seen him before.

Harry tossed his new agreement on the pile of unopened mail. "I'll handle this later." A large envelope slid off the pile. "Do you want some food before your flight?" he asked, scooping up the parcel. "You still have a few hours."

Sara's hand was warm when she touched his arm. "I think I'll stay a few days longer. If that's okay with you."

"Oh." He'd imagined she might say something. *I was wrong. Tell me more about your job.* He hadn't expected this. He fumbled for a moment, then went with the only thought in his head. "That would be nice."

"I misjudged you. I didn't understand the entire picture."

"Forget about it. I'm glad I can finally come clean. You're right about how dangerous this can be. I didn't want to do anything that would get you hurt."

"Harry, you're unlike anyone I've ever met."

His mind flashed back to a comment she'd made right before he and Joey got into a tussle at the restaurant. A comment he hadn't understood at first. "Now I know what you meant before. *That's* what you thought when you first saw me in Germany. Before my amulet." He offered a grin. "I *am* a bit unique."

Sara rolled her eyes. "No, dummy. The first thing I thought when I met you was that you were handsome. A bit arrogant, but handsome."

"Oh." He scratched his chin. "I'll take it."

Harry looked down at the parcel in his hand. He blinked. Sara spoke, but he didn't hear it. "This envelope is from Rose." He looked up. "Rose, my contact for fencing items. She promised to send me anything she could find on my mother's death."

"My goodness. What did she find?"

"No idea. I didn't tell you this, but I never really knew what happened to my mom. She died around the time my father started working for Vincent Morello." He took a breath. "A lot was changing then."

"I understand." She seemed to mean it, and better yet, she didn't ask questions. Proof he worked with Nora Doyle had put him squarely in the good-guy column for Sara. "I'll keep reviewing the mural photos."

Sara turned to her folder as he opened the envelope. A ratty folder fell out, dust blooming when it landed on the table. It was depressingly thin. It took him a second to realize it was the police report on his mother's death, along with the autopsy notes. A handwritten note was on the front, written in the elegant script that was unmistakably Rose Leroux's. *Hard to find this – supposedly "lost." Never trust the police.*

His breathing turned shallow as he leafed through the pages, the dry paper shaking in his hands. Finally knowing more frightened him. His mother, Dani, had been described to him as enchantment personified, a woman with whom Fred Fox had fallen madly in love. Beyond that, Harry knew very little of his mother, and nothing about what had happened to her.

The police report laid it out in cold, unflinching detail. The body of an adult female found on the banks of the Hudson. She had drowned. No signs of foul play. The body had been underwater for several days, making identification difficult, but the deceased was determined to be Dani Fox, an English immigrant with dual English and American citizenship. The police had made little effort to figure out what happened beyond that. Fred Fox had claimed the body and the medical examiner had ruled the manner of death to be accidental. That was it.

He flipped through the pages again, searching for answers to questions he couldn't even articulate. He found nothing. She had drowned, but there was nothing about how or why, and the cops couldn't even say where, beyond a general area and timeframe. Perhaps she had fallen off a bridge. Maybe she'd jumped. Dani could have fallen into the water any number of ways, might have hit her head on the way in, and that was it. A sad, forgotten tragedy that registered with only a handful of people.

An overwhelming emptiness took root in his gut. He hadn't known what to expect when Rose said she'd try to get the file. Something. Anything, really, but not this. Not a clear lack of interest from overworked cops, a bunch of underpaid guys who had quickly thrown their hands up, happy to close one more file. It was all so final, yet not the end at all. It was nothing, and that tore him apart.

He closed the file. A single sheet slipped out and fluttered onto the table. He picked it up. The autopsy report, a scribbled mess of a paper. As Harry pushed it back into the folder, a notation caught his eye. He lifted the sheet close to his face, turning it to catch the light. His stomach dropped.

The decedent has not previously given birth.

This woman had never had a child. It couldn't be Dani Fox.

Sara smacked the table and he jumped out of his chair. "That's it!" She lifted a photograph of the mural and turned it towards him. But Harry couldn't focus on anything, let alone the picture.

"Look at this," she said. "The necklace. Cleopatra was sending a message, and I can read it."

THE END

Author's Note

It is a fact that two thousand years ago, an upstart Celtic Briton Queen waged war against the most powerful military force on the planet. Boudica destroyed three Roman cities – including modern-day London – killing over seventy-thousand people along the way. Boudica commanded an army of over one hundred thousand soldiers, though they were ill-equipped for combat compared to their Roman adversaries and had little in the way of training, an obstacle which proved insurmountable *(Prologue)* when Boudica faced ten thousand hardened Roman soldiers at an unknown location – I purposefully left my battle location vague to account for this – and were crushed by Nero's legions. Boudica died shortly after the battle, though the historical record is not clear on how, either committing suicide or falling ill. Her revolt died with her, and Rome would rule Brittania for over three hundred years, until Germanic and other local tribes forced a fading empire to abandon the island for good.

Why did Boudica wage war? It was personal. She was married to a King of the British Celtic tribe called the Iceni, a man named Prasutagus, who upon his death stipulated his kingdom should be ruled jointly by his two daughters and the Roman emperor. Rome ignored Prasutagus's will, annexing the kingdom upon his death. Boudica and her daughters were horribly abused by the local Roman leaders, setting a fire in the Queen's heart that could only end when the Iceni people were free of Roman rule. Boudica gathered the oppressed people in her homeland and took the fight to their Roman overlords.

The otherworldly relic at the heart of this story is said to have ties to

Aristotle *(Chapter 2)* who witnessed the relic's power on his travels to Celtic lands to study the mystical tribes far from his homeland of Greece. Aristotle died in 322 BC. By this time Celtic culture had extended far beyond their island, as archeological evidence shows Celtic influence as far away as Greece. While not documented, it is possible Aristotle not only knew of the Celts, but may even have met a member of the Celtic peoples during his lifetime. As to if they discussed the legend of Dagda, history is silent.

Jane White is able to identify the Isle of Wight as the location Nero referenced *(Chapter 10)* with the phrase tin isle, and it is true this isle was a rich source of the valuable metal for centuries, including when Rome ruled Britain. Part of the reason Rome desired the island was for the abundant natural resources needed to sustain an empire. Tin was found almost exclusively in the southern part of Britain, including the Isle of Wight. The tribal songs Jane references as the source of her knowledge are my invention, though the method of passing knowledge down through generations by using song is well-documented and a vital component of how many civilizations around the globe educated their young about the history of their people.

The town of Brading *(Chapter 14)* is not truly located on the English Channel, though it is only a few miles from downtown to the cliffside overlooking the water. The ruins of a Roman villa were discovered in 1879 on a farmer's land and have been continuously excavated to some degree through the present. Today the site is a museum showcasing the incredible mosaics and remaining original walls of the twelve-room structure. Fortunately, there is no church on the site for the Germans to have bombed. There are no subterranean caverns, and as of yet, any hidden temples or places of worship dedicated to Celtic gods remain undiscovered. However, excavations are ongoing, and who knows what is left to find?

The Rollright Stones *(Chapter 18)* are possibly named from a Brittonic saying which references a narrow valley, or *rix*, and a description of "The King's Men" circle of wheel enclosure, or rodland.

The site is comprised of three megalithic monuments as detailed, with "The Whispering Knights" situated several hundred yards away from the other two monuments. The only changes I made for story purposes were to add a fifth vertical stone to "The Whispering Knights" and to create a written clue on the stones – no such writing exists. The stone monuments were all constructed at different times over the course of several thousand years, with the most recent monument being "The King Stone", which was likely built four thousand years ago, or at least two thousand years before General Quintus would have buried anything beneath one of the monuments. The legend of a witch turning a king and his soldiers into stone is real, so if you should happen to visit these monuments, be kind to any pointy-hatted ladies you meet with a broom in tow.

The mythical gods Dagda, Nuada and Lugh *(Chapter 22)* play an integral role in this story. They are prominently associated with Irish mythology, but as with nearly all religions, appear in some form or another across multiple belief systems to a certain degree. Dagda, our most prominent mythical being, was said to be as described in this story in Irish mythology, a large bearded man who often carried a magic staff. Dagda can also be seen in the god Odin – central to Germanic and Norse mythology – as well as in the Gaulish god Sucellos and a Roman underworld god, Dis Pater. It is well-documented that at times Rome allowed conquered peoples to continue worshipping their gods, so it is not inconceivable that a man such as General Quintus would worship Dagda and his fellow gods in spite of the Roman affinity for their own deities. Christianity did not become the official religion of Rome until the end of the fourth century, so there were almost certainly followers of Dagda in the Roman military during Nero's reign. Perhaps hidden temples were built, and secret quests laid out, hidden so only a true believer could find them. It wouldn't be the first time.

The final confrontation on Harry's path occurs at Tintagel Castle, which has been a popular tourist destination for over a century largely due to an association with the legend of King Arthur...with which readers of Harry Fox's earlier adventures may be familiar. Geoffrey of Monmouth gave Tintagel as the place of Arthur's conception *(Chapter 22)* in quite the imaginative tale. Archeological evidence suggests the site may have been inhabited during Boudica's time, though the oldest remaining structural evidence dates to the fifth century, five hundred years after Boudica's rebellion. The oldest standing portion of the ruins date to the thirteenth century. However, the long bridge Harry and Sara must cross does exist, though it is quite safe and modern. Merlin's cave is real, though to my knowledge it is not indicative of a larger network of caverns which exist under the surface, where those of a mind to conceal their illicit worship may do so in private.

Excerpt from *The Achilles Legend*

Visit Andrew's website for more information and purchase details.

andrewclawson.com

Prologue

Windsor, England

The flying spears nearly got him.

Harry Fox stood rigid as a statue. One of his feet hovered millimeters above the ancient stone floor. He'd foolishly looked everywhere but down as he entered the hallway. It was hard not to get distracted by the intricate carvings covering the walls. Ancient stone deities watched over him, ever vigilant against intruders who dared trespass in their dark lair. Harry was definitely a trespasser, one who'd nearly gotten himself killed just now because he wasn't paying attention to the floor. That's why he missed the tiny lines underfoot, grooves in the floor that told him the floor wasn't solid. No, it was one big, lethal trap.

Harry carefully pulled his foot back. A warm breeze drifted down the gloomy passageway. He knelt, laying flat on the ground. From this close he could see a line of pressure traps stretching the length of the passage, all the way to where it twisted at a ninety-degree angle ahead. Harry looked to either side where holes had been carved into the walls, holes which he suspected held something rather unpleasant for anyone who stepped on the wrong part of the floor.

Harry stood and wiped his brow. He pulled out the notebook containing every bit of information he had about this hidden temple. The only notebook like it in the world. His research indicated the passageway was booby-trapped, but he hadn't known how, or where it started. He needed to think like the person who built it. A person whose only goal was to make sure no one but them made it through the gauntlet alive.

Too bad for them Harry Fox was here. He'd done his homework and knew where most of the traps waited, which parts of the floor to avoid and what steps led to his doom. At least he thought he did. He frowned. Nothing he'd read mentioned these floor traps.

No matter. He hadn't come all this way to stop now. Harry touched the amulet under his shirt. The answers his father sought may be just ahead. Answers his father never found.

White light fell through openings in the ceiling overhead, enough for him to see in the gloomy passageway. Moving on soft feet, he skirted the barely-visible pressure traps on the floor, hopping between them until he was halfway down the passage. Another thirty feet and he was in the clear. Eyes down, he readied to move when he noticed the wall had changed. Harry looked up. The holes were gone. Holes in the wall he suspected sent thick spears hurtling out if you stepped on the wrong part of the floor. Maybe the spears would miss. Most likely, they wouldn't.

Why did the holes stop halfway down? The man who designed this wouldn't give up his treasure so easily. No, there was a reason, but darned if he knew what it was. He'd skirted the faulty steps coming in, big and wide steps that might hold you, or they may collapse beneath your feet and dump you in a spike-lined pit. Now the passageway which seemed to give up partway through. Harry squinted at the wall. *No, not there.* He looked up. *Uh-oh.*

Archways ran the entire length of the ceiling, curved stone supports which kept it from collapsing, and which until now had been undecorated stone. From this point on, the arches were intricately carved, with decorative holes punched through each of them. The carvings were all along the bottoms of the support arches, cut so they almost looked like handles along the bottom of each. And they were closer together. Much closer.

He knelt again to study the floor. The same pressure-traps ran the length of the floor ahead, only now they seemed to be everywhere, so close you couldn't possibly walk between them. Along the bottom of the walls he spotted more holes, the same size as before but now running at ground level like some kind of deadly baseboard decorations. He closed his eyes, recalling the notebook he'd procured, the only existing document offering a clue on how to survive this gauntlet. It contained crude diagrams, some direct and easy to understand. Others hadn't made sense, seemingly random warnings of impending doom if you tried to enter this protective temple, but he'd studied them nonetheless, committing it all to memory.

One image jumped out. A diagram of a man swinging through the air as though he were on a giant set of monkey bars.

The arches weren't decorative. They were his way ahead. He skirted the floor until one was above him, reached up and grabbed the decorative carving. Which functioned as a perfect handhold. Grabbing tight, he eyed the next arch. Not tall by anyone's definition, it would be a stretch, but he could make it. Probably. One way to find out. Harry took step back, arm stretched to its limit, then launched himself at the next arch.

He got it. Latched on, he swung back and forth, building momentum until he let go of the first arch and used the second one to swing himself forward to grab the next one in line. On this went for a half dozen swings until finally he reached the last one and flung himself ahead to where the passageway ended. He landed softly and held his breath. No spears flew from the walls, no blades sliced him open. A look behind him revealed his heel had cleared the last pressure trap by at least six inches.

That was close. He couldn't help but grin. Things usually were in his business.

Checking the floor for traps ahead and finding none, he crept forward to where the passageway turned. Reddish light flickered across the stone floor. Harry peered around the corner and found lit torches lining both sides of the passage, the flames pushing away the dark and leading directly to the reason he'd risked his life to come here. Only Harry didn't have eyes for what lay ahead yet. The torches had him spooked.

Normally he'd worry about why torches in a stone passageway with ancient traps were lit. Never in his years hunting artifacts had the original owners been alive to keep the lights on. Usually they'd been dead for centuries. However, nothing about this was normal. Harry Fox may have been avoiding lethal devices meant to protect a priceless relic in a place that looked thousands of years old, but it was all a mirage.

The stone passageway was in the English town of Windsor, better known as the home of Windsor Castle, the Queen's main residence. The traps in this ancient-looking hallway still worked because they were scarcely five years old. An eccentric Russian oligarch installed them as protection for his antiquities, a world-class collection acquired mostly on the black market. Evgeny Smolov had made a fortune in his homeland after the Soviet Union collapsed, then run afoul of the tyrant who ruled in Russia. Forced to flee, he'd built a massive home in Windsor which housed his acquisitions. To protect them, Evgeny designed his own security system, one inspired by every deadly temple trap mankind had ever built.

Yet it was not foolproof. Harry had managed to sneak into the facility without the guards spotting him, and given Evgeny didn't want to spoil the look of his exorbitantly-priced ancient display building, cameras weren't installed in the passageways. Evgeny could disable all the traps by pressing a button, and assuming no one would ever be bold enough to sneak in and actually test the traps had made been his downfall. Harry Fox had the guts to do it. And for this prize, there was no question. It was Harry's destiny.

He peered through the gloom, light dancing across the walls as he peered ahead. An object waited, resting on a circular stone platform, lit by recessed lighting that made it come alive. A golden crown that once belonged to Mark Antony. The Civic Crown.

The gold gleamed with a familiar sharpness, though it was the precious stones dotting each of the woven oak leaves that sparkled the brightest. The Civic Crown was most often associated with Julius Caesar, partner of Cleopatra before Mark Antony. Harry took a moment to appreciate the brilliant red, green and blue light washed over the smooth stone walls of the display chamber. The stones were exactly as he'd seen them in a mural preserved in the ruins of Pompeii. A mural that served as a marker on the mysterious path he now followed, one laid out by Antony and Cleopatra.

Why it was important he had no idea. He'd figure that out later, after he stole it from an exiled oligarch and got out of here alive. After he got back to Brooklyn and a woman unlike any other. A woman he'd lied to about coming here. He couldn't die, not yet. Not when they were so close.

The torchlight revealed a smooth floor bereft of visible traps. Harry had acquired the notebook of a single craftsman at great cost. By design, the man only handled pieces of the entire project, which is why Harry was running semi-blind here. The notebook revealed Evgeny didn't have a single modern alarm in the display housing the crown, one of many rooms housing the entire collection. Beyond the stone platform another hall ran on, at the end of which a stack of cut stone and modern saws stood in one corner. Evgeny's collection was ever-expanding.

Harry rubbed his chin. This last part didn't seem right. It couldn't be this easy. Nothing stood in his way, which is why only a fool would stride up to the platform and snatch the crown. Harry took a single step forward, then another. His foot edged ahead until the first flickers of torchlight reflected dully on his boot. Harry stopped. A sound caught his ear.

To continue the story, visit Andrew Clawson's website at andrewclawson.com.

GET YOUR COPY OF THE PARKER CHASE STORY
A SPY'S REWARD, AVAILABLE EXCLUSIVELY FOR MY VIP READER LIST

Sharing the writing journey with my readers is a special privilege. I love connecting with anyone who reads my stories, and one way I accomplish that is through my mailing list. I only send notices of new releases or the occasional special offer related to my novels.

If you sign up for my VIP reader mailing list, I'll send you a copy of *A Spy's Reward*, the Parker Chase adventure that's not sold in any store. You can get your copy of this exclusive novel by signing up here: DL.bookfunnel.com/uayd05okci

Did you enjoy this story? Let people know

Reviews are the most effective way to get my books noticed. I'm one guy, a small fish in a massive pond. Over time, I hope to change that, and I would love your help. The best thing you could do to help spread the word is leave a review on your platform of choice.

Honest reviews are like gold. If you've enjoyed this book I would be so grateful if you could take a few minutes leaving a review, short or long.

Thank you very much.

Also by Andrew Clawson

The Parker Chase Series

A Patriot's Betrayal

A dead man's letter draws Parker Chase into
a deadly search for a secret that could rewrite history.

The Crowns Vengeance

A Revolutionary era espionage report sends Parker
on a race to save American independence.

Dark Tides Rising

A centuries-old map bearing a cryptic poem sends Parker Chase
racing for his life and after buried treasure.

A Republic of Shadows

A long-lost royal letter sends Parker on a secret trail
with the I.R.A. and British agents close behind.

A Hollow Throne

Shattered after a tragic loss, Parker is thrust into
a race through Scottish history to save a priceless treasure.

A Tsar's Gold

Parker follows a trail through the past toward a lost treasure
which changed the course of two World Wars.

The TURN Series

TURN: *The Conflict Lands*

Reed Kimble battles a ruthless criminal gang
to save Tanzania and the animals he loves.

TURN: *A New Dawn*

A predator ravages the savanna. To stop it, Reed must be
what he fears most – the man he used to be.

TURN: *Endangered*

Tanzania's deadliest gangster is after everything Reed
built – and will stop at nothing to destroy him.

Harry Fox Adventures

The Arthurian Relic

The Emerald Tablet

The Celtic Quest

The Achilles Legend

The Pagan Hammer

Check my website AndrewClawson.com for
additional novels – I'm writing all the time.

About the Author

Andrew Clawson is the author of multiple series, including the Parker Chase and TURN thrillers, as well as the Harry Fox adventures.

You can find him at his website, AndrewClawson.com, or you can connect with him on Twitter at @clawsonbooks, on Facebook at facebook.com/AndrewClawsonnovels and you can always send him an email at andrew@andrewclawson.com.

Made in the USA
Monee, IL
27 October 2022

16674243R00154